THE CRIMSON BEARS

THE CRIMSON BEARS

Part I

Tom LaFarge

Sun & Moon Press

Los Angeles

Sun & Moon Press
A Program of The Contemporary Arts Educational Project, Inc.
a nonprofit corporation
6026 Wilshire Boulevard, Los Angeles, California 90036

First published in paperback in 1993 by Sun & Moon Press
10 9 8 7 6 5 4 3
FIRST EDITION
© Tom LaFarge, 1993
Biographical information © Sun & Moon Press, 1993
All rights reserved

This book was made possible, in part, through a grant from the California
Arts Council, the National Endowment for the Arts, and through
contributions to The Contemporary Arts Educational Project, Inc.,
a nonprofit corporation

Cover: Douglas Messerli
Design: Katie Messborn
Drawings: Wendy Walker

LIBRARY OF CONGRESS CATALOGING IN PUBLICATION DATA
LaFarge, Tom
The Crimson Bears (volume 1)
p. cm — (New American Fiction Series: 26)
ISBN: 1-55713-074-4
I. Title. II. Series.
811'.54—dc19
CIP
Printed in the United States of America on acid-free paper.

The Slizz

ONE. **The Slizz.**

*E*dgar and Alice, brother and sister, one morning set out from their room to walk across an entire country. Their room was in the City of Bears, and they were bears; Edgar a dark brown, Alice more russet; they were both about half-grown. The country they were to walk across was called the Commonwealth of Bears, not because only bears lived in it—of course there were many hundreds of other speakable kinds besides—but because bear law governed it, and because bears owned most of what was worth owning, and because everyone in it used the speech of the bears. Edgar and Alice knew that there were other countries where bears did not rule; they knew, for instance, that there was a Republic of Seals, far to the North, presently ruled by a despotic walrus. But country did not press up against country, in this world. There were large waste spaces in between, dangerous to travellers. Restless for something different from what they were used to, Edgar and Alice had known without asking that it was out of the question for them to travel outside the Commonwealth of Bears; nor was it necessary. They had seen almost nothing of their own country. They could go to Bargeton to visit their uncle without setting foot outside it, and in so doing, put the whole width of the Commonwealth between them and their ordinary lives. For the City of Bears was in the far West, and faced out to sea, but Bargeton looked east over the Flood to the desert, across which no bear had ever walked.

There were other reasons why Bargeton attracted Edgar and Alice. It was now only three generations since Bargeton had fallen under the dominion of the bears, conquered by Maximo, last of the great generals. It was, however, an old city and a center for trade, the most important market of the Flood, the great continent-draining river. Creatures travelled there from the far North and South, down-river and up, creatures that you would never meet in the City of Bears; moreover, Bargeton had a large population of other kinds in permanent residence: merchants, brokers, bankers, factors, and artisans, but also actors, dancers, singers, jugglers, tumblers, mountebanks, zanies, story-tellers. Any kind of food at all was to be had from Bargeton's cookshops. All sorts of books turned up in the stalls there. And yet the city was under the peaceable rule of the bears, whose Senate regulated all aspects of life and business; and their father's brother, Claudio, was the President of the Bargeton Senate. They would be privileged visitors and could see everything. They were done with their schooling—bears do not hold with too much schooling—and could stay as long as they liked, since it was an influential relative they were going to visit. Edgar's father was a magistrate, and it was understood that Edgar would put some time into studying the laws of Bargeton, whose constitution was in many ways a curious one. Alice's mother was simply her father's loving wife, and a proud dam, just at this time, of two new cubs whom she had to lick into shape; but Alice needed no one to tell her what to do. Being fond of stories and poems, she had formed her own little project of an Anthology of the Literature of Other Kinds. Neither Edgar nor Alice meant to let these undertakings stand in the way of their explorations through Bargeton, nor of their enjoyment of its pleasures, but they knew enough to agree when it was suggested to them that such researches might lend their visit some point and shape.

In high spirits, therefore, they climbed the leafy suburban lanes above their house till they gained the crest of the ridge behind the city, and looked back down into the demi-bowl of hills, curving around an island-dotted bay, that had contained their lives so far. The two young bears spared the familiar scene no more than a glance before turning eastward to survey the way before them.

On the reverse side of the perimeter hills, as they made their way toward the road, they crossed a herdsbear with a small flock of Slizz. The Slizz were busy cropping the grass in a little dell, while their guardian snoozed beneath a twisted live oak, his feet projecting from the pool of black shadow it cast. The Slizz are wool-bearing lizards of large size, about as long as Edgar and Alice were tall, but so low to the ground on their elbowy legs as to come no higher than a young bear's knee. Their wool, for which they are raised, is feathery-fine and grows in rippling shags of various brilliant hues of green—brilliant when washed. Their muzzles are long and delicately tapering; their eyes large, liquid, and flecked with gold; for such dirty, stupid beasts their features seem unsettlingly expressive. It was heads such as these that all swung around to watch the two young bears as they passed by, and there followed a few brief coughing *yarks*, "as if we would want to come any closer," said Edgar to Alice. "Especially from downwind," Alice replied.

They forgot the Slizz, and made for the Bargeton road, which ran out from a gap in the hills alongside a lively torrent. Although they were only the thickness of a hill away from their home and the bear capital, the world they had entered in crossing the ridge was so thoroughly pastoral that the only way to get over this stream, as they must to reach the road, was by means of a fallen tree, its boughs awash in the current. It rocked as they walked it. A short slope of woods lay ahead, but before they could begin to climb, they heard a strangled cry from behind them. Turning, they saw that the tree had rolled over; something alive was caught beneath a branch on the downstream side. They both jumped into the chilly water and managed with much labor to right the tree. Straddling the bole, dripping from every shag, a sodden Slizz clung to the bark.

Edgar exclaimed impatiently, for he was not only soaked but slimy from wrestling with long-submerged branches. "It must have followed us down from the dell. Now we'll have to take it back."

Back they went and woke the Slizzherd, whose sleepy bad humor and gruff incomprehension delayed them further. Finally he came and pried the Slizz loose from the tree-trunk, and carried it off beneath his thick arm, its head gaping back at them. Edgar and Alice mounted to the road and started off again. They had gone perhaps a mile when Alice, stopping to adjust the straps of her pack, felt something collide softly with the back of her leg, and staggered forward. It was the Slizz. Edgar was furious, but they had no choice but to take it back again and lose all the ground they had gained.

"Well," said Alice, "we've got two months' walking ahead of us, so we're not in a hurry."

"I am," Edgar complained. "I came on this trip to see new places, not to walk back and forth over this same dull stretch of road." But Alice had already looped a strap around the

Slizz's neck by way of a lead. Back they went once more. The Slizzherd was asleep again and more surly than before at being awoken. Once again they started, looking behind them from time to time, but they saw nothing. Edgar's spirits began to rise again. By lunchtime they were well out in the broad blonde plain, and the sun had dried their fur. They found a grove by the road, and sat to rest and eat. Just as he was unwrapping his sandwich, Edgar caught, in the tail of his eye, a movement in the shadows.

"O hell!" he yelled. "It's that blasted Slizz again!"

It was. It came trotting and curled up in the grass at Alice's feet. Alice worked to calm her brother down. Finally she came up with a solution.

"It's too far to take it back again," she said, "and that herdsbear will do nothing to hold it. We'll let it follow to the next farmhouse, and explain our problem to them there. We'll ask them to keep it tonight and send it back in the morning."

Edgar could think of no better plan, so they carried it out. The bears at the farm seemed exceptionally slow to grasp what was wanted of them, until Edgar mentioned whose son he was, and produced a small piece of money. The two travellers saw the Slizz shut yarking in a shed, then went on their way. At Edgar's insistence they put a good ten miles between them and the farm, walking on for a few hours after dark, and then slept in a field of sweet timothy. At dawn Edgar woke with a cramp in his side, sat up, and stared in disbelief at the Slizz stretched out alongside Alice. She had an arm wrapped around it, and it was snoring.

They decided to let it follow them for a while. A few days' travel farther east they would enter a wooded upland and leave the open pastureland behind; and there, Edgar reasoned, the beast would quit them, rather than stray beyond the range of its usual food. But the Slizz was more intrepid than he had reckoned. Three days down the forest road, deep-sunk between huge leaning beech and oaks, and the little beast was still dogging their heels, a frond of fern trailing from its mouth. At times it would cough up some indigestible combination of mosses, fungi, and bark, but it found enough of what it needed to keep going. Later, when they took to the rivers in barges, it followed trotting along the tow-path, pausing at locks to browse on cresses. They had at one point to sail across the width of a very long lake; Edgar thought they had surely shaken the Slizz. But it had secreted itself in the hold, and there was carriage of kine and a spoiled sack of oats to pay for on the far shore. By this time Alice was getting ideas of her own about the beast.

The Slizz as a kind have a trait that is remarkable, indeed, unique: although they are languageless, and kept as cattle by the bears, every ten thousandth hatching will produce an individual capable of speech; whether because of some intellectual or some merely physiological superiority, Alice had never learned. Each year some score of Slizzherds are startled to hear one of their woolly charges return to them the rather injurious epithets that these pastors so freely mete out. From that point on the law admits no doubt or deviation. The speakable Slizz must be washed and clad; from then on it will be treated as no beast but as a creature and a citizen. It, or rather he or she, must now be despatched to the nearest city that holds one of the Colleges specially set up and endowed for the education of such anomalies. There they are brought to full language, taught their letters, and trained to one of the handful of trades legally open to them. The goldsmith's is common. Agile forepaws, intricate sensibilities, and a love for what is rich and rare often combine to direct their talents this way. Upon completing their studies, they are released into the custody of others of their kind, a small colony of whom exists at every major city of the Commonwealth, and at Bargeton the largest by far. Henceforth they are Slizz no longer, but known as Ceruk; if female, Cerugai. These words are borrowed from the Old Lacertic, a dialect of which the Ceruk have adopted so as to have a tongue of their own.

Nowhere else in the creaturely world is this amazing transformation seen. With this one exception the line that divides the speakable kinds from the dumb is absolute. Edgar and Alice had seen Ceruk in the City of Bears, but had never known or spoken with any; they had learned the rest in school. Alice's hope was that this Slizz, "her" Slizz, would eventually speak, and that she would hear its first words.

Edgar gently ridiculed the idea.

"If it had anything to say," he pointed out, "it would have said it by now. But it only opens its mouth to put something in it." His point was well taken; the Slizz—they were presently skirting a pond—was sampling lily-pad, a huge crescent of which hung from its mouth like a green bib. Nevertheless Alice stubbornly held to her contention. Often, at evening, when dinner was done, she would talk to the Slizz and try to raise topics that she thought might engage its nascent intellects, and provoke it to reply. But she had not met with the least success by the time they reached Bargeton.

Bargeton was huge, like nothing they had ever thought of before. It grew out of the fields that fed it. As they approached through the miles of tall corn, a glaring white knob appeared above the tasselled horizon, and rose, and rose with every mile they walked. It looked like a rough-hewn dome but was far too large. Then, slowly, a brick-red wall followed, and grew, and grew to the height of cliffs, and the slant cobalt stippling turned, as they came nearer, to shadowed casements. There was no symmetry about their placement, nor about anything else they could see, nor any proportion, nor hardly any limit. The closer they got, the farther Bargeton seemed to stretch to left and right, and if that great barrier turned a corner, they could not tell where. To make the task of imagining it still more difficult, Bargeton sent its business out to meet them; hours before they reached the gate they were being jostled in the press of creatures that thronged the road, all heavy-laden, most of them leaving the city. Edgar and Alice hardly had time to mark the moment they entered it, they were so preoccupied with fighting their way forward through the crowd; and now it was dusk, and the walls had lost what little form they had in the shadow and glare of sulfureous lamps, waving torches, blue flares, swinging lanterns. They were on a wide street jammed from wall to wall with creatures, whose strange cries and strange smells pressed on their nerves like unfriendly fingers on a sore place.

Edgar got them out of it. He had a good map sense, and he had realized that the great white mound they had seen from afar must be Citadel Hill, where their uncle Claudio lived. He took them by ways that led uphill to the right. Soon Alice grew aware of the huge mass of rock looming ahead of them. The ways wound and twisted ever more crazily as they got closer, till at last the streets all turned to staircases and started to climb.

They did not leave the crowds behind until they were well up the stairs. The streets had been alive with agitation and bustle; creatures, bent under burdens, had hurried down the lanes that they were coming up, and still they crossed a few whose hand-barrows, piled high with goods and offspring, came jolting down the steps out of the darkness above. This seemed like more than the normal frenzy of commerce to Edgar. He thought of the crowd surging out of the city gate, and wondered.

The stairs led to a street that flanked the hill, the street to more stairs. Then there were more streets and still more stairs, level after level of them. They had to climb to the very top. Edgar had thought to get there by suppertime, but it was long past that when he and Alice stood at last before their uncle's door in a narrow lane, both nearly fainting with hunger and fatigue, their calves like wood and their knees like wrung-out rags, their eyes feeling bound about with wire from staring at strange sights under lamplight. The outermost side of the lane showed the roofs, chimneys, and attic windows belonging to the houses of the next level down. Claudio's house presented no glorious facade but like its neighbors on either side showed six plain stories of smooth stucco, white in the light of the moon that had risen while they climbed. There were six windows to a floor, all shuttered. No other feature, no balcony or ornament, varied the surface of the housefront. They would never have known it without the bright brass 4 on the black door.

There was a bell-handle, and they pulled it. After a while they pulled it again. A tiny metal shutter opened with a screech, then closed with a snap. A series of clicks, clanks, and rattles issued from within, and continued long after Edgar had explained to Alice that locks were being undone, so long that he began to doubt his own explanation. Then the door opened an inch, and the tip of a snout, not a bear's, extruded itself and sniffed. The door opened wider. A porcupine stood on the threshold.

"O, so yer come at least, are yer," it snapped. "Get in, get in."

They raised their packs and stumbled forward, wondering at the brusqueness of this servant—for a servant they knew him to be, his kind being commonly so employed—when they heard a small commotion in the street behind them and, turning, saw half-a-dozen bears where none had been a minute before.

"Hoy, Antony!" one called, "When's your master going to give us some news?"

"Not tonight," the porcupine snorted. "Tomorrow, mebbe. Go home!" And he slammed the door and began to reset an amazing array of locks, bolts, chains, and bars.

The two young bears looked about them. The only light came from a single thick taper which the porcupine had set down on a table; it showed them little, but that little was luxury: a patch of bold tapestry, a silver ewer, a marble table-top inlaid with arabesque flowers. The vestibule was vast, the walls and ceiling out of sight. Edgar could not square its dimensions with those of the housefront.

"So," said the porcupine, rounding on them suddenly, "so now you know my name. Antony, *An*tony," he growled, pronouncing the name with such an inflection as a peremptory summoner might give it. "I'm his butler. Please to pick up yer feet and follow me." He paused and stared. "What's *that*!" he exclaimed in disgust. It was the Slizz he was quizzing with his little black eyes. The loyal beast had stuck to them through all the crowds and climbing, and had whisked in through Claudio's door after them. Edgar and Alice each groped for words of explanation in the fog of their weariness, but before they could frame a sentence, Antony sniffed and said, "Is it clean? Let it come! Follow me!" and, seizing the candle, marched hunch-shouldered away.

They followed after the sheaf of black-tipped quills, and the Slizz brought up the rear. Alice felt as if she and her brother had taken the place prepared for them in a little procession. There was to her wearied imagination something disturbingly tomblike about the dimensions of the noble, windowless corridors and galleries through which they passed. A somber magnificence of gilt and jet winked out at her as Antony's taper carved a wavering trail through the darkness. Behind her she heard a dry, quick, rhythmic tapping like a snaredrum-flutter, marking the Slizz's advance across uncarpeted marble. Her brother beside her was lost in thought. Alice guessed that he was puzzling about the house, trying to map it. She had long since given up on that, it was the kind of problem she left to Edgar, but she realized one thing with distressing certainty: they had not climbed any stairs, except for a short, formal flight leading up from the vestibule, and they must therefore be walking into the middle of Citadel Hill; and all that great white brow lay overhead.

They came to a pair of bronze doors set in a deep alcove. Their surface was alive with figures of salamanders in high relief, leaping and twisting among molded flames. They had to wait while Antony opened the doors. Alice sat down on the floor and went to sleep leaning on her pack. When Edgar shook her awake again, the doors stood open. Their inner side, plain and polished, dimly reflected her candle-lit form as she passed. She did not see how they were closed.

There followed much smaller rooms with soft carpeting. Then they came to steps: long, spiral courses up which the porcupine inexorably plodded. Alice strained after him, staring at the shapes woven into the stair-runner, vivid fish-forms that jack-knifed their way up the risers. Then they were at a wooden door, which Antony pushed open.

"Go in and wait," he said, and stumped off down the hall.

TWO. **Claudio's Robe.**

*T*he room they gazed into was long, low-ceilinged, brightly lit, and empty; still it invited them in. Bold and subtle colors danced on the surfaces of things. Through five high arches that pierced one long wall a garden air blew in; its freshness was edged with pungent smoke by the blaze on the hearth.

The carpet's moss-tinted pattern suggested a landscape seen from a great height. The mountainous forms of chairs dotted this fertile plain. They were such *caquetoires* as bears prefer: splay-legged, broad-seated, with high, narrow backs, and draped, every one, in cascades of alpine green. This color was varied, here and there, with a darker coniferous hue. There were also ridge-divans, sugarloaf-sofas, and *chaises longues* like glaciers' tongues; foothill footstools crouched nearby; tableland tables dropped their skirts in geological folds. From a spout in the wall a stream dropped to a small inland sea.

The coffered ceiling was painted indigo as a deep twilight sky. Fleecy arabesques of silver uncoiled there: clouds catching the moonlight. Within each coffer stars of inset crystal caught the winking fire; except above the greatest mountain of all, a throne half-encircled by a rosewood writing desk. There a long-horned moon dangled. The walls were panels, each frame containing a painted view: imaginary cities, unvisited forests, vast expanses of sand or ice.

The Slizz broke the threshold spell by trotting across the acreage, three fields to a step, to drink its fill from an estuarine gulf of the sea. Edgar and Alice ventured a few paces. Alice trod lightly, fearing for minuscule agriculturists. She did not dare to drop her pack.

Then a door opened and slammed shut, and Antony came at them, his short arms swinging at his sides, a huge, high-piled tray on his head. He halted by a rosy-hued mesa, stared at them, then pointed at the pool.

"Go wash. Then come eat," he ordered, and began to unload the tray. It was still on his head; he had to reach up to snatch articles from it. Since his arms were short, he stood on tiptoe as he reached, which of course did not bring the tray any nearer. Edgar splashed into the pool. Alice stepped in gingerly, thinking of flood-tides, but felt clean sand between her toes; she threw some water on her face. Drying themselves with a shake, they went to the mesa and sat on wind-carved chimneys of black rock. Antony served them swiftly; then he turned on his heel and waddled off, the empty tray careening wildly.

"*He*'ll be along soon," he said as he walked away. "If you want anything, shout. 'Antony, *An*tony!'" he bellowed, and was gone through a door.

Alice continued to look about her as she ate. Her eye was soon caught by a column of polished red wood that stood a few feet from the wall. It was shaped like a tree and rose to the ceiling. Its base simulated knotty roots, its capital an unravelling crown whose branches gradually changed color and shape till they melded with the beams of the coffering. Though the tree's trunk was straight and smooth, five feet from the floor it extended two limbs which formed a cross-bar.

Just as they were finishing their meal, they heard a noise of feet and raised voices in the passageway. They jumped up; the door shot open, and in stalked two bears in warm debate.

"Damn them, I won't have them here at all—not on any terms," one of the bears was almost shouting.

"Then you will have to deal with an invasion from without, and an insurrection within, and what you hope to use for soldiers is more than I can guess," replied the second. He was a jet-black bear, not old, brisk in his movements and erect where the other shambled; his eyes, flashing white as they darted about the room, soon found out Edgar and Alice, and fixed the intruders with a challenging stare.

"You have visitors, Claudio," he crisply declared.

The other, startled, followed his gaze. This was a much older bear, his tawny pelt streaked with grey. He squinted down at Edgar and Alice through a large pair of spectacles rimmed with green jasper. From his thick throat, ruffed in lace, all the way to the floor, his body was swathed in canary satin. It was embroidered with figures so lively that Alice could hardly attend to the wearer, her uncle, she so strongly desired to study the robe at closer quarters. The lower lip of its sleeves ballooned to the ground, and surely that was a whole watercourse of silver thread that fell in cataracts from shoulder to cuff. A glaucous ocean of needlework, roiling round the hem, surged as the bear stepped forward to take a nearer look.

"What the devil are these?" he muttered, not quite beneath his breath. Then his expression cleared. "Why, it is my brother's children, from the City of Bears: my nephew and my niece. Tell your names to Senator Julio, my loves, for I have forgotten them."

When they had done so, not without a qualm—it did not seem that their uncle had made those preparations for their entertainment that they had hoped for—the black bear smiled in a brief blaze of well-kept teeth, then turned again to Claudio.

"Not a very propitious time for a visit," he said.

"No," Claudio replied unhappily. "To tell you the truth, I had intended—you might as well know this, my dears, for it does not at all reflect upon my feelings for you or your excellent papa—I had meant to send to put you off. It is rather troubled times in Bargeton, just now. Another time, next year perhaps, would have been better." He stretched out a reassuring paw to each, and as he did so, a flock of fly-stitched parrots made as if to take wing from the elbow on Alice's side.

"Say last year," Julio grimly remarked. "Next year we may not be here."

"Why not?" asked Edgar, feeling it was time to claim his part in the conversation. "What is wrong?"

"Wrong?" replied Julio sharply. "Do you mean to tell me you have no idea? How did you come here? On foot? Got in today? And you didn't notice the horde of creatures fleeing the city, or stop to wonder what they were running from?"

"Wait a bit, my dear Julio," their uncle put in. "I must get settled and comfortable before we go any further. Antony, *An*tony!" he roared, a door slammed almost the same instant, and the porcupine, followed by two others, was once more racing towards them. But Claudio turned away from his servants. Going to the tree-column, he laboriously mounted its bunched roots, turned himself around to face the room again, and stretched out his arms. The two subordinate porcupines quickly scrambled up behind the tree, between it and the wall. Then they gently drew the embroidered robe from off their master's shoulders and arms, while Antony ducked this way and that, grunting terse directions. When Claudio was free from the garment, which seemed to grow larger and larger as it left him, he stepped back down onto the carpet, dressed now in plain but costly black with gold threads running through it. They all watched in silence while the servants carefully slid each of the robe's long sleeves onto one of the tree's branches. When this had been accomplished, and Antony had ceased straightening the precious fabric, Claudio clapped the two young bears on the shoulder.

"Come! Back to table, children," he said, smiling benignly, "and Senator Julio and I will join you, and have our little supper—and some wine—" he nodded at Antony, who whisked his underlings away—"and hear your news of the City of Bears. You see, I have put off the fearful magistrate and hung him up," he added, pointing to the robe lest they miss his joke, "and now I'm only your old uncle Claudio, for a while."

"If only the cares of office were as easily shed as the badge," remarked Julio, as they went to sit.

"For a while, they shall be!" Claudio energetically declared. "And here comes our food! Now, boy, how's your father?"

Edgar had not gotten very far when Claudio, interrupting, began to relate the days when their father and he were cubs together, and then went on to remember at some length how he, when scarcely older than Edgar, had come to Bargeton to make his fortune, and the various stages by which he had done so. None of it meant very much to Alice, nor, as it seemed, was it intended to. Since her uncle addressed himself exclusively to her brother, and Julio with equal singleness to his plate and cup (no very edifying spectacle), Alice felt free to direct her attention where she liked. It did not take long to settle on the robe.

It hung by the door, full and glowing; it spread its sleeves and loomed above the landscape of the room as if it held that world's forces captive in the images on its surface. The overwritten yellow satin shone with power.

Alice got up and went over to the robe. She inspected it from every side, even climbing onto the roots to peer at the collar and shoulders. She found herself comparing what she saw to the room, where three giants sat talking at their mountain, while a shaggy dragon stretched out along a promontory that thrust into the sea. This was a peaceful scene; not so the robe.

Nature's forces at their violent work were embroidered in many places. On the back of the skirt, a fleet of ships was driven along the hem by gusts of stumpwork. The ships' hulls were picked out in horizontal stitching of umber silk. They scudded toward crags undercut by curl-headed spouts. Across one shoulder a fire ate a forest, sending up overlapping billows of silver needlework, and threatening a city hard by the collar. The fleeing inhabitants, blue weasels, were caught in postures of dismay by sure feather-stitches. On the left pocket fat clouds, rimmed with violet bullion-knotting, shed snow on roebuck, who watched their grazing disappear. The snow whistled into drifts that overhung a jade swamp, home to a score of tiny, apprehensive frogs.

The robe was crowded with life. Indeed, the whole unseen population of Claudio's study appeared to have taken visibility there, to lead their lives among upheavals. By the banks of the great watercourse that tumbled down the right sleeve Alice could find: seven dog-sages laughing by a pool; a fishing rhinoceros; a baboon stepping into a boat just above a waterfall. It plunged, a shimmer of pale threads couched at long intervals, from wristband straight down that deep cuff. Then there were the parrots she had noticed on the other elbow, roosting with wings at half-spread on palm trees; those had been raised by the fishbone stitch. But Alice was most delighted when she found, sitting by a buttonhole, an olive salamander that wielded a bright needle and looked back at her.

The two breasts of the robe were covered with scenes which she thought must be drawn from Bargeton's history, but she did not have time to examine them closely. Julio had interrupted her uncle; he was speaking to her.

"Well, Miss Alice, you have looked long and hard at your uncle's robe. Seen any crimson bears on it?"

She turned. The big black bear was grinning at her. She shook her head. Edgar rose to the bait.

"There's no such thing as a crimson bear."

"Ha!" retorted Julio gleefully. "Nevertheless, the business your uncle and I have to talk about, if he's done with his memoirs, is crimson bears and nothing but crimson bears. Strange sort of business, eh?"

"There's a nursery rhyme about crimson bears," put in Alice.

"Is there! Well, let's hear it!"

Alice recited: "If a russet bear you see, Give him kind regards from me. But if you see a crimson bear, Throw some toad's-milk on his hair."

"I never heard that! Did you, Claudio? Odd little rhyme. What is *toad's-milk*, anyway?"

"Heavens, Julio, you know what it is," said Claudio. "The dyers use it on Slizz-wool, to counteract the dye. It's made from toadstools."

"O, I see. Rather technical, your little rhyme. But why is one to throw toad's-milk on a crimson bear, Miss Alice, do you suppose?"

"Because his color can't be real," Alice replied, resisting the temptation to add, "I would have thought that implication rather obvious."

"Ah! Because there are no crimson bears at all! Well, folk wisdom fails us here, I'm afraid. There most certainly are crimson bears. Some I have seen myself. Others—thousands of others, an entire army of others—are said to be marching on Bargeton at this very minute. They are extremely large, they have enormous teeth, and they are crimson. Where they come from, no one knows. They were first sighted northeast of here, across the Flood, where no bear of any color has business being. What they want appears to be this city. Why they want it is anyone's guess, but I think it's because we're rich. So now you know, Master Edgar, why everyone was running out of Bargeton, and why your arrival was untimely, and what it is your uncle and I have to sit up and talk about. Is that enough for you to take to bed, or do you want to hear more?"

THREE

The Crimson Bears.

"**M**y good Julio," Claudio protested, "I am not sure if I think this topic really suitable for young ears—"

"Don't be silly, they'll find out all about it soon enough. Much better hear it from bears they trust. It all began two months ago. A laundress, a bandicoot, went rowing across the river to pick some berries for making her soap. She climbed up the bank to the bushes that grow on the very edge of the desert, and was moving along through them, picking away, when she nearly walked into an enormous figure standing up to its shins in the sand. She says it was a bear, but one so large and menacing she could not even frame a proper greeting; she simply sketched out a courtesy and scuttered away. As she rowed back across the Flood, she recalled that the bear had been red—not a nice, normal russet like you, Miss Alice, but a deep blood-red. By the time she reached the shore the monster had developed huge teeth and black glittering eyes. He stared down at her without so much as blinking or nodding—as if, she said, he hadn't no power of speech. Probably he simply had never seen a bandicoot before. Anyway, she and her kind talked it all over around the mangle, and they decided to report the matter. She appeared before the Senate and quavered out her tale; I can't say any of us was impressed, because, as you yourself pointed out, Master Edgar, there is just no such thing as a crimson bear. And since those same berries she was gathering are also used to flavor a rather potent *eau-de-vie*, we thought, perhaps, some of that got mixed in her report, coloring it, as it were. But as the entire bandicoot community had become exercised about the business, and as they are hard-working, honest, loyal citizens, with none of the pretensions some other kinds entertain, we decided to take her story seriously and sent her back across the river with a squad of our civil guards. Well, they found no crimson bears, but they did find some very large footprints, sunk deep in the sand. They led away northward. The members of the Senate showed marvelous ingenuity in thinking up explanations for those prints, the next time we met. The most popular hypothesis was that the Clowncats—some of Bargeton's more disreputable characters—had played us a practical joke. We wound up praising the laundress' vigilance, and sent her home with a medal around her gullet.

"After that we forgot all about crimson bears. We had plenty of trouble to keep us busy: those Clowncats had been making a fuss since we threw one of their rowdies into the clink, and we had to deal with a flood of 'demands' from the Ceruk—do you know of them?—speaking Slizz with table manners. They've scraped together quite a few pennies in the gold trade and must, unfortunately, be paid heed to. So we had their long-winded delegations to hear, and their pompous depositions to read, and the Clowncats to keep in their place on top of that. So we really were sufficiently occupied without hunting for giants in loud coats."

The senator was hugely enjoying himself, Edgar thought. The black bear sat back on his stool, one leg crossed over the other, and made elegant flourishes with one paw as he spoke. His gaze rested just above his listener's head; you could not meet his eye. Alice was nodding and leaning. Claudio, who stared at his wine-glass, betrayed a certain restlessness during

Julio's narration. Now he suggested they move to more comfortable quarters before hearing the rest.

"Antony, *An*tony!" he shouted; Alice sat up with a jerk. Julio looked displeased. The porcupine and his two helpers arrived in a trice, crowned with trays onto which they all but tossed the supper-service, and then disappeared again.

Claudio led them down the room to the fireplace, where the sweet smoke lay heavy on the air. He brought them in between a pair of high divans, or rather two ranges of hills. They faced one another across a valley that opened towards the last arched casement. The hills were stepped in cushioned terraces. The various bluffs and escarpments wrought out by the upholsterer's needle were so clad as to create, here, a tweedy swath of ling, and there a velvet meadow; in another place the summer rains ran off a rock-face in shimmering moiré. Once inside the valley, Edgar found himself cordoned off by rounded peaks from the rest of the room. Only the archway loomed beyond the valley's mouth. Beside him, Alice fitted herself into a glen between two swellings of heath, and fell asleep.

"Now, do go on," murmured Claudio to Julio. "My nephew is eager to hear the rest of your story; but speak softly, won't you, my dear fellow." And he pointed to Alice sleeping, and smiled a fatherly smile.

Julio sprawled along one range of hills like a colossus at ease; his black feet canted up above one furzy knob, his black ears above another.

"It was just a week later we received a message from the Thoog," he continued. "Know what they are?" Edgar shook his head. "Well, if you cross the Flood and then turn upriver, after a few weeks you come to a savannah that stretches north and east no one knows how far. Very dry, yellow country, not much more fertile than the desert itself, but adequate grazing for some kinds of beast. There the Thoog live: saurians is what they are, big reptiles, big as bears. They keep to no fixed place but range all across that country, driving their flocks of wingless, sightless *avox*; these birds serve as steeds and as meat. The Thoog weave clothes from their long feathers, and no doubt use the bones as well, being a canny tribe who waste nothing. In winter they go down to the skirts of the desert, in the summer they troop far to the North. There they graze the avox on pastures near the great redwood forests. In the normal course of things we have little to do with them. Most bears don't trust them; for one thing, they smell rather high. But they also own a reputation for ruthless ferocity that is not completely undeserved. Like most nomads they feel their honor very keenly; they make no secret of their dislike of mammals. Having little use themselves for cities and city-dwellers, they consider us flabby and deceitful—a view that also has something to be said for it. In winter you can find a Thoog or two in Market Square, trading the feather shawls their females weave for such small luxuries as they permit themselves. But most lead austere, rather military lives; salt is a big treat, sugar unheard of.

"I travelled up that way once, when I was a bit younger than you," he went on. Edgar noticed how Julio's whole demeanor changed then. His gaze fell from the ceiling to meet Edgar's; he smiled. "I went with my father. He was one of Maximo's sergeants, a veteran of the Battle of Bargeton. He never got over the habit of shifting from camp to bivouac, so he turned pedlar. He tramped off to every point of the compass with a few avox to carry his sacks. He didn't often venture towards Thoogland—they're not very welcoming to strangers—but from time to time he needed a new bird. One time he took me along. I sat beside him as he bargained, trying not to choke on the stink in the tent. The Thoog were civil enough, but *I* simply didn't exist. As for my feeling about them, I found them less like creatures than mountains, which in their robes they rather resemble. They cover themselves up head to foot, except for their snouts and their claws. Those are their weapons—teeth and talons—but otherwise they look like hewn rock or cast metal; at least when they're still. And they don't move much. But one day I watched them ride. It was a feast-day, and there were all sorts of races. You have never seen such riders. They stretch themselves out on those birds' backs till you can't tell which is which, and they *fly*. They also perform acrobatics a-fowlback. You'd think they were made of rubber and weighed nothing. The Thoog have huge, heavy tails, you see, but they use them as counter-weights. I've seen one hike out from the flank of its galloping bird and snatch in its jaws a bone ball hung a good six feet away.

"They do another trick, it's really a test of their prowess. They mount a bird that's all plucked, and ride a mile-long course. And as they ride it, they eat the bird bite by bite. They must tear bits from every part of its body, taking care not to cripple or kill it till they cross the finish line. This demands that they swing themselves every which way while preserving perfect trim and a straight course at top speed. Never since have I seen such agility, such grace."

"Sounds like rather a grisly sport to me," remarked Claudio.

"Barbaric, certainly, but beautiful," Julio retorted. "And it's not done for fun. As I said, it's a test. The males must pass it to become full members of the tribe. The consequence is, there are no soldiers like them. Bears, even Maximo's army, look like puddings next to Thoog. Heaven help us if we ever have to fight them."

"Well," said Claudio thoughtfully, "I suppose that's what we have walls for."

"You can't always sit behind walls in a war. However, this is not getting my story told. Where was I?"

"Skaling's message."

"Right you are." Julio's eyes once more rose to the segmented welkin. His voice took on the same dry lilt as before; Edgar listened only fitfully. He was very tired, and wanted to go to sleep. Above all he did not want to hear more about the Thoog. He did not want to know about them, he could make no sense of Julio's admiration. To eat your steed as you rode him: this offended Edgar more than anything he'd ever heard. Julio prated on, and Claudio commented shortly from time to time. The Thoog were somehow tied up in the business. Edgar began to inch his back up the slope of the divan. Gradually he realized that neither his uncle nor the senator was paying him the least attention; then he turned and scrambled to the padded ridge. He wanted to look at the room again.

He liked this room immensely. It was clean, bright, and endlessly various. He felt very glad of the walls dividing it from the waste lands. If he saw no more of Bargeton than this room, the trip would have been worthwhile. He wished he could take a closer look at the scenes on the panels, at the robe.

Now the Crimson Bears were back in Julio's story. Too tired to follow it closely, Edgar still could not hold it completely at bay. To his great discomfort, the story worked into his survey of the room and spread across the carpeting, where he was forced to watch it enacted. A vein of blue wool, meandering through the woven lands, became the river Flood, and all that side of it lying towards the windows, the eastern shore. Thoog were abroad there, driving their flocks. Then from the darkness through the archways, in tramped the phalanxes; these crimson arrowheads aimed towards the river in the rug whose deep pile, ruffled by the night breeze, evoked tall grasses pushed about by oceans of free air. Now darting atomies hurtled towards the bloody wedges. From every corner of the plain the agile specks came riding, converging upon the enemy, circling tighter and tighter. Then a clash; out in the garden a shrill bird supplied the battle screams; then the Thoog-motes dispersed, and the wedges came on again. This time the phalanxes turned till they aimed for Edgar. He dropped back down into his seat and lay there by Alice, eyes closed. He had been robbed of the joy of the room; now he wanted to put everything away from him.

But the voices still rolled around his brain. The Crimson Bears had defeated the Thoog and were marching on Bargeton. This news had been brought by a Thoog-lord. His name had been mentioned; then he heard it again—Lord Skaling. Lord Skaling wanted help from the Bargeton bears, and advice. Julio was appalled. The Thoog had never been known to ask for help! The Crimson Bears must be formidable indeed. And their goal was Bargeton, to which they'd come closer than even the Thoog had supposed. There was the bandicoot-laundress' story, but worse had followed. While the Senate had temporized with Lord Skaling, a whole squad of Crimson Bears was sighted across the Flood. Julio and Claudio themselves had seen them, from an upper window of trained; they had not the size for it. Hadn't the Thoog tried their strength against them, and failed? The Thoog, premier soldiers of the world! So what could be hoped from a rabble of mole-booksellers, owl-plasterers, and caféwaiter stoats?

The Thoog must be admitted to the city and allowed to man its walls and their gaps. Lord Skaling's own regiment stood by, across the Flood, ready to undertake this duty at once, should the bears consent. Edgar, almost weeping, heard Julio declare that this offer could not be refused.

"Damn it, why not?" the senator snapped, for Claudio had been making weary little shakes of the head all during the black bear's peroration.

"My dear Julio, you know why not. I have no new reasons to adduce. I simply do not trust the Thoog, nor want them in control of Bargeton."

"They are perfectly honorable!" Julio began to shout, but Claudio cut him short with a click of the tongue.

"They are also perfectly hostile to mammals. By their own account they have taken a drubbing from one set of bears; what makes you so sure they will not want to ease their minds by passing along their shame to us?"

"Then you would hand the city over to the Crimson Bears?"

"The Crimson Bears are bears, when all is said and done. There is some common ground; we must share some blood and instincts with them. There may be some accommodation to be made."

"Bah! Accommodation with savages?"

"If not, we still need not stand alone."

"O, come off it, Claudio. You're not looking for help from the City of Bears? It will take them months to get here, and what will they send? More lawyers? There are no more soldiers since Maximo died."

"Well, I was not thinking of the City of Bears, no. As you say, they would come too late, although a fleet sent up the Flood . . . but you are right. No, I had other help in mind, to tell the truth."

"What help? Do you think to hire a regiment of rats to nip at their enormous heels?"

"I'll tell you, my dear fellow. It has seemed to me that we ought to trust ourselves to our own kind. This is a contest of bears against bears; bears must resolve. Now perhaps you can guess in what direction my thoughts have turned?"

"I can't for the life of me imagine."

"Why, I would have thought it obvious. We must look to the Great Golden Bear."

Edgar jumped to his feet. Alice stirred and awoke, looked dazedly about her.

"Why, for goodness sake, look at these children still awake at this hour," said Claudio, holding up his paw to silence Julio, who stared at him agape. "We must see them put to bed at once." He loudly called for Antony.

"Antony, Antony," came an answering grumble almost at once.

"The Great Golden Bear!" murmured Julio. "You want to send for *him*?"

"Yes," replied Claudio shortly. "Indeed, I have already done so. I expect him here tonight. It was to meet with him and hear his views that I asked you home with me. But we will discuss this business presently. Good night, my dears," he blandly smiled to the two young bears. "I am sorry I could not have given you a more . . . uncle-ish sort of welcome.

Antony will take you to where you can get a good, long rest. Tomorrow we must begin to think about sending you home. You know which room they are to be put in?"

"Yes," said Antony. "Go get your gear, then follow me."

They picked up their packs where they had set them down.

"Not that way," Antony barked. "Over here." Edgar had taken a step towards the door they had come in by. Beside it the gleaming robe spread its arms to bar his way. He turned and followed the major-domo around the flanks of the throne-desk past the pool.

"Edgar, where's the Slizz?" asked Alice suddenly. Indeed, the beast had disappeared; Edgar had not seen it go. His mind was now so full, he could hardly spare it a thought.

"It can't have gotten far," he said. "Go tell Antony." He wanted to be alone. Alice trotted ahead to speak to Antony and stayed beside him for the whole twisting voyage they made along back corridors and narrow stairs. At last there were only stairs, and he was plodding up and up them. His tired brain swarmed with images. Amidst them all one stood out: red giants, mounted reptiles, and the Great Golden Bear approaching Bargeton's gates.

FOUR. **The Citadel Gate.**

*A*lice awoke once during the night, feeling her legs pinned. She was about to give her brother a kick, but then she saw that the Slizz had come back. It was lying at the foot of the bed, and its weight had pulled the bed clothes tight across her knees. It blinked at her as she stirred.

She lay in an attic room, running her eye up a roof-post into vaulted darkness. The bed was in the middle of the room; the room was square; three walls had windows open wide. The light of the stars shone in, illuminating a wash-stand at the intersection of three shadows. Two of them were faint, but the third struck upon the floorboards distentions of ewer, bowl, and pot. The moon shone on her right hand. When Alice had washed, she looked out, but nothing attended the moon's sinking but flat emptiness. She crossed to the window opposite the bed and looked down upon a jumbled roofscape, hard to comprehend; so she turned her attention to the last window, that toward which the densest shadow pointed.

There was a balcony, and she stepped onto it. Below her a sea of tree-tops swelled into spikes and shifting domes. This sea spread throughout a vast enclosure around which many houses, including Claudio's, formed an unbroken ring. The thin moon bathed a white wall of distant stories, picking out loggias and gables, terraces and turrets. Though a full mile away, these features appeared distinctly in the clear dry air.

The ground was far beneath her. Fountains in many places caught and played with the light. Alice looked directly down into a garden room proportioned like a shoebox, three walls keeping out the forest; the fourth lay in the house's shadow, but windows let in light from some late-watcher's room. There were bushes in tubs on the raked sand; there was a little pool, and in one corner what she took for a colossal statue of a bear, till it stirred. Then two other forms stepped out into the garden, one black, one glimmering, both casting bear shadows: Julio and Claudio in his robe of state. The third bear dwarfed them. Alice had never seen anyone so large or so bright. His shags caught the ruddy light from the house and turned it into flames. With each movement he made they flared and died. This must be the Great Golden Bear, but just as she thought to wake Edgar, the three walked back into the house.

Edgar was furious when she told him about it in the morning. He rushed out onto the balcony and craned over its broad coping. Alice, beside him, surveyed with sleepy interest the green world circumscribed by lofty mansions. Where under the moon's light she had seen only trees, now she noticed many sizable buildings dotting the enclosure, and even discerned near its center a crossing of wide avenues. Bears in gay robes were pausing to salute one another. Other bears now began to emerge onto balconies and terraces. With a startling clatter the shutters flew open on a window not far off; a tubby old gentlebear waddled onto his balcony, which so matched the one where she and Edgar stood, Alice supposed it must belong to Claudio. He was followed by porcupines who managed to lay three trays of steaming breakfast upon a tiny table. The gentlebear made Alice a courtly bow, then sat down and faced away.

With a snort of annoyance Edgar stalked to the next window. Alice knew better than to intrude upon his waking humors, and crossed the room to the other window.

She found herself looking east, toward the rising sun. Beneath it stretched a coarse sheet brushed with ocher wash and touched by a green nib: this was the desert. The breeze and the heat conjured glittering twists that whirled for a second and dissolved. At the limit of sight a blonde ocean surged into dunes.

Her brother joined her at the window, as she knew he must; he was no hoarder of miseries. For a while he looked at the desert in silence. Alice awaited some severe utterance. Then Edgar pointed down at the far bank of the Flood.

"Look at that line of bushes," he said. "That must be where the bandicoot saw the first Crimson Bear." He said this in such a here-our-troubles-began sort of way that Alice peered where he pointed. They looked like ordinary enough bushes. To tell the truth, she was rather hazy about these Crimson Bears, though she remembered hearing them spoken of; but she reckoned that Edgar would soon be more forthcoming, and turned her gaze another way. Her eye travelled back across the Flood to the near shore, pausing a moment on the broad, smooth sheen of the river, hardly at all like water as she knew it, the wind-chopped bay at the City of Bears. There was little enough of fabled Bargeton between the river bank and the orange tiles that fanned out below her window. But beyond the lowest roof she could see houses arrayed on a noble square opening on the river. A double row of trees lined the bank. Each house rose in tiers, like a cake, to some fanciful pinnacle: a campanile, a widow's-walk, a slotted observatory dome. The houses stood free from one another, yet were somehow joined at the ground floor. There, scores of doorways let onto the square, many more doors by far than houses to be entered. Alice grew confused till she realized that what she had taken for doors was really an arcade. Then the rest of the puzzling picture fell into place: behind the arcade the houses abutted; the whole ground floor surrounding the square was roofed with a terrace; and the free-standing higher stories grew up from this. It was an intriguing plan. The terrace would be common to all the residents of the square, yet more private than the open agora below. Under the arches the shade must be cool at noon; perhaps the ground floor was all shops; she wondered what they sold; it seemed an agreeable way to live, with the sun and breeze off the river.

Beside her Edgar was fidgeting in such a way as to claim her attention. "What did you see?" she asked him, and then submitted to being led to the middle window to have things explained to her. This window looked northwards (so Edgar claimed) over the tops of the next few houses and towards a slice of Bargeton that lay along the river; not a very wide slice, for the Flood here opened into a great half-moon basin cut from the city side to make a port. While Edgar pointed out the shipping, the river, and the desert, all fairly unmistakeable objects, Alice looked at the picture in her own way and saw how it split into a foreground of white and orange planes and a denser-textured background of city, river, desert. The city-swath contained forms too distant for particularity. Only the thick brake of masts pointed, a sign that read "shipping." Miles upriver, above the houses, if those were still houses, loomed an enormous bluff, if bluff it was; a certain regularity suggested that it might be a building, ancient, stained, and that the poor beast had had nothing to eat since their arrival, and further, that it was not house-trained. Into the feelings of compunction that now overtook her there crept a certain calculating coolness, as she reflected that the Slizz should be taken outside. Perhaps they would be able to explore the park within the ring of houses. She was choosing the right words to suggest this, when Edgar suddenly blurted out,

"Antony, is the Great Golden Bear still in the house?"

"Not he," said the porcupine shortly, between puffs. "Got business."

"And my uncle?"

"Him too." And Antony once more fell silent, except for the horrible sucking of his pipe.

"But surely we don't have to stay in the house all day?" cried Edgar.

"I really think we ought to take the Slizz outside," added Alice meaningfully. Antony swung round, leaned against the balustrade, and fixed the Slizz with a baleful eye.

"What you want one o' them for a pet for?" he gruffly asked; but, as no reply other than beseeching looks came from the two young bears, he took his pipe out of his mouth and grudgingly went on. "All right. Here's what I been told about you two. It's bad in the city. Them Crimson Bears got everybody running. Everyone's either locking up or leaving. That ain't all of it neither. That Clowncat. You may have heard him spoke of. The one we had locked up in the cells for a rowdy and a rebel. Someone come along last night and let him out. Now them cats will be up to trouble too. The Ceruk may join in with it. That's what yer uncle's worried about, anyways. He's off to tend to all that today; you won't see him. I'm to look after you, he says. Yer not to be let out into the city. But," he added, softening a little at their evident dismay, "you don't have to stay in the house. You can come and go within the Citadel, 'slong as yer back for supper at sundown."

After a pause Alice asked, "How do we get there?"

"Get where?" replied Antony, pipe in mouth.

"Into the Citadel."

The porcupine stared through the thick smoke that billowed from the bowl of his pipe.

"Yer don't have to *get* there. Yer in it now," he simply said while the smoke coiled sardonically, then humped like a shrug and dispersed. "This here," he went on, "is Citadel Hill. So called on account of the Citadel what is on it."

"But citadels are fortified places," Edgar protested. "We didn't pass any sentries on our way up here last night. There wasn't even a wall."

"No *wall?*" exclaimed Antony. "D'yer mean to say, Hisself never spoke to you about no wall? What, never a word, eh? Filled yer ears with tales of Crimson Bears and Thoog, and never mentioned the good stout wall yer got 'twixt them and you? Ah, so he left it to me, then. I see. Antony, Antony," he sourly muttered. "All right, get washed up, while I load this here tray. I'll show you the way out into *that*," jerking a thumb back over his shoulder at the broad enclosure, "and I'll show you the wall and the gate." And he began to toss crockery onto the tray.

He led them to a pair of great bronze doors at the end of a gilt reception room many flights below their bedchamber.

"The gate," he announced. He grasped a wall sconce as if it were a lever, and pulled it smartly down. The doors swung easily inward. Their other side was wrought out in writhing salamanders; Alice exclaimed,

"We came through these doors last night!"

"This," said the porcupine sententiously, "is where you two first set foot inside the Citadel of Bargeton. Now as to that wall what you inquired about," he went on to Edgar, "that wall is here. You will note the twenty-odd foot what must be traversed afore yer properly in the next room. Them twenty-odd foot is the thickness of the Citadel Wall."

"It lies inside the house!" cried Edgar.

"Inside the house. From cellar to roof. From one side to the other side. Cuts the house right in half; this here's the only way in or out. But does the wall stop at the party-walls 'tween this house and the ones on either side, no it does not. It continues. It cuts them two houses in half as well, and then it cuts in half the two beyond them. Where does it stop, it doesn't stop. This here wall," he said impressively, "continues right round the ring of superior residences what enclose the Citadel Gardens, them what you seen from off yer balcony. Right through the heart of all them houses runs this wall twenty-odd foot thick. One hundred houses—one hundred gates. No other way to get in or out. Now, as to guards, there's a team of vigilant owls, creatures noted for their night vision, what take it in shifts to watch upon each gate from a secret hiding place. Anyone comes trundling up that hall out there, the owl rings a bell, and I gets out of bed—Antony, Antony—and come along to see who it is." He raised the sconce again; the doors swung closed with a little sigh. "Now take that Slizz out into the gardens afore it fouls my carpets. I got work to do."

The gardens, once Edgar and Alice were in them, seemed rather marvelous, and if they had been older or younger, they could have easily contented themselves with this confined little world, secure in the great hidden wall that ringed them round. But having tasted the pleasures of wandering at large, they were now eager to explore the city they had come so far to see. Edgar had gotten over his tremors. He wished no more than last night to encounter Thoog and Crimson Bears, but Alice and he were to be sent home, it seemed. He longed to go while he could to see sights that would surprise him. Intricately beautiful though the Citadel Gardens might be, they would not surprise him. Alice could have told him why, for she figured it out in the first half-hour of their aimless ramble. She stood on a sculpted knoll, as the Slizz cropped herbs, and looked around at the circle of houses, and saw how much it resembled the City of Bears. At home, the mansions of the well-to-do grew out from caves in the hillside to form handsome pavilions and porticoes. These opulent homes studded the flanks of the demi-bowl that contained the bay. On a clear day each was visible to each, and flew a family pennant that flapped in the breeze. At night one could number the lights and group one's neighbors into constellations. So here likewise the houses turned on the city a featureless false front, reserving their splendid faces for one another alone. From the little world they gazed into, all were excluded but wealthy bears and their servants. But Alice had come to Bargeton to see the lives of other kinds, and to taste of the city's variety. So as they ambled she pumped her brother for an account of all he had learned the previous night about those creatures with the exciting names.

The gardens were cut up by walls and hedges and high-mounded ha-has into a series of rooms, each kept as tidy and fresh as a salon. Each continued some master stroke of artifice. One held an orchard of twisted trees that bloomed in a violet so dark it looked black; another was paved in interlacing colors of cobbles. One room held a pool choked with weeds in which a quincunx of stained bronze frogs revolved, squirting. Many rooms had pools and fountains and statues. Some of the statues startled them by moving: a flamingo raised a copper hat as they passed by, an enamelled dolphin switched its tail. A leopard made a stiff pas-de-chat, and then, as they halted, extended a paw as if to point their way. Edgar, when he recovered speech explained to Alice that they were driven by water.

They met few other bears in the gardens. On one sward a dozen cubs frolicked demurely, while their nursemaids gossiped in the shade. Here and there they came across badger-groundskeepers plying trowels and shears. Along an alley of stately old limes a number of stately old gentlebears stopped them, asked their names, and having heard them, welcomed Claudio's nephew and niece to the Citadel; never to Barge-ton. "Your uncle's a capital fellow," they all said. "Haven't seen him today. What's he up to?" Edgar and Alice politely replied that they did not know, then took their leave. As they turned a flowering corner, the Slizz would pop out of the shrubbery; it seemed shy of bears older than they.

Some of the garden rooms contained small buildings; some were roofed in glass. Sometimes in passing from room to room they had to go down a tunnel with doors, and it was not always a simple matter to tell which one led to the next lawn or glade. In fact, it became all too possible to confuse the indoors with the out-of-doors, they so intermingled. After only a few impulsive choices, Edgar and Alice found themselves roaming the corridors of a strange house, one they had never been conscious of entering. The elderly porcupina they met at last, dusting the stuffed fish in a long room, greeted them courteously, but she was so deaf they could not make her understand their questions. To escape her respectful ducking and bobbing, they continued into the next room. This was a hall occupied by glass cases displaying single shoes. They were sorted, it seemed, by the kind of foot, paw, hoof, claw, or trotter each was designed to fit; thus in a few minutes, as she passed among the cases, Alice saw eagle-buskins like gloves, a shrew's dancing pump (beneath a magnifying lens), a fastidious mud-turtle's chopine, and the heavy, zigzag wooden boot of a fox-postilion. At the far end of the hall they recognized a pair of great doors, one of the Citadel's hundred gates. They were closed.

Just as they turned to retrace their steps, one of the doors shifted with a groan; then with ear-rending tremors they opened to reveal, first, a straining porcupine, who set his shoulder to each in succession, and then, behind him, a file of blindfolded monkeys. At length the doors stood half ajar. The porcupine led his charges through, each grasping the tail of the one before; they were monkey-merchants from the southern jungles, clad in ballooning trunk-hose and slippers with curling toes. They chattered noisily as they bumped among the display cases. The porcupine usher had so much to do with keeping them on a steady course that he never noticed Edgar and Alice. At the entrance to the room of stuffed fish he called to his fellow-servant, the porcupina with the duster:

"Hey, there, old Mab! Come lead these guests up to the Opal Parlor so's I can go close they dratted gates!"

"Eh?"

"Guests! Opal Parlor! These here monkeys! You take them on up to master! GUESTS TO MASTER!"

"Can't dust no faster nor what I'm doing now, dern you. Like to know why yer playing party games with all them fancy apes in here, anyway. Get 'em out, afore one of 'em puts his foot through they eels!"

The guide made a plosive noise expressive of vexation, and dragged the file of monkeys brusquely through the room, calling out over his shoulder, "Mind the gate!"

"The skate?" She gave a few indignant flicks of her duster to the evil-looking ray mounted in simulated flight above a tub of sand. "Why, he's just where he should be. Who said he was missing?"

While Edgar and Alice were still smiling at this exchange, they felt a small commotion at their feet. Looking down an instant later, they did not find the Slizz. They hunted for it in every direction. At last Alice cried out: "There!" An olive blur winked among the shoe-cases halfway down the hall. The two young bears pursued it, but by the time they reached the spot where they had last seen it, the Slizz was standing on the very threshold of the Citadel. As they rushed towards it, it blinked its gold-flecked eyes, twitched its tail, and disappeared between the half-open doors.

FIVE. **Through the Market Square.**

*W*ith only a second's hesitation they stepped through the portal and ran down the long, dark hall that lay just outside the Citadel of Bargeton. Its walls were panelled in pier-glass to the floor; three pairs of candle-stands, crowded with smoking tapers, stood at intervals of twenty feet down its length; thrice, therefore, they glimpsed a line of Slizz spread out to left and right, loping away from them with sprightly step.

They followed through room after room. Though they had broken their uncle's prohibition, they could hardly be in any danger while they were still in a rich bear's house. So they jogged down tapestried corridors and smoky staircases, following the ever-receding brush of olive wool, and were surprised to round a huge stone column and find themselves blinded by sudden daylight. And when their eyes had grown accustomed to the brilliance pouring in through an open door, they looked out and saw the Slizz in the street. It stood gazing back at them, then set off to the left at a smart trot.

They could not pause; they had to follow. The city was no place for a silly beast raised in the open fields. For all they knew, there might be creatures out there who would look upon Slizz in the light of dinner. Besides, they had already disobeyed Claudio. To continue would add nothing to their crime, nor to their punishment, since it had already been decreed that they should be sent home. At least they might take a look at the city till suppertime. Then the worst they had to fear was a scolding from old Antony, who could hardly grow much more cross than he already was. So they set out in pursuit.

Though they sprinted after the nimble little beast, it easily kept its lead; they never came within ten feet of it. For a while it held to the middle of the street that ran around the brow of Citadel Hill, but just as they had begun to hope they would not have to chase it down one of the long flights of stairs, the Slizz jogged sharply to the right and dived downhill. As quickly as they dared, they followed down a staircase so steep that a house on its margin might have three front doors stepped each above each and opening into as many "ground floors." Through open archways they caught rapid views, as they dashed by, of courtyards where hens pecked or flapped in the dust. They glanced into black holes of cellars from which there wafted a sour smell of wine-lees or an earthy savor of mushrooms; once a goat's pale face thrust out of the darkness at them. Just a few steps below that cellar's little low door they glimpsed through a gap in the wall a rooftop where washing, faded and shapeless, was strung up between two dusty orange trees in tubs.

All this while they saw few bears and met none on the stairs to whom they could cry out to hold the Slizz; in any case, they hardly had breath for such a cry; both Edgar and Alice were gulping air and clutching their sides. Still the Slizz ran undulating downwards, pouring itself as easily from step to step as if it had been a mat of olive weed borne on a torrent.

They had crossed eight or nine transverse streets, and descended as many hundreds of stone steps, when a building grew up across their path, and they hoped they might have

51

reached bottom and trapped the fugitive in some cul-de-sac. But the staircase plunged them precipitously down a tunnel that opened beneath the house, so that they carried on the chase amidst slapping echoes and a musty smell of mold. By now, Edgar reckoned, they had gone down further by far than they had climbed the night before. He was growing increasingly anxious, and wanted to turn back; but they still had met with no one, and the Slizz still hopped from step to step just as far ahead as they could see. It was not quite dark in the tunnel, whose ceiling was pierced at intervals by shafts that let down a little light swimming with flecks and twists of ash. The stairs were slick and crumbling. In places the larger holes were patched with broken boards that tilted when they set their feet down on them. Two hundred steps down, they began to see heavy iron-studded doors that muffled sounds of hammering, grinding, shouting; along one stretch, of frantic gobbling squeals. A greasy glow bloomed from iron-grilled slots. Circular openings low in the tunnel wall would cough and emit a noisome, viscous flow into the gutters.

Still they kept going. The further they descended, the darker, danker, chillier the tunnel grew, till Edgar began to wonder if they had missed the city altogether, and dropped straight from the lofty hill into some cellar world. Now lateral tunnels began to open to left and right. He prayed the Slizz would not veer off down one of them, for he had in his mind the image of endless ramifying borings spreading beneath Bargeton, places where even Claudio's nephew and niece would not be wise to lose themselves. But the Slizz kept straight on down the steps. At the bottom it led them over a railingless span across a dark canal. They gagged on the reek as they threaded a path between holes in the rotten planking.

A layer of floating matter corrugated the surface of the canal; a barge, piled high with casks and tuns, cut a swath of unreflecting black.

Beyond the bridge the tunnel turned sharp right and debouched into another, much larger way. All at once they were caught and carried along in a rushing crowd. Crooked creatures were all around them: laborers jostled them with chitinous elbow and oily wing-case. Arms, jointed oddly, held burdens aloft. At many a door parcels were being loaded into panniers slung across the broad backs of scarabs. Edgar, with a quiver of disgust, watched the claws reaching from doorways to drop the bundles in, but Alice noted how the scarabs twitched their antennae at each fresh addition of weight, while patiently abiding their masters' pleasure. The parcels, she saw, wrapped forms of elaborate workmanship, and Alice caught many a glint of silver and gold amidst the folds and twine.

They had no choice but to go forward now, the press about them set onward so strong, though they had lost sight of the Slizz. Edgar was faint with fear and revulsion; Alice kept her wits well enough to record some of her impressions: the acrid fetor of these workmens' sweat; the dry rustle of their movements; a high sibilance just on the border of hearing, which seemed to have no distinct origin. The creatures seemed to pay no heed to her; she saw her image floating in no more than a few peripheral facets of their great compound eyes. They all were driving or driven, heavy-laden. Everywhere she looked, she saw burdens humped on rounded backs above a scurry of bent-stick legs. She wondered whom all these laborers carried for, as she guided her brother forward, his eyes screwed almost shut.

The young bears were nearly pulled by the crowd past the narrow side tunnel before they noticed the silvery patch of daylight shimmering at the end of it. They had to fight their way across the flood of traffic to reach the opening; when they finally stood there, they were winded from being so knocked about, and coated with gummy oils from brushing against so many bodies. But the light was all that mattered to them now, though Edgar could scarcely believe it was truly the light of day, they had plunged so deep below the hill. When they emerged into fresh air and sunshine, however, he was amazed to see that the city still lay beneath them. They stood on a sort of landing, and two long flights of steps were still to be descended before they stood in Bargeton's streets. Edgar looked out across three rows of houses to a vast open space flooded with the light of noon. Far to the left he saw stately buildings gleaming white. Far to the right he saw masts of ships and the winking of water in motion under the sun. Between buildings and ships, stretching away from him into unguessable distance, the ground was covered by an inconceivable throng of creatures. He was still staring at the pearly radiance made by the mingling of colored dots in that vastest of crowds, when Alice, peering down the stairs, cried out, "Quick, Edgar! There's our Slizz!" and dashed away down the steps.

A minute later they were at the bottom of the two flights. The street was choked with creatures, carts, and barrows. Then Alice saw the Slizz go wiggling between the legs of an ass, and they were off again. Through a narrow alley—across another street—into a majestic lobby where uniformed wolves prowled with pompous malevolence—up broad stairs—through a waiting room past knots of turbaned hyenas, who blinked at them before resuming their urgent, swooping colloquy of cackles—out what they thought was a window, through which the reckless Slizz had hurled itself—across a bridge above another street, in through another window—then dodging a legion of disgruntled stoats in black jackets and white aprons down the length of a dining room full of the hubbub of eating and drinking—down one last pair of stairs and out one final door—and they were standing on the verge of the Market Square, confronted by more kinds of creatures more frantically engaged in more varieties of business than either had ever witnessed before. But the little Slizz was nowhere to be seen.

Now Alice hung back, anxious to find the Slizz, terrified lest some harm might overtake the silly, affectionate beast that she had brought to Bargeton, yet seeing no way to insert herself into that vast crowd, wherein she hardly could make out individual forms, or tell merchant from buyer, or either from the wares being dickered over between them. She looked back at Citadel Hill, hoping to fix her position somehow, hoping also for a sight of something familiar, finally simply wanting to see an object far enough away to take on some distinctness of character. She saw it and knew it well enough, but the noon sun was burning in windows all around the great white dome, and they reminded her uncomfortably of the insect-carriers' eyes. She saw Citadel Hill then as the head of a great amorphous body, which was Bargeton. That head contained as many dreams as rooms; for all the glittering windows, there were more thought-chambers that never saw the light than ones, like the attic she had slept in, that let in sun and air. The hill had swallowed her whole; now she held back from the border of crowd, fearfully resisting her final ingestion into the gorged tissues of the city.

Edgar, for his part, was glad to be free from the tunnels that honeycombed the base of Citadel Hill. To him the packed market seemed rather inviting. He didn't at all mind the idea of getting good and lost there for a while; it was not as though one could possibly miss one's way back to the Citadel. Of course they had to search for their Slizz. He was not really as concerned for it as Alice was, reckoning that the worst that could befall the beast was to be thrust into some flock of its kind and so get itself sold. But he, as a carefully nurtured bear, was naturally sensitive to the welfare of beasts that could not speak, and all the more strongly so for one whom he and his sister had more or less adopted and made a pet of, even though it was only a Slizz. He had grown attached to it; its very contrariness in following them when they did not want to be followed, and running away from them when they did, had won from him a sort of admiration. But more than that, he knew how very upset Alice would be if they did not find it and bring it home. His last thought, far more cynical than his real feeling, was that the search for the Slizz would give some point to their wandering about the colorful turmoil of the great bazaar. Besides, he felt hungry, and wanted to inspect some of the hundreds of foodstalls whose smokes, charged with savors, drugged the air above the sea of creaturely heads. So he took his sister resolutely by the paw and led her up to the wall of massed bodies. He cast about this way and that, searching for a breach that would admit them, but the crowd on this side of the Market Square was packed so densely that a space opening between any two volumes of bargaining creature was sure to be promptly filled by a party to yet another transaction, if not by the goods themselves. They came up at last behind a pair of bulky buffaloes arguing with a sea elephant who sprawled in a tub of brine, surrounded by baskets of coral and amber, as well as select ornaments in mother-of-pearl. In the course of a few minutes' histrionic haggling the buffaloes tossed their long, low-curling horns, and made as if they meant to lumber around and plod away, while the wallowing merchant mimed immense indifference. Edgar seized the chance thus offered and pulled Alice after him through the gap and into the crowd.

It took them half an hour to squeeze their way a hundred yards forward; Alice was certain she would be crushed or trampled, and only Edgar's teasing and the thought of the hapless Slizz kept her going after an elephant nearly put his hind foot down on her. But thereafter the press thinned out a little. They found a cart from which a civil-spoken tapir was selling cakes made with honey and ground nutmeats, which raised her spirits, though she had to turn her back on the noisy gormandizing of some long-lipped gazelles. When the two young bears had thus refreshed themselves, they joined a circle around a troupe of dancers who had cleared a patch of ground with cries and shoves and now were swaying sinuously in a ring. The dancers were apes from the North; their silver-white hair grew long and fine from every part of their bodies, and floated about them like veils as they danced. One of their number scraped endless arpeggios from two little fiddles, fingered with his feet and bowed with his hands. Just as the pace of the music grew hottest, and the apes were beginning to hurl themselves in the air and tumble down on the ground, Alice clutched at Edgar's arm, for she thought she had seen, in a split second's gap before a fringe of silver hair fell across it, the tapering olive muzzle of their Slizz.

For the next two hours Edgar and Alice moved across the Market Square in circuitous ramblings broken by starts as they bore down on the spot where Alice most lately imagined that she had seen the Slizz. It was never there when they arrived. Edgar often was able to point out what it was that had deceived her eye. They had stood amidst a cloud of glossy ravens, all trying to shout them into the purchase of sundry lurid rugs. The ravens displayed each rug by grasping its corners and rising into the air with a furious clatter of wings, never ceasing to hoarsely extol the fine points of the article's knotting and the brilliance of its colors. In the midst of all this clamor Edgar still managed to show Alice how the humped folds of a moss-green rug lying rolled up on the ground did a little resemble the line of a Slizz's back. In the same way, Alice gave some momentary annoyance to a peacock driving a brisk trade in tiny tree-frogs. He claimed they were trained to sing. The peacock kept the frogs in spheres of osier stuffed with frondage, and offered them as pets to water-rats off the barges. His neighbor, a gopher selling footwear, likewise had to break off his patter when Alice ran around both merchants in figure eights, crying out that she had seen her Slizz's eyes. In actual fact, it had been nothing but two of the golden ovals in the peacock's tail. Alice had glimpsed these "eyes" reflected in the mirror the gopher had set up on the cobbles for a caribou customer, that he might consider the spectacle of his hoofs and pasterns encased in galoshes. Another time, Alice muscled through a party of touring wombats and left them in stertorous confusion behind her, as she descended on a vaguely tail-shaped feather duster being demonstrated by a raccoon. Edgar had to make their apologies all around. He found the whole business not a little embarrassing.

Still, though they zigzagged from side to side of the Market Square, rebounding between the Flood's embankment and the stately buildings opposite, the spasms of their search carried them ever northward, away from Citadel Hill. Edgar looked over his shoulder from time to time, to reassure himself that he would be able to get them home once the Slizz was found, or else given up for lost. What he saw always set him at ease, for the farther from it they travelled, the more clearly Citadel Hill stood free from the clutter of buildings that tumbled together about its feet, a mob in masonry and orange tile. So they plowed on through the gradually thinning multitude, and on their way saw reindeer-conjurors, acrobatic ptarmigans, mountebank boas declaiming their fustian as they looped and coiled about one another, as well as wrestling iguanas and mantises equally skilled at thimble-rigging, legerdemain, and picking of pockets; they listened to ballad-mongering spoonbills and choral kangaroos, to bag-piping wildebeests and lute-twanging pandas whose plangent trills and quavers made the head ache. Gusts of cooking-smoke from stalls where pumpkins turned on spits above a brazier; blasts of musky scents purveyed by civet-cats to gaudily decked-out armadillos; breezes off the wharfs from nets abulge with silvery crescents, swinging between hold and pier; nougaty zephyrs awaft from the booths of toucan confectioners; whiffs of coffee, catspaws of cumin, beery blasts, straw-dust simoons; these and other winds blew them from sighting to sighting until they found themselves at last with only one last row of booths between themselves and the houses on the far side of the Market Square. Most of the booths were shut up and locked, though it was now only two hours or so past noon, and the market was still in full swing. A sickly stink hung in the air. The crowd had pulled away;

Edgar and Alice were standing nearly alone beside one of the weathered booths.

The sun was hot, and they stood together in the bit of shade cast by the booth. They were each pondering what to do next. Alice was doubting whether she had really seen the Slizz as often as she had thought, and wondering how her brother would react to the idea of searching back down the length of the market. Edgar, meanwhile, was surprised by a movement within him of greater concern for the Slizz than he had ever been aware of feeling. He had been rather taken aback to reach the end of the Square without finding the beast, though he had never consciously expected they would find it. Thinking about this for a moment, he realized that somehow there had grown upon him the curious idea that Alice and he were being led. A lingering question in his mind about the beast's intelligence; its holding for so long just within view as they chased it down the stairs of Citadel Hill and through the tunnels at its base; finally, the fact that Alice's sightings, false as they had seemed to him at the time, consistently led them farther and farther from the Hill—all this taken together had put Edgar in the way of thinking that they ought to find the Slizz waiting for them on the far side of the Market Square: waiting to lead them on. But this, thought Edgar, would imply purpose. How could he have harbored such an impression without growing suspicious? An intelligent Slizz, playing the dumb beast, inserting itself into their company, and so worming itself into the very heart of the Citadel, overhearing the deliberations of the bears' two most influential leaders, then disappearing for part of the night—it all made up a sinister picture, yet they had blithely followed the Slizz out of the Citadel and down into the ferment of the troubled city. Why? Edgar, searching his morning's mood, came up at last with the faint outline of a rather childish hope: that the Slizz had somehow been sent, or had appointed itself, as a means to help them past their uncle's prohibition, to be their guide into the adventures they had come to Bargeton to seek.

But the Slizz was not standing by to lead them farther into the city. Edgar was glad to find his fancy exploded, though he now felt singularly exposed to all the strangeness around him. The whole of the Market Square stood like a wall between him and Citadel Hill, which he must find some new way to climb, for he would not a second time enter those dark tunnels. He supposed they ought to start back. At least they would have seen something of Bargeton. Tomorrow, no doubt, they would begin the long trudge back to the City of Bears, in some respectable company. Edgar turned his thoughts to the Slizz once more: since it was proven to be the silly beast he first had thought it, he ought to try to find it. The one place they had never thought to look was in the cattle-pens, which should not be too difficult to locate. He was not entirely sure that he would recognize the beast among a number of its kind, but Alice might, or else the Slizz itself might come to them. There would be explanations to be made, but they would be dealing with bears, amongst whom his uncle's name would carry great weight.

Edgar was about to speak, when a sinuous something stirred low to the ground in the shadow of a booth farther down the line from their own. They both saw it at the same time; without a word spoken they set off after it at a run. As they came up on it, it moved out into the sunlight and kicked its length around the corner of the booth. They could see it was no Slizz, though about the right bulk and color: but it was naked and owned no arms or legs that the two young bears could see.

They slowed to a walk and rounded the corner. The stink in the air grew suddenly much stronger, it buffeted against their nostrils and nearly stopped them dead. The thing they had chased was lying half out of a peeling door that stood just ajar in the side-wall of the booth; it lay there like a fat sausage tapering to a point, legless, browny-yellow like lustreless tortoise shell. Alice wanted to turn back, but Edgar drew her a few steps further on, just to have a look down the other side of the row of booths, and also to satisfy his curiosity about this booth, since it evidently was not empty.

The front of the booth was open. A pair of horizontal shutters made a sunscreen and a shelf-ledge whereon there rested a short, thick arm that ended in a club fist; the arm was the mottled color of old bronze, and looked like a decaying joint of meat. What was inside could not be told, but it filled the entire structure, and it was alive. Edgar and Alice, coughing in the sweet, musty reek that burgeoned out of the booth and enveloped them, saw fold upon fold of dirty leather bulging in pouches and knobs, or crawling, one wrinkled layer across another. A twisting movement brought a long yellow grin into sudden view, a saw-toothed set of chops with no eye near it. Next, the fist that lay upon the ledge slowly unfolded, as if they were delicate petals responding to sunlight after rain, four gnarled fingers each ending in a sickle of lead-hued talon six or seven inches long. The fingers flexed themselves in the air before the young bears' noses, while from the booth there proceeded a rhythmic creaking panting. The bulk inside the booth shifted again to let a second claw appear on the ledge, holding a log of cinnamon wood. The first claw jerked towards the log, one talon extended while the rest were folded back against the wrist. Slowly, lazily, the single talon slid down the length of the log until, with a thud that made them jump, a third of the wood's mass detached itself and dropped to the hard-baked ground. It had been sheared off as clean as if by a razor; behind it there lay exposed a bloody oval of heartwood. Again the talon rose and effortlessly fell; another slice of wood dropped off. Now the talon began to work in shorter, quicker movements. As it gathered speed, the log shrank and took on more definite form, amid a spray of chips and sawdust. In the end, what was left was so small, compared to what it had been, that it was engulfed in the leathery fist, which closed around it tightly before they could see what it was. The windy moaning from within the booth now divided into staccato hiccups un-recognizable for laughter, till they heard the sound repeated behind their backs.

Whirling, Edgar and Alice saw themselves surrounded. There had grown, while they watched the carver, a circle of mountainous shapes around the booth. The intruders stood motionless, like robed and muffled pyramids, swaddled from top to bloated base in shimmering stuff: angled iridescent planes of gold and copper, oiled-metal blue, and peacock green. From beneath the radiant hems uncoiled fat, razor-back tails; from out of the rainbow folds thrust dun snouts split into crocodile smiles. Every least movement of these prismatic masses dispersed rank waftings.

The creatures closed in around them with spastic wheezes of glee. They could not be anything but Thoog: Edgar could see their fowls behind them, that Julio had told of, the blind and flightless avox. Saddle-backed bodies, propped in the air by a pair of legs like dandelion stems, white-haired, slender, ending in splay-toed feet; from their rumps and the tips of their useless wings, a spray of extravagant quills of metallic sheen that hung to the ground and swept the dust; the avox' heads, bald, bobbed in the air above their riders'; the eyes of the avox, their round, blind eyes, were totally white.

As Edgar and Alice choked and stared, a Thoog-shape appeared behind the ring of mockers, looming above them as high again as they were high. Its jaws opened, and a thin scutter of syllables cut short the wheezy laughter in a second.

"Well, gentlemen," the little voice said. "Aren't you going to let me through?"

At once the saurians shifted and parted, opening up to the bears a view of the newcomer, who rode forward on his avox. From beneath the cowl of his hood, the long snout seemed to consider them with flaring nares; eyes they could see none.

"What's the joke, gentlemen?" the voice said again, when the avox, stepping high, had brought the Thoog to within a few feet of the bears, bathing them both in a swirl of sweet stink. "Won't you let me in on it, so I can laugh too? All I find here," the voice went on after a short silence, "is a couple of young bears. Now, if someone can inform me what's so darn humorous about *that*, I'll be most appreciative. Perhaps—I can't say for sure, of course, not having been here to see it—but perhaps old Iskabang in the booth there has been having a little game with our two young friends? I don't say he has, mind you. Maybe you gentlemen were joining in it too? I'm not *accusing* anyone; but then again, you *were* all having a jolly old time when I came up, now weren't you? Drop that thing in your fist, Corporal Iskabang."

The gnarled fist on the booth ledge opened, and a crimson block fell to the ground. Edgar and Alice stared at it where it lay in the dust.

"What the devil *is* that thing, Corporal?"

An answering voice came scraping uneasily out of the booth.

"It . . . it's a toy, sir, a little toy I cut out of a bit of scrap wood, General, while we were waiting for you. Like a sort of dolly . . . just a little bear-dolly, d'ye see, sir."

It was a little carven Crimson Bear. Its rear legs were bent as if it meant to leap forward, its forepaws were pulled up next to its head as if it meant to claw, its lips were drawn back from its teeth in a most Thoog-like expression.

"Why, that was thoughtful of you, Corporal!" the dry voice said, a bit more affably now. "To make a little doll they might enjoy."

"That's it, General!" the voice in the booth eagerly affirmed. "I just . . . I meant it as a sort of a gift . . . just a little present for 'em."

"Well, you two should feel quite honored! You may not be aware of it, but Corporal Iskabang is famous as a carver among us Thoog. Some of your little friends will be quite jealous when they learn where you got that little doll. Why don't you pick it up?" Alice did so, scooping it quickly up from the base of the booth. "Now, tell me where you come from."

"From the Citadel," said Edgar; and then he thought to add, "Senator Claudio's our uncle."

"Claudio is your uncle? Well, isn't that odd. Wouldn't *that* put a kink in an avox' neck! I've just now come from speaking with your uncle. Well, what a funny coincidence. Why, Corporal Iskabang," the mounted Thoog continued roguishly, "I'm going to have to suspect you of being a subtle courtier! You certainly know whom to give your presents to. Claudio's nephew . . . and his niece, I think? Well, isn't that something. I'm delighted to meet you two. When you see your uncle next, please give him my compliments—my name is Skaling—and also those of Corporal Iskabang, of course! Now, you gentlemen, make way there, so that our guests can get through. Where are your manners? Good-bye!" he called after the two young bears as they walked, hurrying as slowly as they could manage, between the Thoog.

"We'd better thank him," muttered Edgar.

"You do it," Alice gasped. "If I take one more breath, facing towards him, I'll be sick."

They turned around. "Thank you!" Edgar called back to the mounted Thoog.

"Not at all. You're quite welcome. Don't get lost, now!"

"Good-bye!"

"*Good*-bye. But we'll meet again, I'm sure. Hey!" They stopped. "Have you still got it?" Edgar stared, blinking; still got what? He couldn't mean the Slizz? "Corporal Iskabang's carving! Hold it up!" Alice slowly raised it above her head, its crimson grimace turned upon the Thoog.

"Very good!" called the mounted commander. "*Thank* you! *Good*-bye!" He sat on his fowl in the middle of the rank of Thoog drawn up before the booth where Iskabang's claw and grin were still visible, framed by grey wood; Skaling sat on his bird like a heap of lustrous mud on stilts, smiling towards them; but from all around him there grew up a rushing noise of rising wind, as if the sight of the little Crimson Bear had unleashed a tempest there, on the far side of the Market Square. Alice slowly lowered the carving. Then she turned, and Edgar turned, and they ran.

SIX. **Clowncattown.**

*T*hey had left the Market Square behind them; and when at last they slowed, free from the stink and laughter of the Thoog, they no longer knew where they were. They stood in a broad, elegant street lined with shuttered windows. Not a creature was abroad to direct them. Edgar, searching down the streets that met in this place like the spokes of a wheel, saw nothing but more vistas of shutters. It was Alice who caught sight of the Slizz, at the mouth of a lane, and set off after it.

Edgar followed, suspicious. He asked himself again, was the Slizz leading them on? Where? As for Alice, she was determined to catch it and carry it home to the Citadel. She was not going to have it roaming a city in which there were Thoog at large. The chase was hot, for a while. Both bears ran, yet the Slizz remained, easily, always in view, never in reach. Twenty times it slowed to pick its way; each time Edgar thought he had it, but it sprang askew and left him clutching at air.

"Edgar, you're frightening it with your puffing and cursing!" panted Alice, after another such failure. "It thinks you're angry and want to hurt it. Of course it runs away."

"I *am* angry! Damn the stupid beast! Where in hell is it taking us?"

"*It*'s not taking *us* anywhere. It's you who are driving it farther and farther from the Citadel. Now, let's move up on it slower and let me go first; stay back, and stop swearing."

67

Edgar did as he was told. Alice moved forward more gently, making coaxing sounds. The Slizz slowed but did not stop or turn; the chase continued as before, though at a more leisurely pace. Edgar forbore to comment.

Now they entered narrower streets of shabbier houses; still they met no one. They crossed a sullen green canal and, looking down it, saw in the distance a flash of sunlit water; perhaps the Flood. Then on through more streets. The houses past which they jogged were clearly not the homes of bears, nor of any kind near them in the roll of creatures. There was one lane so narrow, they had to squeeze down it sideways; the houses came only to their chins. It released them into a meadow-boulevard, bordered by barns, sown in fragrant timothy. Alice spotted the Slizz ducking down the bank of a glen in the middle of the street, but when they pushed through spiky growth to where a stream bent down the weeds, the Slizz was no longer there. Struggling out again, they walked along this tussocky avenue. Smells of hay and dung were strong in the air.

The Slizz once more came into view, brandishing its tail like a flag. The beast would not be caught, yet would not stay lost. But perhaps it was simply hungry for some special food it missed? Edgar hardly cared anymore. He loped along and presently thought to admire his endurance. His two months' march had knocked him into shape, it seemed; the old Edgar of the City of Bears could no more have kept up such a pace than he could have turned bird and flown. His wind was good, his body hard and lean. He was just thinking how well suited this sort of fast-paced sightseeing was to a city in danger, when his right knee buckled, and he went tumbling. Hearing his bellow, Alice hurried back and searched him for injuries. It turned out he had wrenched his knee, not badly, but enough to constrain him to a limping walk. The chase was cut short and the Slizz clean gone.

It was now midafternoon, and they must start to search out a way back to their uncle's. Citadel Hill still made no part of any horizon they could see. Edgar, nursing his knee, at last worked out a course by the sun that should bring them in sight of the Hill, he thought. It lay along an almost respectable street; Edgar hoped it might lead them to bears, among whom he might invoke Claudio's name.

This hope was ill-founded. The street soon shed its propriety, becoming first raffish, then absolutely wild. Before they had gone five hundred yards, they had entered a stretch so utterly decayed that had it not been deserted, they would have put about at once. As it was, they went on with misgivings that Alice did not keep to herself. Along either side of the street had been planted, at some ancient date, a row of larch for shade. Many, though dead and broken, still groped with heavy limbs. Some in their day had seeded small forests of saplings around them; beneath their fresh green the pavement buckled. At the end of this street Edgar and Alice walked into a plaza half-drowned beneath a lake. Fringed with cattail rushes, the dark waters encircled a basin; the tall thing set atop the marble dish was now so draped by vines, its shape could not be told.

Streets stretched forking in all directions; the bears had twenty choices of way. The two or three great thoroughfares that seemed to continue their route could be seen to branch furiously, every offshoot veering toward unknown districts. Alice waited trustingly for Edgar's celebrated map-sense to come into play. Edgar rubbed his knee and stared around him, hoping for a hunch. This time, he angrily thought, the Slizz had really betrayed them. He knew he could not guide his sister through this endless slum. So he chose as perversely as he could, in the end, and took the seediest street yet seen.

It split and split again. Shadows lengthened, and Edgar still kept plunging down whatever way seemed most uninviting. Alice followed, swallowing protests. There was no chance now of getting back to Claudio's by suppertime. She could only hope that her brother would not lead them into some dismal waste; Bargeton seemed quite large enough to hold a wilderness within its walls.

But wild indeed was the district into which they were plodding as the sun sank. The avenue was broad, and had been paved once, but it was houseless now. On either side untended shrubbery made a ragged palisade. Perfumed dust gusted around them as they trudged. Then through gaps they began to glimpse houses and gardens after all: huge houses, sprawling plantations, all in ruins and overgrown.

They reached a crossroads canopied by the embracings of four elms. Beneath this roof the shade was green and cool. They stopped to drink the water that rilled from a tarnished lion-mask. The basin that should have caught the trickle was cracked, the mossy floor damp underfoot. Here they conferred about their route. The road ahead looked to grow even wilder; that which crossed it was hardly less so, but broader and better used. Alice insisted they should take it, and Edgar, for once, agreed. He hoped that by turning away from the sun they might find the Flood, whose course they could follow to Citadel Hill. Alice thought of the desert beyond, and of the Crimson Bears, but she let Edgar have his way.

They set off in this new direction, and soon their spirits began to rise, for the vegetation thinned, and the houses drew nearer to the street. As they passed them by, their pace faltered; soon, whenever a clear view offered, Edgar and Alice stopped dead.

They were very large, these houses. Some were true palaces. At ground level they were ordinary mansions enough, in spite of anomalies—a wicker minaret, a leaning arcade—but as they mounted, they struggled into shapelier life. Window-embrasures swelled, making masonry lids around watchful panes. Columns crooked knobby shafts and struck down hooves, or clutched at their bases with claws. Bays and dormers turned, on the upper floors, to bony protrusions. Who had lived in these houses, Edgar wondered? What must it be like to look out through one of those eye-socket windows? To stare up from one's bed into the seamed underside of a skull?

The roofs were the greatest marvel. The two bears cried out at a hall whose wings were covered by fanning feathers of slate that showed all the colors of a pigeon's throat. But this great bird was molting. Alice, surveying the ragged gaps, pitied it, flightless and empty. An elegant pavilion, next along that street, supported a charging boar in terracotta, twisting as it galloped. Its splayed legs embraced the building; its long tusks were waterspouts. Across the street a gull-headed bat spread leathery wings to roof a wide veranda. And one whole house was nothing but a pine-shingle-scaled codfish. Edgar might have laughed at this fish so far out of water, but for the way it lay broken among tall trees in the dull red light. The householder who raised that cod, would he have felt, on stormy nights, the tug of ocean currents?

The district seemed abandoned at first. But as they walked and gawked, Edgar and Alice grew aware of eyes within the glassless eyes of upper stories. Shapes darted from tumble-

71

down porticoes, dropped from oriels, slipped across weedy piazzas, took cover in collapsed colonnades. The bears quickened their pace. They began to hear, as they hastened, a confused but rhythmic murmur, mounting to a steady chant. It seemed to run, "Hurlaboogle, roolaburgle, burgleoogle"—sounds that conveyed little meaning to them.

Suddenly a lithe form bounded out of a thicket. It crouched, still swaying, lashing a long tail in time to the pulsing chant that grew all around them from masses of privet, jasmine, and bamboo. Before they could make out the dancer's kind, a second joined it, and a third. Streaked, speckled, splotched with orange, brown, tan, and gray, the three shapes interlaced with a speed and agility that baffled the eye. The two young bears halted. Turning, they saw the street blocked by a writhing wall of bodies. As the *burlagoobles* swelled to a bellicose pitch, Edgar and Alice fought their fear while watching the antic throng. At last Alice caught sight of one in a moment of comparative repose.

"O, Edgar, look!" she cried. "They're cats!"

And as he desperately stared, he too was able to make out hairy cat-faces appearing and vanishing beneath flailing cat-arms or between capering cat-legs: faces cross-eyed or upside-down, or showing an end of tongue from one side of a grin. Padded paws beat at the pavement. Teeth and silvery whiskers flashed. Alice and he soon were standing in the middle of a ring of cats, while *ooblegurbles* throbbed all round.

"Come on, Edgar," said Alice. "Let's dance. There's not much else we can do."

And indeed there was not. The street was choked in either direction. The beat was infectious; the two young bears began to shuffle about, bear-fashion. The cats promptly picked up the tempo and soon had them leaping and cavort-

72

ing, in spite of their fears and fatigue. The ring dissolved, and the bears were part of a horde that danced madly up and down the street and overflowed into the gardens. There were no set figures; one simply flung oneself about and trusted the cats to get out of the way. Their fluid mass molded itself to the bears' least movements, rubbing against them in ceaseless soft pats. Alice, as she pranced, changing partner for partner second by second, felt a warm back press her back, a limber leg coil round her leg, an arm stretch lovingly across her shoulders, a spray of whiskers tickle her jowl. This friction was always caressing, yet after a few minutes she felt sore. But there was no avoiding it. She closed her mind to the soreness and danced.

Edgar was not as nimble on his feet, and his knee still troubled him; he was not at all clear in his mind about this impromptu carnival. Were the cats friendly to bears? He kept as close to Alice as he could.

All at once they felt their arms caught from behind, and they were spun around to face a figure remarkably tricked out: a long, lean cat, emerald-eyed. His lemon pelt, so short it seemed cropped, thinly mantled his ribs and broad skull. From the neck down he was festooned with hundreds of azure, garnet, lime, amber, daffodil, amethyst shreds and rags of striped, printed, brocaded, flocked, tasselled, sequined silk, canvas, corduroy, linen, velvet, buckram, dimity, taffeta, drugget, satin, baize, and lace; and he was wearing a purple tricorne several sizes too small. While he held Edgar and Alice, looking them over coolly, the surrounding riot died down, and the chanting stopped.

"Intromit me to perduce myself," said the rag-draped cat. "I am Dionisio the Outragioziferous; I am the Chief Hooburg-aloo of Clowncattown. Yes," he went on dreamily, "Dionisio is my name, no two doubts about it; but you may call me—nay, you must and shall call me 'Mister Dizzy.' Try it now."

"'Mister Dizzy,'" repeated Edgar and Alice.

"Nicely spoke like a pig in a poke. And now, little porkers, may one know by what cognomen, agnomen, or just plain pignomen you dis-stink-which one another from the rest of the swoony swine?"

"Excuse me?" said Edgar and Alice in unison, not to say perplexity.

"Your names, little piggies, prithee let me know your sow-briquets."

"I'm Edgar."

"I'm Alice."

"O, delightful, enrapturacious!" Mr. Dizzy purred. "Such fine, short, baconomical names. And yet, all the same, not, you know, very suitable; not sty-lish enough for me. No. *They*," and he indicated the rest of the Clowncats with a sweep of his arm, "might not divine, from such names, that you were of the porcine race. They do not love the unporcine guest, when they hold their revels, prudent brutes that they are—or do I mean brutent prudes? I'll have to root up something better for you, something more oinktuously swinsome, something that cries the sty. Now, you," he said to Edgar, "I will baptize Gruntusculo. And you, my sweet sowlet, will henceforth be known as Wallowine. O rashers! Very fine names indeed for a very pignificent pair of young porkers."

What sort of joke was this? Edgar was starting to protest, "But, Mr. Dizzy, we're not pigs at all," when the Clowncat cut him off peremptorily.

"Pigs you are, without a snouty doubt. Don't be hoggravating. Say 'Oink,' this minute."

"Oink," they both said, alarmed at the stern note that had entered his voice.

"Melodiously oinked! And now, my pigturesque Wallow-ine, and most supersquealious Gruntusculo, will you do me the signal, pignal hognor of bearing, or I should say *boaring* me company to my jungle-o bungalow, and sharing a spot of grub with us cats?"

There was no way to refuse; and anyway Edgar was very hungry. But he could not decipher these cats: they shed waves of good humor and anger at once. Alice felt this too. Better than Edgar she saw that in naming them pigs, the Chief Hooburgaloo had given the Cats a clownish pretext for accepting them; two young bears would have received differ-ent treatment. So she sensed danger, but still she was ready to play along. Fatigue and overexcitement, above all the shock of their encounter with the disgusting Thoog, had pushed her into a reckless frame of mind. As a bear she could do nothing; she was willing to be a pig for a while. Moreover, she liked the Clowncats, liked their nimble nonsense, which seemed to be the best way, now, to deal with the immensity of Bargeton. She made their acceptances with a warmth that earned her a glance of amused approval from the chief of the Cats.

"Ho!" he snorted. "Most hamiably replied, my Wallow-ine. Then let's be off to swill our fill!"

From all around them the chant arose once more. The mob formed into a swaying, bending file, to the head of which the bears advanced arm-in-arm with Mr. Dizzy, past cats who respectfully-satirically knotted themselves into the most skeleton-defying of bows. Then the column set off, still to the rhythm of *gulaburloogles*, down the street.

Soon they began to wind in and out around the ruinous palaces and through their thriving, tangled gardens. There they saw stiff rows of trees, reaching with root and branch to block the alleys they framed. They skirted a hedge-maze turned solid hedge, then climbed some broken flights between bomb-bursts of yew and box, their trim shapes exploded by time and storms. Leaving the animal-palaces behind at last, the column danced through parkland that was very jungle-like. After the heat and glare of the city, the bears were glad of the dim hush.

They didn't enjoy it long. Just when they had grown used to darkness, they stepped once more into light; Bargeton was waiting with another of its masks.

Across waste flats arose a sandstone cliff. The sun, now behind them, raked the tawny facade, filling its cracks with violet shadow. In these crevices pines had rooted, that twisted out and up into the glow of sunset. But against the darkening eastern sky the top of the cliff made a perfectly straight though notched horizon. Was it the city wall, Edgar wondered? But that had been higher, redder. Alice remembered the bluff she had seen from her window in the Citadel. Had they come so far?

The greatest wonder lay between them and the cliff. Piles of trash, heaped to the height of trees, spread all across the ground. On the apex of each sat a cat armed with a flail, driving away the magpies and jackdaws that circled, excited by so much glitter. These were no stinking middens like the shell-mounds down the coast from the City of Bears. Everything hereabouts was clean and dry. It all, Alice realized with a thrill, had been made: made and then discarded, some of it worn out or broken, some outgrown and replaced; but all of it had been in use, and then thrown out, and then collected and saved by the Cats. Their way led them among the trash heaps. Mr. Dizzy took them dancing around the bases of these manufactured hills, as if to dazzle his guests by a display of treasure. They saw there more things than they could ever remember, things and the half-hidden parts and pieces of things, each of which assumed, in those piles, a virtue of its own, so that there grew around it a sense of the life into which it once had fitted. Nothing that they had yet seen in Bargeton gave them so overpowering a feeling of the city's age, of the number and variety of lives that had been led there, of the generations of making, buying, using, then discarding; nothing had brought all this home till they saw the trash heaps of the Clowncats.

Coming out from among the mounds, they saw ahead a cluster of dusty trees near the foot of the cliff. More cats stood silently at the grove's edge, observing their approach.

"Way! Make way, there!" shouted Mr. Dizzy. "Way for their most hogust pigcellencies, the lady Wallowine and the porciform Gruntusculo! They dine tonight in Clowncat-town!"

SEVEN. The Chief Hooburgaloo's Throne.

*T*he cats at the grove's edge stood aside, as the column of dancers wormed its way in among the trees; they did not join the dance but watched it pass, placidly settled on haunches, and moving no more than the tip of a tail. These cats were soberly dressed, in coats of fawn, dove-gray, or black. They seemed better fed than the others.

In amongst the tall old trees the dim light fell aslant, making a salmon glow. It spotted the warty trunks and the floor with unsteady orange, and tipped naked boughs with coral. Edgar and Alice danced, staring, into a clearing and down its length, along the brink of a trench lined with lustrous mosses, toward a structure that rose at the clearing's end like an attenuated wedding cake in teal blue lattice-work. This temple, or gazebo, or pagoda, grew up in diminishing stories from a terrace at the top of a fine stone stair, on whose steps a group of poised figures now shifted around to quiz the dancers; and it was before these cool exquisites and beneath their incurious survey that the *harroobigargles* finally died away, and the two young bears came somewhat self-consciously to rest.

In the midst of the group on the stair stood a small, portly cat, liver-colored except where his fur caught the light; there it shone silvery. His olive tunic was faced in cranberry and cut so as to mold into chevaleresque dignity a noble *embonpoint*.

More than his own quiet, expectant demeanor, the attitudes of the cats around him made plain that he was a personage of consequence. A sudden pang of embarrassment knotted up Edgar's tongue at the thought that he was about to be presented as Gruntusculo the Pig.

His wrist was caught by Mr. Dizzy, who led up Alice on his other side; the introductions were soon performed, just as Edgar had feared, wreathed all about with tendrils of the Chief Hooburgaloo's characteristic nonsense. All the while Edgar shamefacedly, eyes watering, waveringly met the grandee's gelid gaze, confessing and beseeching at once, until he thought he could discern a little gleam of comprehension and amusement. At the conclusion of Mr. Dizzy's flowery rigmarole Edgar and Alice made such obeisances as well-brought-up young bears are taught to make to their elders, and received in return an affable nod.

"I am indebted to you, Chief," said the important cat in a deep, wet, richly resonant voice, "for making me acquainted with our young guests. I had not expected, I confess, to meet new friends here and tonight, but I applaud your initiative. Signior Gruntusculo, Donna Wallowine, you are welcome to our revels. My name is Equivair. Your presence honors me and all Cats. You are not, I think, from this city? Perhaps you have come here on some errand of pleasure (for I think you are too young for business)—a visit, I guess, to some distinguished relative here in Bargeton?" Edgar nodded, controlling his excitement. This Equivair seemed to hint that he knew who they really were, though Edgar did not see how he could. Had Claudio already missed them, and sent out word through the city? If so, this dignified lord, who apparently stood at the head of a party of far more civil and sober cats than Mr. Dizzy's crazy rout, might be the means to return Alice and himself to the Citadel.

"Well, you have come to us at an interesting time. I am overjoyed that you will share in our banquet and witness what is, for us, a rather important occasion. Chief Dizzy will please me, I know, by making sure that you are appropriately seated and kept perfectly . . . comfortable." Mr. Dizzy here involved himself in obsequious knots of compliance. "You must forgive me if I turn my attention to business at hand; I trust we shall enjoy further speech at some later time. Chief, if I may offer the suggestion, perhaps Signior Gruntusculo and Donna Wallowine might enjoy to be shown your Throne? It is, my dears, a rather remarkable artifact. The feast, Chief, the feast will soon be set; it is fast nearing the time when you must take your proper place to preside over our festivities." And with another nod, the lordly Equivair moved off with his retinue, and vanished among the trees that bordered and overhung the mossy pit.

Edgar looked after him as at a receding hope. There had been something comfortably familiar in Equivair's self-assurance. If Edgar had not sensed that a conscious charade was being enacted, to save appearances of some sort, between Mr. Dizzy and the other, and that it would be untimely and even hazardous to question it, he might have run, as he felt tempted to do, now, and told all to Equivair, used Claudio's name on him, which he was sure would weigh with this magisterial cat. But he watched him sink into the gloaming, then turned to follow his sister up the steps towards the gazebo-pagoda, led thither by the Chief Hooburgaloo. The glow in the air was now duller and redder, as evening came on. The dancers had all vanished, all but a few who loafed about the clearing, but there were lights and movement in among the trees on either side of it. The first fireflies began to carom, winking, about the glade, and Edgar heard the whine of a mosquito hovering by his ear, and struck at it. He could smell spicy-oily-fishy cooking-smoke from somewhere nearby. The last thought to cross his mind, before he joined Alice and Mr. Dizzy at the top of the stair, was a question why this Throne they were going to look at was assigned to the Chief Hooburgaloo rather than to the lordly Equivair.

The terrace before the gazebo-pagoda was paved in a chessboard pattern of black and white squares. Mr. Dizzy stationed them on two of these and bade them not to move, "neither trotter nor eke hock," while he went off behind the strange construction. They waited there rather a long time, and Alice was starting to wish she could sit down and not be shown anything more that day, when they heard a low hissing and then a series of dull pops. From the top of each of the cast-iron ornaments—alternating pineapples and cabbages— that studded the railing around the building, there started a pale-green flame. Then wisps and plumes of steam began to boil out around the edges of some of the squares in the pavement; this quite frightened them. They would have retreated off their stations if the black square four in front of Alice's had not flipped back, and let out a walnut curio-case. It came rushing up to teeter and then stand still; its shelves were crowded with snails who clung, as well, to the diamond panes of its doors. A knight's jump to the left, by Edgar, a tall clock ascended stately through another square hole. When it was quite out, it emitted a complicated machine-noise, a pair of little doors flew open above the face (unmarked with numerals and innocent of hands); a crudely carved parrot

tion in some other quadrant of the Throne. Nowhere that Edgar looked could he see anything that did not seem capable of being set into motion. There was, as far as he could tell, no fixed skeleton at all; the great and small systems depended entirely on one another for support. Then how did the Throne hold its shape? Even as he framed this question, the whole machine began to move and its contours to change. The crest of it sank, its flanks bulged and spread, while the ground beneath their feet throbbed. A long arm of gleaming steel tubing extended itself towards the two young bears, section by jointed section. It reached its full length just in front of Alice, by whose feet it set down, with a musical crash, a great disc of brass that had once, Alice guessed, been a cymbal. Other such arms reached out in all directions and clapped down other discs—wagon wheels, table tops, capstan heads, well covers—to give stability to the whole (so Edgar reckoned), as the metamorphic Throne sank and distended like a great lump of mechanical dough.

Down the middle of its now much easier slope there arose from within, with much noise and shaking, a cogged track that ran from crest to floor; and as soon as it was securely in place, a thick belt whirred till its markings were lost (it was marked like the skin of a snake), a wheel went around, a bellows set on a vertical rod began to open and close, directing a stream of air across the necks of a row of bottles filled to various heights with water; as the bellow's nozzle switched from side to side, the bottles in turn sent each a throbbing note to its place in a tune, a halting but lively march. At the same time the weighted end of a balance arm, such as might once have raised a little drawbridge, sank down out of sight, the rising end lifted from the apex of the Throne an inverted bathtub, and Mr. Dizzy was discovered, at ease among purple cushions, in a sort of car at the head of the cogged track. As soon as the tub was lifted clear, the car began to descend the track. It did so by halting stages, while the bottle-organ filled the air with triumphant tremulous *poots*. At every stage of his descent, the conformation of the Throne would change, on one side or the other of the track, to bring forth some offering to the Chief Hooburgaloo. Thus, an extending tongs shot out to release in his lap a bunch of fat black grapes. At the next station, spidery arms came waving forth, each tipped with a miniature rake, to scratch the Chief wherever he might itch; the lemon cat rolled around luxuriously while the rakes searched his fur. At the next, a ceramic whale broke from the works and shot an amber stream of beer from its blowhole to fill a large mug on a salver that had swung itself out on the opposite side, and Mr. Dizzy drank deep and smacked his lips. A woven tube snaked forth as he passed, and he snatched it and put the end to his mouth, emitting a fine blue ring of smoke; but he made no selection from a shelf of books that slid out like a tongue from the suddenly yawning mandibles of a copper coal scuttle.

As Mr. Dizzy's car neared the bottom of the track, Edgar saw that it was made from the bottom half of a great tun, upholstered within in rich purple. There was a legend stamped across the staves; he read: "Best Ignalian Anchovies." When the car finally came to rest, the machine fell into fresh throes and regrouped itself around and above the gaudy couch until Mr. Dizzy sat inside a sort of articulated grotto. Four lamps were lowered from its ceiling now to light it: the white, translucent skull of a fish; a great ruby egg glowing like a coal; a tall, thin coffeepot with a flame aquiver at the tip of its spout; the last was a lump of something on a string. It possessed no luminous properties, but it was not many seconds before Alice noticed fireflies darting around it, at first a few, then dozens the next time she looked, till she cast a glance over her shoulder and marvelled to see, at various heights from the ground, the long, snaking files of fireflies making for the dangling lump from every quarter of the glade. Soon the grotto was lit by their flickering incandescent green, by the dancing yellow flame at the lip of the coffeepot, and by the refulgence of crimson and hot white from egg and skull. In such a light the cat, wrapped in his shreds and bandages of motley, asprawl on his purple couch, nearly lost form altogether; only his eyes held the young bears' stare. Meanwhile, all around him, the grotto's inner surface shuttled and slid in a shifting mosaic of oiled metal parts: the Chief Hooburgaloo's Throne rested but did not sleep.

"Goolaburloo," murmured Mr. Dizzy, deep in his throat. "Such, O hambassadors, is the state of the Clowncats." He allowed their wordless admiration to continue for a few seconds longer, and then said, "About snouts, now, my piggies, and train your porkspicacious gaze adown the glade."

Edgar and Alice turned. All down the clearing, on either side of the mossy trench, torches were burning in brackets on the tree trunks, to light the feast; and the pit was filled with cats. They sat facing outward down its two long sides, whose lip was their table, set out in an array of crockery, vessels, and utensils that was very far from making a uniform dinner service—more gleanings from the trash heaps. The cats that lined the left-hand wall of the pit were those same Clowncats with whom they had danced so madly that afternoon, but those opposite, their backs to the others, were Equivair's

EIGHT. **The Banquet in the Clearing.**

*A*s a great hubbub of cheerful noise broke out down below, Edgar and Alice walked back to take their seats on the stepladder and the rocking horse, respectively. All the other articles had sunk back through the chessboard parquet, but two small tables mushroomed up before them as they sat looking down at the revelling cats. Alice's table was set with a footed iron pot, a large clamshell, a soup ladle, and a leather dicing cup; Edgar's, with a candle snuffer, a mustard pot in the shape of a swan, three finger bowls, and a loaf pan. All were empty. Edgar wondered when they would be served, and with what sort of food.

He did not have to wait long to find out; a calico cat came up through the floor, lugging a great tureen. He hefted it over to the two young bears and began to dish out its contents, meticulously filling the pot, the shell, the dicing cup, the finger bowls, and the loaf pan with skillful tilts of his serving spoon. When they thanked him, he winked, and swung the tureen away, to serve the Chief Hooburgaloo.

"What is it?" whispered Alice.

"Some kind of stew," Edgar hissed back.

"But what's in it?"

Edgar shrugged. He poked around in the loaf pan with his candle snuffer. "I have a fish head."

"I have a peach."

"I can smell garlic."

"I can smell brandy."

"There are raisins in mine."

"In mine too—unless these are peas—or capers. Have you got a dumpling?"

"If you mean these squashy blobs, I have three—one in each finger bowl. They're solid, though, not stuffed. I think they're turnip. Or shortbread. Here's beans."

"Here's olives. I have pineapple rings."

"I have onion rings *and* pineapple rings. I have banana."

"I have sardines. I have rum cake—a whole big slice."

"Alice, are we going to *eat* this? Will it be safe?"

"I don't know. It smells all right to me. I'm too hungry to care." Alice picked up her ladle and started to eat. She caught Edgar's eye as he stared, and made a vague motion of her head. When her mouth was free again, she said, "It's all right. It's not bad at all. I think the trick is to take small mouthfuls from different places—it doesn't seem all to have completely blended yet." She fished with her ladle. "Cheese!" she exclaimed with pleasure, and ate it.

Meanwhile the feasters below were being served with quite different ceremony. From the trees on either side of the dining pit there advanced a team of servitor-cats with a barrel mounted on wheels. As each great firkin was trundled along the marge of the pit by two straining cats, a third, scampering in advance, caught up bowls and held them in the air to be heaped high with steaming dinner by the fourth, who rode the barrel's rim and wielded a broad, black shovel. Edgar watched the square blade sink and rise, blindly flip a perfectly apportioned cat's-appetite-worth to hit dead center in the bowl that was equally blindly held aloft, while the butler groped for the next. In this way the pit-diners were all served in a matter of five minutes without a drop spilled that Edgar could observe. The Clowncats on the left set to without delay; but Equivair's retinue, over on the right, made only a few fastidious sups at the mess in their bowls before dropping their spoons and pushing their dinner away. Edgar, who was now filling and raising his candle snuffer with greedy alacrity—for the stew was rich and satisfying, and every snufferful brought a new taste, as spearmint, onion, chocolate, lentil, fennel, orange, oyster, horseradish, almond, pickled egg, wine sauce, caramel, chervil, chard, and nougat—saw many a disdainful frown pass over the faces of these sleek gentry, though Equivair himself was all polite composure. He noticed, further, pairs of eyes like twinned lamps that shone out for an instant and then extinguished; he thought these glances were not friendly. As they were repeated, his apprehensions grew. The courtiers nearest to Equivair now leaned towards their leader, who gravely heard their murmurs. At last he turned and bent his gaze on Edgar, opened a smile, and then turned back to his followers, who shortly straightened and once again sat still.

It was not long before the Clowncats had despatched this course, those of them that had deigned to partake of it; there was no second to follow. The left-hand side of the dining pit was abuzz with conversation and more: the cats on that side had eaten and drunk well—all at the same time, of course, the dinner having contained sundry liquors—and seemed riotously disposed. Bursts of song rang out. Tipsy cats came clambering out of the trench to prance on the greensward, while their less mobile friends beat spoons on bowls and called out rhythmic insults. The elegant cats on the right-hand side were silent and stiff. Some few looked over their shoulders, regarding unblinking the commotion behind them. Suddenly the moon rose above the Throne, small and bright white, just one thin crescent paring. Alice had seen the same moon only the night before, from her uncle's window, seen it set over the desert. This was her second night in Bargeton.

A throb underground, a clash of meshing gears, announced a new change in the Throne's configuration. Edgar saw all the Clowncat eyes gleam out just before he himself turned to see the illuminated grotto's roof slide back, the cogged track tilt forward, the Chief's car joltingly climb till it rose above the mass of machinery, and Mr. Dizzy stood in silhouette against the sky. He stretched out an arm. A bank of levers rose beneath it. Seizing one, he pulled it down; then they heard a succession of hissing *fwhoots* as missiles darted skywards from various points of the Throne. Next, the whole slot of night sky above the clearing was filled with twisting blue-white comets spreading from several centers; then followed a tattoo of rattling reports. The Clowncats on the left gave a lusty cheer. When the last of the comets had snaked its way to extinction, the air overhead was suddenly cut by plummeting shapes of white. One sank down a foot from Alice to clang on the pavement: it was an enamelled sauce pan, suspended by threads from a spread of white silk. A brocaded cushion landed near Edgar, and on his other side, a green felt bag split to release a cascade of tin spoons; these too were braked in their descent by luminescent puffs of silk. Another salvo of *fwhoots* from the Throne, and the sky was bright once more with crisscrossing lines of orange that left the image of a hexagonal grid on the staring eye. More artifacts came hurtling down, and again the clearing rang with the clamor of Clowncats, who now leapt out of the pit to seize on these treasures dropped from the skies. Against the fulgent sliver of moon Mr. Dizzy's black arm was seen to depress another black lever; stars exploded in rays of icy green; Clowncats howled in awe; Edgar jumped aside to duck a massive iron lock, its thick-shanked key projecting, that bounced off the top of his step ladder and fell to the pavement, trailing its silken shroud. He heard a few loud guffaws from the pit.

"Silence for the Chief's Music!" roared a hoarse voice from behind them, and again they turned to see the Throne performing a new evolution. From behind its back it brought forth a circular platform that spun as a tray spins on the nonchalant waiter's finger. Its edge was slotted; as it went round and round, behind the bears and above their heads, they saw pairs of objects leap to fit themselves into the indentations on opposite sides of the disc's circumference, till twelve of them revolved there. They were all the pieces of a set of luggage, and they each emitted music. A huge brass-bound trunk breathed an oboe's caressing notes; a handsome leather bandbox vibrated to the plangent throb of a viola da gamba; snare drums hissed and clattered within an upright portmanteau; a harp sounded from a carpetbag, and a flat case for the transport of epees rang with chords struck out from mellow chimes. To various tempi, in several keys, the members of this musical baggage came dancing around to shower sounds over the two young bears and down the clearing, while the Throne's machinery kept up a clackety whir beneath the whole cacophony, making further nonsense of each music that came lurching forward to take its turn.

Abruptly the concert ceased; the action of the orchestra reversed as the pieces of luggage fled the stage, in pairs as before, and the platform swung back. Before it was out of sight behind the Throne, a new clamor broke out that drew the bears' eyes around again. Masked cats were running out from among the trees. The hoarse voice once more loudly croaked: "Silence for the Chief's Comedy!"

The actors—there were four—came bounding up the steps so fast that Edgar and Alice feared for a moment that they were to be made a part of this performance. But the cats stopped short of the terrace, bowed to the Chief Hooburgaloo (the moon now hovered a foot above his long-whiskered head), and turned to face the crowd in the dining pit. The Clowncats on the left greeted them with uproarious applause; even the fine gentry to the right stirred and showed signs of excitement. There had been a constant passing, up and down that side of the pit, of small, rounded shapes—flasks, Edgar guessed—and the mood of Equivair's retinue had subtly volatilized over the last few minutes. Now, as the actors made their courtesies to the audience, it was evident that some eagerly awaited entertainment had arrived. Equivair himself maintained perfect poise, and a calm, polite, attentive air; his long-muzzled face caught the light of moon and torch, variously showing gleams of silver and deep, rich brown; but many a neat, stiff-whiskered visage behind him showed as evident an appetite for pleasure as any mobile phiz across the way. Edgar wondered at this awakening enthusiasm, for it seemed from the actors' preliminary antics that this was to be a performance typically Clowncattish in its uncouth vigor, but Alice had noticed that one of the four was a she-cat, long-bodied and silver-furred, and had observed the beauty in the strong lines of her face. She moved with a kind of agile languor, as if in dream she followed a skein of many lines of feeling, whose nodes made moments of turbulence, they in turn prompting just those shuddery gestures and quick swirls, those brief interlockings with others in the company, that part and scene demanded. Whenever she moved, whenever she slowed to rest, her spirit then seeming to retreat down secret ways, her form was held by the eyes of all of Equivair's party and by Equivair's own eyes, lambent, unwavering.

The other three were Clowncat males, small, lithe, and tiger-striped. Their humorous leaps and posturings the eyes ranked along the pit's left side eagerly followed, winking with mirth; and sharp-fanged Clowncat jaws continuously gaped to give issue to great bellows of laughter.

The comedy was wordless. Mime quickened to jig or froze into tableau. One of the cats was always three stairs higher than his fellows; he wore a sort of mask, an eyeless lion's head, that covered all of him but his prancing legs. From it there issued, Alice could not tell how, a grating, halting, skirling tune, sour as a bagpipe, scratchy as a fiddle, tremulous as a keening voice, fitful as a hurdy-gurdy's ever-repeating melody, though no two sequences were ever quite the same. To this music, three steps below, the other three played out a series of scenes in quick succession. They had a great sack from which they pulled festoons of costuming and mask after mask as these were needed. For a while Alice could not make much sense of the scenes, particularly since the actors were playing towards the pit, so that much of their pantomime was lost to her; she found herself nervously attending as often to the audience's responses, the clamorous yowling of the cats on the left, the silent stares of the cats on the right, as to the performance itself. But presently she thought she saw a pattern. Each scene began with an encounter between a pair of the actors, who moved about one another with stiff, spasmodic motions, while the silver cat danced somnambulously by herself to the fretful tune that the lion's head sang without pause. By degrees the action of the pair built into manic fury. Then there was conflict. Then the silver dancer was drawn into it, and the three bodies writhed through impossible figures to freeze, all of a sudden, in a grotesque tangle, while the Clowncats below whistled and stamped. Then there was changing of robe and mask, and the scene began again. But Alice could not make out what, if anything, it was all meant to represent.

Edgar, who was slightly better placed to see the bits of business that were gone through by the pair of actors, thought he could tell what these were about. Each showed a comic quarrel unfolding between a noble cat and his clownish servant. The servant was forever aping his master's graceless formality, while the original of this burlesque copy fell into writhings of rage each time he caught his disrespectful flunkey out. As snarls, blows, shrinkings, and duckings multiplied, the quarreling pair moved nearer and nearer to the silver cat, whose favor each of them variously invoked—or so it seemed; but here Edgar began to lose the thread. At last she was caught up in their madness, and the whole scene turned to feverish dancing. Edgar was baffled to know what this could mean, but in what had gone before he was sure that he could see a pointed comment on the several miens of the two very disparate castes among the cats. He had not been blind to the tension growing between the parties on either side of the dining pit, brought together this evening in unusual and forced conviviality. He, therefore, at certain broadly farcical passages in the acting, began to grow anxious lest Equivair's followers take offense. The parody of their manners could hardly be mistaken, and implied that their dignity was no more than a cover for an underlying clownish flux of mood such as the vulgar sort of cats made no secret of, but openly displayed. Edgar too kept a worried eye on the audience, especially the cats on the right. But all those eyes remained greedily fixed upon the silver cat.

When he looked at her to find out why, he saw her beauty at last. This was no mere pretty, round little puss-face. Its lines and planes were clean and strong and almost coarse in their simplicity. Elegance and refinement were absent from it; mischief too, or malice. Her brow was narrow, her muzzle longer and more squared than any other cat's Edgar had seen. Her green-gold eye caught his as he stared, and she gave him a wry little smile. At the end of the scene it was she who first disengaged from the comic three-headed monster into which the performers had braided their bodies, and went to the gunny-sack whence the costumes and masks were haled forth. At that moment the lion's head ceased to play. The actor who wore it took it off and laid it down, with much ridiculous ceremony, at the top of the stairs facing towards the Throne; after lavishing caresses and obeisances upon it, and many other tokens of exaggerated reverence, he left it there and ran back down the stairs. Seen from so close, the lion's head looked a flimsy thing, built on a wire foundation that in places showed through the peeling layers of painted papier-mâché. Its mouth hung foolishly agape; two banks of ivory pipes stood in for teeth, but Edgar could not determine how they were played.

Below, the silver cat was distributing gear. Two of her colleagues had already tricked themselves out in cape-knotted pelts of livid green wool; on top of this one of the actors now pulled a tight, long-skirted gown of golden cloth. Innumerable rents and slashes let the shags of wool show plainly through the brilliant fabric. Next this same actor slapped upon his crown a sort of stocking-cap or Phrygian bonnet, red, with a drooping peak. Then suddenly he slammed his foot down an inch away from the second cat's nose, and the latter, he who wore only the woolly pelt, scuttered away on all fours, belly low to the ground, exclaiming a series of grunting coughs that precisely mimicked a Slizz's *yark*. There came a great burst of applause from the pit—Edgar noticed signs of amused animation even among Equivair's party— and at that same moment both actors pulled leather masks over their faces, and turned into Slizz.

Or one was a Slizz; the other, in gown and cap, flew into such a torrent of high-pitched squealing gibberish, it was plain to the bears he represented one of the speakable Ceruk. And indeed, throughout the rest of his performance in that character, he never ceased to gobble and squawk his volleys of unintelligible matter that seemed from the pitch and tone of it to be an aged creature's endless litany of grievances. Still reeling it out, this sudden pantaloon hobbled over to the costume-sack, bent over it with much fluttering of the paws and many squeaks of excitement or of rage, and began to twitch things out of it, slowly at first, but then faster and faster, till the air about his head was thick with flying garments and the crisscross trajectories of masks and props. At last with a shriek of triumph, he held up a long, knobbed stick and shook it above his head, lovingly gazing up at it. Then the one long leather snout swung around to search for the other; of course the beast was not easily found. It had followed its master to the sack; with an air of sprightly curiosity that had drawn snorts of recognition from both bears, it had nosed about among the bright clothes that kept raining down from the skies, and shied away from many a falling cup or dagger. While the pantaloon rummaged for his stick, its silly face had peeped out from the bodice or sleeve of sundry garments, and a swell of chuckles grew among the cats. But when the "Slizz" now stirred beneath a cerulean great-coat that had fallen across it, poked its snout between the coattails just in time to meet the other's gimlet gaze, and the two long masks stood almost end to end, while the cudgel trembled in the air, as if in passionate anticipation of the bastinado it was about to deliver—then even Equivair could not restrain himself, and the whole clearing boomed with laughter.

Needless to say, the feeble "Ceruk" was too slow in his swing. The stick arced down in a furious peal of syllables, but the coat was empty. Then the hunt was up. The "Ceruk" was ferreting about in one quarter, keeping up his sibilant cackle, while behind his bent back the Slizz-mask rose to face the howling audience from beneath a beribboned wig. At another time the pantaloon went strolling away, choking down his mutter to a whisper, feigning indifference, whereupon the "Slizz" came blithely trotting after him, all danger forgotten; then came the sudden turn, the gape of horror, the slow swing, the somersault, the *crack* of wood on stone, the gibber of frustrated craft, the roar from the pit; and all was to begin again.

All this while the silver cat was contriving a new identity for the fourth actor, the one who had just left the lion's head. Alice watched her fish around in the litter of costuming that had been strewn about the stairs by the cat who played the Ceruk. First she selected a pair of hairy brown leggings for her colleague, far too long and broad waisted for him; he held them from him ruefully. But in one lazy turn, with three languid stoopings, the silver cat brought him back a pair of high pattens and enough miscellaneous padding to make the trousers fit. When a black coat, similarly stuffed, had engulfed the actor's torso, he was four times as big as himself, and only his head looked incongruously tiny atop the mass of his new body. He shifted his bulk around, tried a few steps, went up the stairs, winked at Edgar and Alice as he turned, and went back down again. Then he squatted. The young bears thought he was sitting to watch the outcome of the latest business played out by the two masked cats. The "Ceruk" had fetched over the empty gunny-sack, and now was pulling handfuls of gold from the pockets of his gown, counting the pieces and fondling them, then dropping them into the sack where, unbeknownst to him, the "Slizz" had hidden itself. When his pockets were quite empty, the pantaloon went to shoulder the sack but could not lift it; his voice rasped hoarse astonishment as he struggled and strained; he dashed his cap on the ground and stared bewildered into his own pockets; the laughter of the cats came in waves without intermission. Finally the "Ceruk" shrugged, opened the neck of the bag; there was the "Slizz," blandly chewing. Nothing could match the old "Ceruk's" rage. He hauled the beast out by the scruff of its neck and flung it away, upended the sack, shook it— nothing fell out. The "Slizz" gave a long, contented belch. Down in the pit the Clowncats were simply falling over one another while Equivair's retinue shouted with laughter. Then suddenly they all froze with open mouths.

The fourth actor had risen to his feet. He wore on his shoulders a new head, round and brown, that the silver cat had just placed there. Edgar and Alice could not at first make out what it was, but then he turned to stump across the stage one stair above the others. The head he wore was the head of a bear, bushy-whiskered, with a great pair of spectacles perched across the broad bridge of his muzzle. Suddenly, with a gasp, they knew him: it was their uncle Claudio.

With his entrance the comedy began to follow a scenario, as the "Ceruk" ran to him for redress against the felon who had eaten all his gold. The silver dancer came on masked as a dog-lawyer to defend the "Slizz," and they won their case in spite of the fact that the defendant, every few seconds, would gulp and strain and shiver, following which perturbations a golden brick would be seen to fall from under its tail. But "Claudio" dismissed the pantaloon's plea with contumely. The "dog" and the "Slizz," following this victory, raised their masks a little and winked over their shoulders at the audience, and the Clowncats stood up and cheered. Then the two actors strutted off, arm in arm, and the "Ceruk" got his gold back, greedily gathering it into the folds of his skirts while "Claudio" mimed immense revulsion at the sight.

From that point on the play developed more rapidly. The cat-comedians shifted masks, went on and off, engaged in business that kept the audience in an uproar, but Edgar and Alice could no longer easily follow most of it. Their long day's exertions and their rich dinner had made them sleepy; the characters now assumed by the actors were not familiar; silver lacings of cloud passing before the moon made it hard to see clearly all of what was transpiring halfway down the stairs. All that Edgar could later remember of the performance was that whenever the pace of things had built to a particularly frantic pitch, "Claudio" would come bumbling on as the representative of authority, to be lavishly hood-winked by a masked Clowncat. Edgar laughed with the rest.

By the time the company had taken their final bow the whole audience was laughing and cheering together. The cats that had lined either side of the pit no longer sat with their backs to one another but crowded together at its hither end; so Edgar judged that the comedy had done its work. The Throne now struck up a new music, a mellow but spirited quacking that issued from the bills of a line of brass ducks, ranged by size and length of neck, that had grown up beneath the Chief's barrel-car while the throng was still applauding. The four actors ran down the stairs and pulled forth members of the audience; the silver cat invited Equivair to dance. Soon the whole clearing was filled with leaping cats. The two parties mingled freely, though most of the dancers chose partners from among their friends. At the end of the reel the ducks blew a long blast.

"Return to your seats!" called Mr. Dizzy in a loud voice. His car descended its track; he walked forth and stood just behind and between the two young bears with a long drinking-horn in his hand. The cats below poured back into the mossy trench; the servitors once more appeared, dispensing goblets and cups of every description; once again the wheeled barrels made their rounds, and the multifarious vessels were slopped full of some sparkling beverage which Equivair's party did not now disdain. Edgar and Alice, looking down the glade, suddenly and uncomfortably found themselves the objects of steady attention for a host of paired green-yellow lamps.

"Hooburgaloo!" roared Mr. Dizzy, and "Hooburgaloo-gle!" swept from the throats of five hundred cats in reply.

"Tonight," the Chief went on, "we meet together for the first time in many years." A cheer a little less than full-throated went up from the pit. "And our face is greased—I mean, our feast is graced—by the presence of two most hognorable guests. Gentlefelines! A toast! Raise your glasses to the health, the happiness, the porkspareribbity, of the squeallustrious Gruntusculo and the hamcomparable Wallowine!"

"Long live Gruntusculo!"

"Long live Wallowine!"

"Hail to the pigs!"

The garden glade resounded to the bravos of the cats and the clatter as they knocked glasses, mugs, pitchers, tea-cups, cans, soap-dishes, steins, bud-vases, jam-pots, salt-cellars, canisters, inkhorns, cream-jugs. Then followed a long pause while every throat rippled to the passage of the liquor. Edgar was just trying to frame a polite reply, one that would be decorous in the mouth of a grandly feted pig, when the silence was broken by a loud, harsh voice from the end of the clearing, crying,

"And death to all bears!"

Then Equivair, smiling, rose to his feet. Behind him, dandies were standing to brandish their feathered chapeaux. They were hurling their hats in the air, they were jumping up too. They were behaving like Clowncats. Now the cats across the trench were on their feet, and Equivair still smiled. All of the crowd except for Equivair were howling, but his smile was like a howl. Edgar could not understand this surge of clamorous rage. He had missed a step, somehow: was this how the cats drank toasts, and did they expect him to rise and howl along with them? The howling turned to chanting. The chant was "Death to the Bears!" Edgar in shock clutched one last time at the thought that had sustained him all that long day: he was still within the frontiers of the Commonwealth of Bears, and in one of its largest cities, where his uncle was chief magistrate. But his uncle was Claudio, whom he had just seen portrayed on the steps. That bubble burst, and then he saw. This place was no part of the city. This place was a forest, and the moon overhead was a hunter's moon. And Equivair was smiling.

Alice turned a look of reproach on Mr. Dizzy; she studied his broad, bony face, trying to read their fate in his expression. Musingly he returned her stare, then smiled.

"Ah, little pigtures of disgruntled dismay," he said softly, "my gamble has failed, and I have lost more by it than you have, but the Clowncats most of all. Adieu, adieu, my little Wallowine, my brave Gruntusculo. We shall meet again, but now we must part. If you value your necks, you will not stir from off your seats. Farewell." He turned, and went back to the Throne. What he did there they never saw, for the cats now came yelling out of the pit towards the stairs, Equivair in the midst of them, giving orders. He pointed at them; and as he did so, the ground beneath them shook and gave way, and they sank down into darkness.

NINE. **The Silver Dancer.**

*T*hey cried out as they went down, calling each other by name, but they were in separate shafts and could not hear. A few moments passed of solitary terror. Then came a time when, though they still sank through total blackness, they grew conscious that they were no longer immured, and that their unsteady perches, Edgar's stepladder and Alice's rocking-horse, had carried them down into some vast space beneath the garden and the Throne. They were in fact no farther apart than they had been aboveground, but when they ventured a whisper, each thought the other's voice very small and far away, as if surrounded by empty immensity. When they called a little louder, echoes came back to them after a long time, reduced to senseless rustling like mice's feet among a litter of small bones; so they fell silent again.

They had no way of judging how far or how fast they were descending. Edgar felt no upward rush of air, yet he could not rid himself of the fancy that he was plummeting to sudden destruction. But at last they felt a gentle bump, and their seats came to rest. A high whine, noticed only after it had ceased, now cut off, and a silence as complete as the darkness enfolded them.

Edgar gingerly climbed down his stepladder and groped with his foot; at once his toes felt the cool stone of a solid floor. He drew a deep breath and set his whole weight on it. It held firm. He took a step, arms outstretched, in the direc-

103

tion in which he thought his sister must be found, if they had kept the same relative positions as above, on the chessboard terrace. At once he smashed into some large object that rocked from the impact; he clutched at its edges to keep it from falling, and screamed, "Alice!"

"Here! Edgar! What are you doing?" Her shrill voice came from nearby but was strangely baffled, as if it travelled through a wall. "I'm coming," she called, and the next moment the thing that Edgar gripped (smooth wood, squared and planed) rocked again, nearly tipping over on top of him. Then his clutching paw found his sister's, reaching around from the other side. As soon as the wooden thing stood steady, they were in each other's arms.

When the warm comfort of touch had restored some calm to each of the badly frightened young bears, they began to ponder what had befallen them, and the nature of the place into which they were come. They slowly grew aware, from attempts to shift their position a little, that objects bulked all around them; Alice suddenly sighed. "Don't you see what all these things are? All the things that came up through the floor! The clock, the case of snails . . . ." Edgar saw it at once, and wondered at the invention, which must have cost some brain a heavy price in calculations, and many hands weeks in the building of it. Why, there must be shafts sunk as deep again in the earth below them as they had already descended, to house the columns that pushed this array of articles to the surface! Had the cats constructed all of this? Why?

They began to grope their way out of the forest of upright forms, a task that grew easy enough when they recalled the quincunxial chessboard arrangement of them. They moved, without at first realizing it, in the direction that would, aboveground, have taken them towards the Throne, and soon encountered a high wooden paling that blocked their path. It curved away from them on either hand; they decided to skirt it. After several dozen steps taken with their right paws on the wood, they began to worry that the fence was a circular enclosure, around which they might have travelled, for all they knew, several times. But then they looked away from the fence and saw the lights.

There were two, very small and far away, two clear pinpoint gleams of hot white like distant wildfire or houses aflame on a steppe. What could they do but go chase these fata morgana? There was no retreat; Edgar thought bitterly that Bargeton never offered a way *back*. Likewise there seemed no point at all in lurking where they were. Neither of them could guess whether Mr. Dizzy, in sending them here below, had meant to save them, or simply to relieve himself of a pair of embarrassing guests, so what should they wait for? "If we don't start to move soon," complained Alice, "I'm going to forget my own shape. You're already no more than a voice, and I can't tell where I stop, exactly; I don't want to puddle out into nothing!"

They moved forward with exaggerated care, whispering cautions to one another, hinting at such perils as might uncoil or yawn beneath their feet, although the floor they traversed, high-stepping, was perfectly plane and smooth, and their toes encountered not so much as a rounded pebble. But without these elaborate fictions of dangers to guard against, it was hard to keep up the illusion of movement at all. So in a rhythm of heart-leapings, paw-clutchings, and slowly returning confidence, they crept across that boundless plain of stone, dividing the immeasurable spread of time into minutes of shock and seeming hours of willed calm. For a long time the lights did not seem to grow any nearer. A fear grew on Alice which she did not whisper to her brother, though it was far more real than any of her suppositions of skulls or rats, that the lights might suddenly go out; Edgar kept the same fear to himself.

Then, after a long, dead stretch in which their pace quickened and their fancies slackened, the two lights began to move apart. Shortly thereafter, each divided into two bright glows; the pair on the right took on a yellowish tinge. Then the bears began to imagine that they could see a huddle of objects beneath each twinned incandescence, catching the light, and they moved still faster; now, if a pit or crack had opened before them, they would have walked right into it. But Alice had seen a gleam on the wet tip of her brother's nose, and two more in his eyes, each redoubled orange and yellow, and she could make out her own paw's silhouette when she held it before her. This return of vision filled her with fresh spirit.

At last two scenes developed in wavering light before their aching eyes, one near at hand, the other divided from it by some hundreds of feet of night; they must pause to study them, and to decide which to make for.

In the scene on the left a robed figure sat at a vanity table between two torches set upon high stands. By their flaring, ruddy light the figure studied its reflection in a large oval mirror. Three others waited upon it in deferential attitudes. Edgar, squinting, made them out to be cats; at the same moment Alice caught a glimpse of the face that floated in the glass: it was the silver-furred dancer's.

The second tableau, far to their right, showed them another figure that sat with its back to them at a long table. Two thick tapers, stuck on iron spikes, raised fat, yellow flames, one on either side of the lopsided mass they took to be the sitter's head. This figure, which they did not recognize, even as to its kind, appeared to be eating. Edgar saw a black elbow lifted and a sparkle as of a crystal decanter tilted; he heard the ring of glass knocking glass.

Alice pulled him toward the cats. As they drew nearer, they saw that the three cats standing like lady's-maids about the robed dancer were none other than the tiger-striped males who had performed with her on the stairs. She rose and let the robe fall from her shoulders. The three began to caress her silver fur, all over her body, while she stood looking in the mirror; then, coming closer still, the two young bears saw that all three males held combs, and that they were lovingly grooming her long coat. Her eyes were half-closed with the pleasure of their ministrations; Alice was once again struck by the beauty of the face in the mirror, but then she was startled to see that those reflected, reflecting eyes held her in their gaze. She seized her brother by the upper arm, and they came to a halt at the edge of the light.

"Come forward," said the face in the glass; its expression was unreadable. The voice was low, gravelly, almost gruff, as if it were not often used. They took a step or two forward into the light. Not sure why he did so, Edgar stole a look at Alice, curious to see her after so many fears and so much darkness. The truth was, he wanted to remind himself of her familiar, comfortable presence, to reassure himself that something in the visible world was still the same amidst all this bewildering difference. He was therefore rather upset to see that his sister had changed, he could not quite tell how. She still clutched his arm, but she was staring at the silver cat with an expression compounded out of various wantings and anxieties.

"Look how you are trembling!" exclaimed the cat; Edgar could feel his sister's shivers transmitted to his arm, and then grew aware of his own shaking. The dank chill of the darkness through which they had walked struck him now for the first time. "Go, fetch them seats," the silver cat commanded, and two of the striped males whisked off to return lugging a wicker settee. "Here, beside me. Now come and sit. What shall we wrap you in? My robe must serve for two. Come, sit! I am your friend. I have been waiting for you."

They perched themselves on the settee. The silver cat caught up her robe and draped it across their shoulders. Alice sniffed with pleasure at the hem of it. The dancer turned away and stepped lithely into a pair of breeches, then held out her arm, half-bent, behind her. One of the striped servitors helped her into a tunic that she then quickly buttoned up the front. Alice noticed how the spring-green silk from which both garments were cut had been sewn in lozenges, the weave of each running counter to those surrounding it, so that glossy was everywhere bordered by matte, and matte by glossy. It fell to Edgar to catch the gleam of tiny white jewels stitched on at the corners of the lozenges. Over one shoulder the dancer tossed a half-cape of coral velvet lined with the same green, put her feet into slippers adorned with salmon roses, and then sat down again on her stool.

"But I did not know by which of all the ways that there are in this palace you might come," she went on, looking slowly at each of the bears in turn. Blinking, not understanding, they returned her gaze, Alice as if enchanted, Edgar in fresh wonder at the strange proportions of her beauty. Beneath the fine, silver fur, around the tranquil, slow-considering eyes, her skull showed its angles and planes; it was, he thought, a perfect face to lie beneath that series of masks he had seen her put on and off. "I could not stop to hear the toasts drunk; I and my company do not use to linger when once our play is done, our magic would be spoilt. And I was stayed for, here below." She gestured toward the distant table where the tapers burned and the dark-clad figure still had not moved. "But I know that Dionisio our Chief designed to drink your health; now tell me, little one," she said to Alice, and leaned forward, "with what success he met? Although I partly guess," she added.

Alice haltingly described the toasts, and the call of "Death to all bears," the furious outcry among the cats in the pit, Mr. Dizzy's last words to them, and their sudden descent.

"Ay, so I knew it would be," the silver cat sighed. "A gamble indeed he made there, to think that Equivair would easily submit to so arrant a piece of Clowncat nonsense. Ay, I knew he had failed, when you both crossed from yonder."

"Excuse me," Edgar blurted suddenly, "but *we* don't understand at all. What was this gamble? Why did Mr. Dizzy bring us to the banquet, if all cats hate bears so much? Did he really hope they would consent to think us pigs? I don't see how he could. I . . . ." He wanted to say that he felt they had been badly used, as if they were pieces in some secret game that cats played against cats; but this too was a cat, and the game might not yet be finished. And he did not like to be impolite to her. Uncomfortably he cut himself short, but the anger he felt must have shown in his face, for the silver dancer replied, with the same wry smile he had seen her wear earlier, above on the stairs,

"You are not native to this city, then, I guess? Yet Claudio is your relative, is he not?"

"Our uncle," they mumbled, Alice timidly, Edgar with a touch of defiance, both wondering how she could know this.

"You must know a little, then, of what broils are toward in Bargeton. You have heard your uncle, perhaps, speak of Clowncats as a lowly rabble? And you saw what sort of a figure he cut in our comedy. He is become one of our common characters, your uncle, a humor unto himself; he has a part in many of our plays. We speak of 'the Claudio'; 'Who plays the Claudio?' we ask when a new piece is proclaimed. It is sometimes a risky part. Your uncle long has thwarted us, young bears. Lately he threw, with no color of justice, one of our best-loved leaders into prison, only for that he came to him with a petition. Had you heard of that? Yes? And then that he was strangely set free, last night?

"Ah! Was your uncle *very* wroth?" she asked, and her eyes gleamed with mischievous pleasure.

"We only heard about it from his servant," Edgar answered, grudgingly. "Our uncle was out of the house on business before we got up this morning."

"Yes," added Alice, "and he stayed up long after us last night. In fact, I don't think he could have slept at all, because I saw him in the garden in the middle of the night, talking with Julio and the Great Golden Bear."

"Alice!" cried Edgar, a second too late, after he had seen real surprise cross the silver dancer's face.

"What? What is it? Have I said something wrong? Edgar, was it supposed to be a secret? No one told me to keep it a secret. It has nothing to do with cats, anyway. He's here to help defend the city against the Crimson Bears—isn't that what you told me, Edgar? Why should that be kept secret?" Alice was scared and upset; Edgar did not know what to say.

"I don't know if it was a secret, but . . . ."

"But news to me," said the silver cat softly. "The Great Golden Bear in Bargeton! None in Clowncattown have yet heard of it; this intelligence will be much talked of. O, do not fret yourself, young bear!" she said rather sternly to Edgar. "Have I not said that I am your friend? Now rise and come with me," she commanded, springing up, "I must bring you acquainted with another friend, he who sits lonely yonder. He knows your uncle; he was his guest till yesternight. Come." They rose to their feet. She took them each by a paw. "You will clear all this away," she said across her shoulder, and led them out. Before they had reached the limit of the light, their shadows suddenly vanished, and all around them was midnight once again. They looked back and saw nothing—it was as if that whole little island of light had sunk into blackness. Only the twin tapers palely burned, a long way ahead of them.

TEN. **Possy Damp Paws.**

*A*s they crossed to the other island of light, where their uncle's recent prisoner sat waiting for them, Alice and Edgar found their thoughts all broken up in free-drifting questions of the most diverse kinds, as, "Where is the ceiling of this vault?" "Why does she dress like a male?" "Do the cats want us for hostages?" "Why was Equivair so civil to us?" and "Are the cats in league with the Crimson Bears?" But since there was no way to know, they let themselves be pulled along through deep night by the now invisible dancer's strong grip. And slowly, for want of answers, the questions themselves, like ice floes, drifted apart and away beyond the verge of thought, leaving behind them only the gently rocking ocean of mind, black and void, ready to float whatever new impression came along. They were both, to say truth, in an extraordinary condition, knowing themselves prisoners of a situation they could not understand, yet detached from it by their very exhaustion, and the super-plenitude of the experience they had absorbed, and also, perhaps, by the fact that they were both in it together. If either Edgar or Alice had had to deal alone with this succession of events, these demonstrations of hatred followed by claims upon their trust, and all the other complex ironies that these cats seemed to take delight in, he or she might not have held out so long. But they were together; and then, they were young, and had both just eaten.

So, joined in the chilly darkness by the thrill of the dancer's touch, they walked on beside her till they stood at the edge of the tapers' nimbus. Their starved eyes battened eagerly upon the thick stalks of the candles, translucent at their tops, decked down their length in strings of greasy tears; upon the waxed boards of the table where the candleshine shed golden pools, in which arrowhead glints from the faceted decanter— itself a mere constellation around a smooth ruby glow— swam like a school of fish stilled in mid-dart. They studied with pleasure the graded tones of pallor in the papers scattered over the table-top, curl-edged like porcelain shavings, and the patterns in their crisscross sepia scrawl. But the cat who sat behind this display of lights, still studying the sheet upon which he was writing, had a face so black that it hardly emerged from the darkness. It was not, like the dancer's silver head, clean of contour; rather, it spread to either side in a thick fan of sable whisker. The features grouped in the center of this dense cloud were delicate and neat, but did not acquire a focus till the cat withdrew his attention from the papers; then the young bears were transfixed by a pair of eyes, pale, brilliant blue; the bonnet of midnight velvet that crowned him seemed to Edgar to figure, in its shapelessness, the boilings of unfettered mind.

Then the cat was on his feet. He swept the bonnet from his head and made them a courteous bow.

"Have no fear," were his first words to them, "although the place be something tenebrous and vasty-gloomy, yet we may shed light of cheer in it by changing loving greetings." The voice surprised Alice, who had expected a deep, full-chested growl, by twanging out in the middle range. Then he came around the table, and she saw that his figure was slight beneath his robe.

113

"Well met, well met indeed, young friends; you are safe landed now on our quiet shore. None of the rout above comes nigh us here; we may be private, and merry together as Fortune's cast-offs, whom the tempest, passing, leaves behind it, glad of their lives, though driven in wrack on desert strand—" he paused to survey the table-top as if it were such an island as he imagined; Alice, then, found herself too weary to resist the suggestion that made of the scattered white papers a landscape of shelving ice or bird-dunged rock—"on desert strand," he repeated musingly. "Which this ring of little light as aptly figures as the darkness about us an ocean to divide us from our hopes. I know whose niece and nephew you are. Your uncle, I thank him, had me lately in's jail. Durance not vile but gentle. He used me honestly enough, did Master Claudio; but still, 'twas prison. Since I am escaped, however, by help of a friend whom you perchance should wonder to hear named, there keeps no manner of ill-will between you and me. You yourselves, I think, are fugitives? For I cannot think that Claudio has willingly enlarged you thus to roam the city at such a juncture, nor to amble into the haunts of gentry so ill-conditioned as the Clowncats." All the while he spoke, he held them each by a paw, and smiled, and gazed.

"Possy, y'are prolix," drawled the silver dancer, who had seated herself lollingly in her chair. "Dionisio's shifts are come to nought. By this time he is deposed, and thy cousin Equivair leads all the cats conjoined along his way. Keep within compass."

"Thanks, sweet," the black cat thoughtfully replied. "Ay me, I guessed it would be so. But now I forget myself indeed! Here I stand prating and yet know not your names! Small courtesy indeed; pray tell me, how you are called?" Edgar and Alice told him. "I like these names! Simple, honest names—indeed, they bespeak the virtues of the bears, to which, believe me, I am not blind, I hope I still can see past privy grievance. But now, to make myself known to you, what shall I say?"

"Not much!" said the silver cat with sudden energy, sitting up in her chair. "By no means, voluble Possy, shall I be party to the slow unfolding of thy lineage, nor lend ear to the tedious bomphiology with which thou art wont to set forth the quarterings and impresses of thy house. Believe me, young bears, the River Flood itself is a sluggish trickle for kittens to lap at, to the all-o'ersweeping tide of Possy's ancestry. Why, let him but say his complete name, and we are condemned to a nine-hours' sitting. Therefore will I present him to you, he is simple Possy, known as Possy Damp Paws, gentlecat of Clowncattown; and I myself am Zawailza, and no more."

"I fear this looks like rudeness," Possy protested. "We ought not to mar our fames by giving ourselves a lesser countenance than what we truly own; but, sure, we must for this await some larger occasion . . ." and, with a touch of regret, he swept them another bow.

"Now you shall sit at your ease," he resumed, drawing out a bench from beneath the table, "and, if it like you, I would gladly hear what you have seen since you have been among us."

They sat, and Possy Damp Paws perched himself on the table's edge. Edgar began the account of their coming among the ruinous animal-mansions. Alice stared from one to another of the cats, and wondered if they were brother and sister. But the silver cat, Zawailza, had not claimed Equivair

115

for a cousin. Was she then not noble? Could she be only a Clowncat? Alice again studied the dancer's long, sleepy face, then shifted her gaze to Possy's raked bonnet, to the ballooning of his dove-gray sleeves, the inky folds of his robe, and the quick sparking of his broad blue eyes. She started to find these suddenly turned on her, and her name spoken:

"'Twas well related, Edgar, you show us to the life. It was well that you joined in the Clowncats' frolic measure, it showed a quick apprehension and a good heart. But, Alice, do you take up the tale, I would fain hear you."

As Alice began to speak of the Throne and the banquet, Edgar sat still beside her on the bench, while muscles deep-buried in his shoulders, neck, and calves slowly unknotted one by one. He had not had so much to tell, but Possy's eyes had made the telling a severe trial; not that those eyes were misdoubtful. No, but Possy was simply the most intent listener Edgar had ever had. The black cat's shifting expression had shown how closely he was following the story's least contours, like a bird flying low across a terrain whose rises and dips its flight must closely mimic. So Edgar had striven to make the landscape varied, as he worked to convey the exact impression made on him by the animal-mansions, by the dancing Clowncats and the Chief Hooburgaloo, by the mountainous trash-heaps, and the courtly Equivair. And as he struggled, he found that his every phrase was followed, its direction noted, its cadence savored, and an answer posted in those changeable eyes. In the end Edgar felt he had come through it well, but he was exhausted. He began to listen to Alice; critically he caught at her words. She had just got through telling of the fireworks and the musical luggage. Now, he realized with a spasm of relief, she would have to describe the acting, with Zawailza sitting there to hear her! He was glad it had not fallen to him to tell that part. But Alice had always been fond of stories. She spoke, he found, in well-measured periods, and placed her emphasis with great assurance. Edgar was amazed to hear how much of the comedy she remembered, and how much more of it she had understood than he had. She even alluded, delicately, to the display of greedy attention that Equivair's followers had made to the silver cat's dancing, and Edgar, watching Zawailza's face, saw her smile a weary, disdainful smile, while one quick yellow glint of remembered anger shot from her half-closed eyes.

"Why, Zawailza," Possy exclaimed, when Alice had finished describing the toasts and Mr. Dizzy's last words to the bears before they had sunk through the ground, "now tell me, where are you, truly, here beside me, or in this lady's tale? Stand Equivair and Dizzy yet above, or do they not rather inhabit the words of this pair of rare expounders? Surely it is but insubstantial shadows that walk the skin of the earth, a ghost-Dizzy and a phantasm-Equivair. They wrangle about the command of shades, for the life of those dancers and carousers, the Clowncats, resides in these recountings. Mistress Alice, well done, you have shown us our very forms in a true glass, I have known them, not without pain indeed; how odd it is that strangers should show us more than we could know of our own selves, and that only in this dark cellarage should cat-kind come to visibility."

"The telling was good," Zawailza said coolly, but both the young bears, hearing an undertone of laughter, caught her eye and were at once made complicit in her teasing of Possy, "and I would gladly hear it grow to limn the portrait of Possy

Damp Paws, that famous orator; but those same insubstantial shadows may soon descend, or else send down, to wrangle with *you*, my lord. What do you mean to do?"

"O, I'll await 'em here," he replied insouciantly. "Dizzy loves me well; he'll come now to take counsel with us, his designs being frustrate. Cousin Equivair loves me not at all, yet he will have need of me, sore need, if one may judge from these." He waved his paw above the litter of curling scrolls on the table, which had already drawn Edgar's eye more than once. From the glimpses he could get, they looked to be drawings or plans of the parts of a machine. This was naturally interesting, but what was even more so was the sheet, half-unfurled, that showed in vertical section the bottom half of some large creature's leg, drawn to plot not muscle and bone but jointed rods and clustered gear-wheels. There was something like a chain-drive too. But Edgar could not begin to guess what this contraption was for, or how it would form a basis for dealings between Possy and Equivair.

"Ay," the black cat growled, "they will both come to me. And you liked my Throne," he said to Alice, with no change of tone. "Mine I call it for that I made it; you did not know that, maybe. Years of patience it cost me, it is of my labors the largest but one. This making has been my life; I have not walked often, there above." Edgar peered toward the invisible ceiling. The world beyond it seemed remote and flat as legend; his own travels, a kind of crawling across a thin crust. "We work within these walls, my helpers and I, by our toil the Throne burgeons over our heads. You gave me much pleasure, my Alice, recounting its several motions, for that I designed them and built them all. From here beneath I directed them; it is why I am here. When Dizzy's car rolled down its track, when the spinning baggage skirled musics, when rockets flew and Clowncats roared, I was at work, at each metamorphosis of the Throne I was at work, I, here below, I touched the keys and stops; from this room I governed the action."

Edgar stared; Alice, to whom most of this harangue was addressed, struggled to conceal her surprise. Yet Possy's words were not boastfully pitched. "Therefore, Zawailza," he went on, after only the slightest of pauses, "the Chief and my cousin have leave to look for me. For now we can begin to move that way I guessed we must. Dizzy has made his venture, and had my service to it; now he must serve mine. Equivair, trust me, only seems to prevail—may his well-looking fortune keep him blind!"

"It may be so," Zawailza replied, "but I am loath that cats should drink dishonor, whereof Equivair fills 'em a brimming cup; and I fear, too, that cats will bleed, some hour not long to wait."

Possy pretended he had not heard her.

"Yet I wonder at Dizzy's policy, in this matter of healths drunk," he went on, "and still more at his making these our young friends welcome at our revels. Pigs, did he call you?"

"Yes," answered Alice, "but I still don't know why."

"'Twas done for your better protection," said Zawailza. "You would have been rudelier used in your own persons, but Gruntusculo and Wallowine might be honored guests."

"But everyone could see that we're really bears, not pigs."

"True, but Clowncats love a jest better, at most times, than they hate a foe, being clowns by nature; and by jests such as these, and many another rank absurdity, has our fertile-witted Chief maintained the ill-mannered rout within the bounds of civil government."

"Ay, but he could not think," said Possy, "that Equivair nor his haughty partisans could e'er consent to submit to his too arrant nonsense and non sequiturs. Then so to propose their healths, at such a time, was not this merely to invite an insurrection? And so Dizzy falls. I tell you, I wonder at it."

"It may be, Possy, he was in this a better politician than you reckon him. For let us imagine absent our Alice and our Edgar; what health must he next have offered, but your own? Then had your cousin made his will fractious and held his cup from his lip, where had you been? It was, I guess, Chief Dizzy's thought to try the wind to see which way it blew. The feasting, the rockets, the luggage-music, all the several actions of the Throne, and last our comedy, all this was done to bring our kind out of their factions and into harmony, fit to consent to common cause and common leadership. This end gained, had it proven tolerable to their patience to look on Claudio's kin, seated among them, Dizzy would have known most assuredly that the cats were apt to take that path of moderation which he and you and I have hoped they'd follow. This was no empty expectation; you must know," she said to Edgar and Alice, "that not all our kind think so ill of yours as to design 'em mischief."

There followed a lull in the talk while Possy digested the dancer's words. It was ended when Alice said, in a troubled voice,

"Excuse me, Zawailza, but I still don't understand why any cats should want to do mischief to bears."

Edgar looked at Possy, and saw his face grow stern. Zawailza also glanced toward the black cat, as if she expected him to make reply, but when he did not, she gently said to Alice,

"Why, thou saw'st the Claudio in our comedy, how stiff he was; so most bears seem to us, those seldom occasions when

120

we encounter 'em, which falls when we run foul of their laws. It is the office we see, never the bear; nor bears see not the cat, but the clown, the miscreant, the pauper, the vagabond, the sturdy beggar, ay, and the thief. You may say these are our offices. So office speaks ever to office, and never creature to creature; so is love lost between us. Here is another reason why our Dionisio should desire to show our assembly two young bears that so far forgot their bearish dignities, that they would jig with Clowncats! This is a phenomenon indeed! The auditors in the pit, that laughed and cried out on the Claudio, might look past him and see you laughing with them. Five more such visits, my loves, would go far to erase the quarrel between our kinds."

"But what *is* the quarrel?" Edgar asked, not happy to be reminded that he and his sister had mocked their uncle before a whole audience of these creatures. Possy looked up from the floor and kindly scanned his face.

"Be assur'd, young sir, 'tis not with you nor your fair sister. Zawailza hath said it: two so courteous and magnanimous bears have not come amongst us here, where we live, in many a long year."

"But, Lord Possy," Edgar began again, and Alice, who had heard a new note in the black cat's voice, now grew anxious at her brother's truculence, "why should there be any quarrel at all? My uncle only does his duty. He *is* the chief magistrate of Bargeton, and this is, after all, the Commonwealth of Bears, whose laws he is bound to enforce." Edgar stopped abruptly. He had somehow said something wrong, for Possy's face had lost its friendly aspect, turned cold and unsmiling. But before Edgar could choke out an apology, though he had no idea what he should apologize for, the cat turned haughtily on his heel and stalked off into the darkness.

ELEVEN. **Felipo's Treasury.**

"*I*'m afraid we've given some offense," said Alice quick-ly to Zawailza. "Please ask Lord Possy to come back, and excuse our rudeness. We didn't intend any impoliteness."

"No, and I'm very sorry for . . . for whatever I said that was wrong," said Edgar, who was really quite angry himself, feeling that he had somehow been put into a false embarrass-ment. What had he said that was not incontestably true? Zawailza's tone, when she spoke, was no less civil than before; but something of a coolness had entered her voice, as well as a sadness.

"Possy must choose his own time for returning," she said. "It is with him as with others of his birth: their rage stands still on the point of a pin, in doubtful balance; the least gust spills it. Now he must walk a while, and mend his tempera-ture. This curse afflicts the best of us, and to tell you truth, Sir Edgar, your words, though veering not from the strict line of truth, raised a motion of anger in my breast also."

"Please forgive me, Zawailza," said Edgar, now com-pletely miserable. "I must be awfully stupid, or I never would have said anything to hurt you—you've been so kind to us."

"Teach us how we have angered you," added Alice, uncon-sciously adopting the silver cat's own language, "so that we may mend our manners."

"Why, your courtesy puts me to shame," said Zawailza, smiling, "and I am embarrassed to show you error where none lies; only the truth you uttered is a hard one for us to hear. We love not to be reminded that we are a subject kind, that is all. For true it is, that our beloved Clowncattown is now no more than a poor, ruinous suburb of your thriving Bargeton, and that we all are client to the bear. Yet was it not always thus."

"Your bearish scholars falter, and their learning decays, if they taught you not that," came Possy's voice out of the darkness beyond the taper-glow. Seemingly recovered in temper, he sauntered back into the circle of light, a jovial if slightly wry smile on his face once more. "Did your historical doctors ne'er instruct you in the matter of Concatena, the Cattish Kingdom, that held all these cisfluminous parts in its claws, north and south?"

Edgar and Alice were forced to confess their ignorance, and Possy showed signs of haughty disdain.

"Possy, be mindful of the centuries that have passed ere this Clowncattown last received her King, or her right name of Concatenopolis, whereof 'Clowncattown' is but the vulgar corruption, twisted in the mouths of the poor strays we are grown to be—nay, gainsay it not, proud Possy, for if you and a few score others have cloven to the memory of what once was, and to traditions of honor and learning, how many others of that rough multitude have turned wholly away, and seek their daily sustenance in the refuse of the bears? What other course than that do you offer them? To what hunt will you lead them in these latter times? Small wonder, then, if our affairs are not the study of the bearish schools.

"Where you now sit," she went on, turning back to Edgar and Alice, "was some time the treasury of the Lion-King of Concatena, and all this hugy vault was filled with his uncounted wealth. Felipo was his name. Come, we will look on him together." Zawailza rose to her feet and plucked a candle from off its spike, then beckoned to the bears to follow her. Possy caught up the remaining taper and followed in the rear of the procession, which now set off through darkness. They walked for a long while without speaking, the candlelight showing no more than a circle of smooth stone floor. Alice kept her eyes on the dancer's figure and her graceful walk. Edgar pondered how so immense a space could ever have been filled with treasure.

By and by they slowed; the glow from Zawailza's candle ran up a wall that appeared in front of them. Coming closer, they saw the living rock, but in places the light was reflected in a dull gleam. Then they made out smooth areas of irregularly shaped blonde tiles, laid in no pattern than they could discern, for in many places the tiles were laid alongside one another, and ingeniously joined so that only the tiniest of hairline cracks showed between them; you had to pass a paw across these edges to feel that they were there. But the tiled areas were bordered by rough rock, the very wall of the cavern. At last Alice guessed that the tiles must compose a picture. But she could not see enough of it to guess what it was.

"Are these trees?" she asked diffidently, pointing to two shapes that mounted the walls like stocky boles.

"By your good favor, my lord Possy," exclaimed Zawailza impatiently, "can you not make us some larger light?"

"Endure, I beseech you, yet a moment this feeble glow, till my powder comes to hand," Possy replied. "A pox on these pockets! A regiment of lynxes might lose their way in one of them. Ah, I have it! Now you shall see Felipo Segundo face to face."

So saying, he shook from a little canister a quantity of fine powder onto the head of his candle, which sputtered and suddenly flared in a burst of strong, white light. An immense sweep of wall loomed up and over them, bending inwards; Alice gasped and leaned back to see. Far above their heads, to the height of ten grown bears, there towered the image of a white lion, its body shown in profile. But its face was turned outwards, and it bared its teeth in a grimace of rage. What Alice had taken for tree trunks were its two front legs. The huge paws now sprang into view at the base of the wall, rising as high as did Alice herself, and the far-extended talons were capable, if they had been real, of tearing open a cast-metal colossus.

"Behold the mightiest of our kings!" intoned Possy, while the light still burned. "The second Felipo, greatest of his house, shown as he was at the height of his power and ours. He it was that built this chamber, to receive the tribute of an hundred subject races; and to the end that no covetous thief nor treacherous minister, emboldened by hope of measure-less gain, seize what not to him nor any private wight pertained, but only to the King, Felipo set his gigant image here to guard, amaze, forestall. So over centuries he has kept ceaseless watch; and now he watches still, where no thief will think to come again, for the treasures of old are lost, and the very place is forgot to all but few.

"To more affright the temerarious intruder, and to display his power," Possy added, "look how his likeness is made. Do you guess, gentle bearcubs, yourselves descended from a race of hardy hunters, what substance that is in which Felipo is limned, as it were by marquetry, here in the living rock?"

"Ivory?" quavered Alice.

"Bones, my little one, bones and teeth, the relics of his enemies turned his quarry, hunted down and slain for their presumption of raising their wills against the awful *fiat* of Felipo! Artisans shaved and trimmed those bones, then set them in the wall with a mortar too terrific to be named. Of a thousand skulls his head is carven, his legs of an hundred thighs and shins. Gaze but upon his eyes!"

They had to step back twenty paces to do so, while Possy's torch fizzed and popped and shed a wavering light that seemed to lend life and movement to that horrible mask. When they had reached a suitable distance and could, by craning, get a clear glimpse of the effigy's eyes, they saw how fierce the two great ovals gleamed; they were evidently not of the same material as the rest of the mosaic.

"The pearly horn of the Narwhal," said Possy, "that great Monoceros of the Hyperboreal Sea, went into fashioning the whites of those great eyes, after Felipo and his hunters tracked the fish across wastes of ice in his northernmost province. The glassy hooves of the winged deer, having glanced the slopes that hedge the sunrise round, found in Felipo's pupils their latest place of rest. And in his irises are packed, an hundred to each, the bronze scales of the river-serpents that coil around weedy pillars in the drowned city of Roum, far in the South. Felipo himself dived to find them, though no cat loves water. Therefore, in emulation of his deed, must those who would be reckoned in the lists of heraldry, though by birth elect, plunge into the Flood and brave the soggy tug of wet confusion even so far as the opposite shore."

"And therefore art thou called Possy Damp Paws," laughed Zawailza, "the sole he of the generation now in flower to practise this clammy rite. Never had honor so bedraggled an aspect as when you clomb the mud-bank, weed by weed."

Their laughter sounded strangely in that place, running off into the vault to lose itself as water does in sand.

"'Tis true," said Possy then, "the custom is antique, and none before me for four lives of cats had satisfied its articles. O, rightly indeed is honor likened to a costly pearl, when both must be dived for! Yet I would not have all the ancient ceremonies disappear from remembrance, nor all the old arts neither."

"Push, my lord," Zawailza replied, looking up at Felipo in the failing sputter of the candle's blaze, "some few of these are worth the keeping, maybe, but for the most part they're worthless thrums, of no service to cats. Even Equivair affects 'em not. You would not have Felipo back again?" Possy said nothing. The bears stared at the lion's fading form. Presently Alice coughed.

"Are any of those bones . . . ?" she asked, bringing her words out haltingly, and stopped.

"I conceive you not," Possy answered, frowning. "What is it you would know about the bones?"

"She would ask," said Zawailza dryly, "if bones of bears be not there intermingled."

"None, none," said Possy seriously. "Lift that care from off your spirits. Felipo's might set ne'er a print upon the history of your kind, unless it were in legend handed down. Nay, long ere the first of the great bears shambled out of the hills and took up housekeeping in a cave by the seas, and licked his cubs to form in the wastes of our long-deserted western province; long ere your forebears rose to speech, and made themselves better than the Slizz, Felipo's power had faded, as his kind had dwindled. You are but latecomers, you bears. Your might increases yet, or would if you would venture forth, or reach your broad paws for the fruit of dominion, ripe now near to dropping. For who would contest your force? Not cats, the era even of our waning empire passed before your memories began, and your tales share no common matter with ours. Who else to stand against you? Not Thoog, no, sure: for though they be strong and subtle and cruel withal, they lack . . . ay, me, they lack what we now keep as the sole legacy of our great age, and that is the quick rage of the hot-blooded kinds. It slumbers beneath your thick pelts, young one, the generous flood of ire, but slumbers deep, coddled by all your quilted reason and close-wove charity. But some day it will awake. Then bears will see the vision of empire, and taste desire for universal mastery. You will raise up your own Felipos in that hour, to hold the world on the broad pad of your paw, and curse to see it so small. But for us that hour is long since fled."

"I muse you would wish it back again," Zawailza said.

"Look how this prancing choplogic puts me to it!" Possy cried. "So, Zawailza, you'd unhusk me quite, and have me blaze my inmost thoughts before the very image of Felipo, and in the presence of Claudio's kin! Yet she is in the right of it," he said to the bears. "I would not have Felipo back again, no, not if all his empire should be restored, and cats have infinite sway, and once more dwell in the conceitful palaces of a renewed Concatenopolis. We have dwindled beyond repair, we're Clowncats all, let my mad baths of honor pass for merest clowning!"

Edgar could not let this pass; Possy had impressed him too strongly. After a pause, in which the light of the candle sank to its natural size, he protested, "You built the Throne!"

Once again Zawailza's gruff laugh wrestled with the echoes.

"Ay, now y'are known, Possy Damp Paws!" she exclaimed. "For all your froth of wounded honor, 'tis a builder you are, and no courtier. Indeed, he built the Throne," she continued, turning to Edgar and Alice, "and built it out of multifarious trash gleaned from the heaps that you saw, built it for his compere and friend, Dionisio, Chief of the Clowncats. This art, not being ancient, is *not* lost, and we cats can make, build, fashion; but this Possy is our subtlest artificer, therefore, good sir, no more of Old Felipo and his glory, let's fashion something new. Let Equivair dream his dream of ancient sway restored; you shall make of the palace, before we are dead, a better place for me to dance in, and a more hospitable receiving chamber for our guests than this barren treasury, this infinite room of no riches. Let's see your shop. Ay, sir, your shop!" She insisted, as Possy stood staring at her, "your secret room, where you work your miracles! Nay, why do you shift about and make mouths at me like a gamesome ape in the Market Square? Let our guests see how you do." She winked at them. "Soon they must leave us, they're missed by now at Claudio's. 'Tis a long road from Clowncattown to Citadel Hill, and a seldom-traveled. Shall these the first bears to walk it in memory be let to go speak of us, without some glimpse of what we are, at our best? Come, they have trusted themselves into our hands; they have danced with Dizzy and eaten the Clowncat *olla podrida*; they have watched us play the Claudio, and heard how we pledge the bears, and been sent down into darkness, and made to hear us brable and chop out our speeches, you and I; shall we not make return of faith in them?"

"My sweet, the cause for why I hesitate is not that I doubt their honors, but this: I mind still that Claudio makes me in's

TWELVE. **The Boneyards.**

E dgar and Alice stared at the black cat's back, half afraid that they had once again given offense; but Zawailza caught their eye, and motioned to them to turn away. Looking out into the void of the Treasury, Edgar felt his brain all a-swamp with puzzles that he must urgently solve: whether these cats were really their friends and meant to let them go; what they expected him to tell his uncle and the Great Golden Bear; how he was going to persuade an angry Claudio that his fool scamp of a nephew should be allowed to relate his escapades to that hero in the midst of the crisis that had brought him to Bargeton, and whether the cats were not somehow linked to the Crimson Bears. He wondered too what Equivair was planning; what course it was that Possy, Zawailza, and Mr. Dizzy meant to pursue; finally, why he and Alice should now be standing facing into darkness, while behind them Possy leaned against the Treasury wall. It was with no small relief that the perplexed young bear suddenly saw the answer to the last, the most trivial, but by no means the least nagging of these riddles. This workshop they were to visit lay on the far side of the wall; Possy was busy conjuring a passage to it, and he desired the means kept secret.

So indeed it proved. When they turned again, a low, square door had opened in the wall between Felipo's legs.

"Our way lies through this door," said Possy in a hushed and chastened voice. "Now, gentle cubs, I must unsay what I

131

have said, and beseech you, as you value Possy's friendship, do not make full relation to your uncle of how you came unto my shop. This aperture you see is little known even to cats, it alone gives access to my quarters, I would not have it commonly known. You may say, 'Then we were guided thither,' or so, omitting to mention the manner how; this prevarication alone I beg of you."

Of course they promised. Possy made them a deep bow, then held out his arm in sign that they should enter. Zawailza went first, shielding her candle's flame against the draft; Alice followed, Edgar entered next, and Possy came last of all. His candle lagged behind a second; Edgar guessed he was closing the door to the Treasury, since the rush of air past his face now ceased. He was not unhappy to be sealed off from that huge hole.

They were in a low-ceilinged tunnel. "Have some care of your heads, young bears," murmured Possy (but the echoes still almost overrolled his words), "for this is a place set down by one of our ancient poets,

> Where all at once one reaches where he stands,
> With brows the roof, both walls with both his hands.

It may be you were best to walk on fours." But Edgar and Alice would not do so, seeing the cats did not.

Edgar hurried after Possy, leaving his sister to follow with Zawailza, for he was eager to put some questions about the Palace. Alice, for her part, wanted to know more about the cats, but also to engage Zawailza, to whom she felt drawn, in any kind of talk. So it was that they both heard approximately the same story: the histories of the cats and of their Palace

were not two different things. Both had grown slowly over a
thousand lives of cats, following no plan, but registering the
imprint of successive rulers' several characters, policies, urges,
whims. Felipo Segundo, the greatest of these monarchs, had
done the most. As Possy launched into a discourse on the
gests of this autocrat, Zawailza fell silent, and Alice was left
to listen as the black cat's grandiloquent periods unrolled;
each travelled back to her garnished by its few yards' journey
with a susurrus of echo that lent it sepulchral finality. Edgar,
meanwhile, walking by Possy's side, was trying to make out
the black cat's attitude. Possy's tone was rather too heated for
an equitable scholar, yet if he was a partisan of Felipo's, it was
strange how many damning ironies larded the string of de-
tails. What Edgar learned, above all, was how dearly the Lion
King had loved power, how much he had done to get it, how
long he had held it. Edgar chewed over this lust of Felipo's.
So personal an empire was not, he thought, much in the style
of the bears. None that he knew, Claudio least of all, would
cut a figure as universal dictator. Bears, he concluded, did like
to have things run by bears, but there they drew the line. He
himself could hardly imagine what it would be like to act
effectively on his own account, even in a much smaller world
than Bargeton was turning out to be. If he could get out of
this Palace, he did not think that he would ever feel the
hunger to build such a pile around him.

A few paces back, Alice had absorbed from the quality of
Zawailza's silent listening a certain critical interest in Possy's
fascination with Felipo Segundo. Clearly, this monarch's power
had endured beyond his death; Possy, at least, it still held in
thrall. He had studied Felipo's life and reign in detail, and the
elegant paragraphs of commentary that he now threw off

were not unrehearsed. Alice too found Possy's tone equivocal; she heard, perhaps magnified by the tunnel's echoes, a note of revulsion in his recitative, which she could not easily square with the intensity of his interest. She knew, however, that Felipo, though he might be Possy's obsession, was not his hero.

Felipo had worked to bring both history and Palace subject to his imperial will. At his behest, architects and scholars had labored over the years of his long reign; but he had failed in the end. There were parts of the Palace, said Possy, and those no mean closets or crannies, but whole wings of rooms and lofty-vaulted cellarages, which had never been charted by Felipo's sages, and on which his eye had never fallen. In the same way his histories, whose goal it was to legitimize his rule, magnify his person, and mirror his conception of what a cat should be, had never quite succeeded in eradicating certain legends, customs, traits, traditions, manners, modes of speech.

"Like clowning?" asked Alice.

"Ay, the clowns," said Zawailza sardonically, "they indeed were the first to go to the wall. They were sent down to dig these tunnels and to raise these foundations. They never saw day again. They were none of Felipo's minions, the clowns."

"He favored a graver decorum, with more suavity of address, yet was no enemy to wit in its place," Possy commented; Alice thought his judiciousness a little studied. "He brought his kind to the very apogee of their powers as builders and makers; no so conceitful architects have flourished since his day, I think. He thought to kill the clown that lurketh in each particular cat; to bury it, rather, beneath more politer manners, greater learning, a sweet reasonableness, and all the gentle disciplines of courtesy."

"This sort of burial he did so well," came Zawailza's prompt reply, "that ten thousands of Clowncats died of it. So many layers of affectation weighed something too heavy a burden on their clownish hearts. And in those that could better sustain such civil entombment, what ensued but continual warfare? The mad fool shut within; the courtier without, prancing, cogging and shifting, making mouths here and obeisances there; 'twas never a happy marriage."

"From such struggles as these grow the finest inventions of art," Possy rather stuffily remarked.

"But the victory went to the clown!" cried Zawailza. "He burst his bonds and danced free."

"Ay, so indeed it fell out, when Felipo was not long dead," said Possy, "just according to the figure of another of our poets:

> as when a Fume,
> Hot, dry, and gross (within the womb of Earth
> Or in her superficies begot),
> The more it is compress'd, the more it rageth;
> Exceeds its prison's strength that should contain it,
> And then it tosseth Palaces in air.

"Though this Palace sits yet on Earth's superficies, yet being thought haunted, it is now seldom visited, save by myself, and I know but a small fraction of all its rooms and ways; nor do I suppose the assembled knowledges of the last ten generations of Clowncats competent to make a map of it. My father knew more than I, but our learning decays apace. The clown indeed is everywhere now regnant."

"Not everywhere; we still have Possy Damp Paws," Zawailza maliciously said.

"'Tis Zawailza's beauty subdues the clown in him," he politely replied. "Else would I yowl and caper like any tom o' th' backyards."

Alice heartily hoped that the part of the Palace they were now passing through was the part that Possy knew. They had begun to pass many archways opening off the passage they were following, but they made no turn. She saw her brother, six paces or so ahead of her, peer into each of the openings as he went by. She herself took no interest in them, did not care what lay beyond them, unless it was the way out of the Palace. But she could not restrain herself from giving a sidelong glance from time to time. She did not see much: blackness, mainly, a familiar sight by now. But Zawailza's taper illumined, each time Alice peeked to right or left, a patch of wall just inside the arch. It was a strange sort of masonry they had used in the building of those walls: pale members laid in horizontal bands to make a rugose surface, like a basket woven from some reed of gigantic girth, or some swollen water-weed dried and bleached in the sun.

"O!" thought Alice, recalling the mosaic on the wall of the Treasury, "I suppose they're bones."

"These are our boneyards," replied Zawailza to her question. "All dead cats are buried in the Palace. Come, if I show you one of these chambers, you will see they hold nor ghosts nor ghouls. It is but bones, Alice." They paused, and the dancer thrust her taper inside an opening. Alice looked squinting into a beehive cavern, not large but lined from apex to floor with white bones. They were far too large for Clowncats. "Of old we were weightier creatures," said Zawailza. Alice spotted one skull near the floor, that sprouted a long arc of fang from its upper jaw.

Then they hurried to catch up with Possy and Edgar, trotting past dozens of the burial-chambers, and past cross-tunnels down which Alice could see the dark mouths of more. She caught herself nervously sniffing the air, but smelt only damp stone.

"Are these the dead from Felipo's time?" she inquired at length, only to break the oppressive silence.

"No," said Possy. "These are older. Felipo's dead subjects rest all beside their king." He paused in the tunnel. "'Tis not far to where they lie," he said reflectively, with the air of one who means to indulge a private wish. "Not far from here; 'twould not lengthen our way by much to visit them, and the hour is propitious. The moon, Zawailza, stands high by now. If we hasten, we shall arrive jump at the time to view Felipo's tomb—what say you? Ought not our guests to see this sight?"

"Lead on, lead on, Possy Damp Paws," Zawailza resignedly replied. "Take my arm again," she whispered to Alice. "It is a cheerless place, but not a dreadful; indeed I take some comfort from it."

"Comfort?"

"Ay; it glads me to remember that Felipo Segundo is dead."

Now they followed Possy through a maze of branching corridors that grew ever larger and more imposingly solemn, till they stood before an enormous pair of smooth black marble doors. At Possy's touch these swung back without a sound. Within was a hall whose walls and roof the light of their two feeble tapers was impotent to show them. Ranked on either side of a central nave stood mountains of bones; they rose high above the heads of cats or bears. The conical piles were girdled by bands of cat-skulls facing outwards, as if to mount guard; the next thing Edgar noticed was that, except for the girdling skulls, each pile's bones were of identical shape and size. A heap of pelvises rose like crockery beside a tumulus of such tiny knuckle-bones as might tip a skeleton's tail. Farther on were rib-cages, a stack of combs.

"Why are the bones all sorted?" Edgar asked.

"O, for an enterprise Felipo conceived that year he perished," Possy answered. "For seeing that cats cleave not to one strait mold, but are most various in their bodies' coinage, some being tigers, some margay, others panthers, else bobcat or puma, he thought to extract the finest, strongest, noblest limb of each several sort, and bring these together into one single, sublimed skeleton. Therefore he set his court anatomists to collect the mortal relics of all that had died in his reign, to put each bone with his fellows, then from each aggregation to choose which peculiar ossment perfectest seemed, and so compose, by their art, the frame of the Cat Ideal. But before this task could be finished, Felipo died. Then the doctors, to save labor and curry favor with his heirs, declared that Felipo himself was the Nonpareil of Cats. Therefore the *membra disiecta* of his subjects were left to stand in heaps, as you see them, to watch over his perfection with their rude multiplicities."

"He should have done better," said Zawailza, "to search out what was noblest in the spirits and intellects of his subjects, and from that to make a model for his own kingship."

"I am of one mind with you in that, my sweet," said Possy enthusiastically. "This is indeed a project that one might still achieve, I think."

"And I have heard," Zawailza went on, slowly, inexorably, "that this same nonpareil of cats, this Great Felipo, was no lion, as he pretended, but a tufty-whiskered lynx of no famous lineage; and that he died of a surfeit of river-eels, in swearing apoplexy."

"Of this I can say nought," replied Possy, with lofty scorn. "It is but one of many foolish tales. His soul was the soul of a lion, whate'er his outward case declared him."

He led them in. They walked a long way past scores of bone-hills; Alice began to pant and grow dizzy from her effort to breathe that heavy air, and she wondered how the ceiling could hold, so broad as she thought it must be and all unsupported by pillars, with the whole weight of the Palace above it. At last Possy halted, and the others came to where he stood in contemplative contrapposto.

"The tomb of Great Felipo," he said.

But there was nothing to be seen. The two young bears waited, standing between the cats at the sculpted edge of a pool whose dark waters, still as a mirror, spread out of sight. There was nothing but candle-flame and cat-profile, to left and right, and the same reflected in the water. Their own two faces were lit from the side. Alice, looking down, saw half her face, half Edgar's. They each had an eye in eclipse; neither demi-grimace could easily be read.

"There!" exclaimed Possy suddenly.

A ghostly column rose up before them, so pale at first it seemed a trick of tortured vision. But then it grew solider; they looked across the water at a shaft of moonshine falling through some conduit far above and striking an island in the lake. There, amidst shapes of stone like young shoots of mountains, stood Felipo's mausoleum. A plain temple, built of snowy stone, it sparkled. None of the animal-palaces' whimsy had been permitted here. Simple and severe, the funeral house had been framed to face that harshest test, the endurance of immortality.

But its roof was broken. Something heavier than moonbeams had dropped upon it.

"Ay, 'twas done some forty years since," sighed Possy, when Edgar had put the question to him, "by a seely clown, one that conveyed trash to the heaps. The hole that lets in the moon stands hard by them; his ox having backed the dray too far, all fell on Felipo, trash, dray, and ox. Do you mark the pediment that's toward us?" Only a fragment remained, but some words had been carved on it. "What says the insculption?"

Edgar squinted and read the chiseled letters: "KINGS. LOOK" was the legend on the tomb.

"'Twas longer than so, none now recalls what weighty sentence Felipo's wisdom left to us that should come after. Ay me, 'tis the least of what we have lost."

"We shall build better in times to come," said Zawailza, "and learn to set our wisdom not so deep nor so far from the light, nor where the accidents of daily living may so bespurtle it."

"So we may do when cats again own strength and their true genius. Some say, young bears, Felipo shall rise once more; that he but sleeps yonder." Alice shuddered.

"He sleeps in one bed with ox and dray, then," remarked Zawailza, "and their common coverlet is trash. Such bedfellows should give one's dreams a humbler color; may it be so with him!"

"Come, we must now take our leave of him, humble or proud, dead or asleep, our road lies long before us," said Possy, rather curtly.

THIRTEEN. **The Butterfly Hunter.**

Whether they returned along the way they had come, or whether Possy followed a new route, Alice could not tell; it was years before she thought to ask her brother, who pointed out that they had not passed any of the beehive boneyards. Even he remembered little more than a long walk down stone halls, and then flights of stairs. But unlike those they had trodden the previous night, upon their arrival at Claudio's, these stairs had no soft runner. They were treacherously worn at the lip by generations of cats climbing and descending, descending and climbing.

As she struggled up, Alice hoped that the next room they entered would be small, not a cell, but a room built to creaturely scale. Claudio's comfortable study was in the back of her mind, though the chamber she envisioned was simpler and smaller. It was warm, it was furnished with carpets and chairs. It had windows . . . .

She got a part of her wish. The room into which they staggered, after Possy had unlocked a heavy door, seemed warm and not too large. There was a carpet on the floor, and ·hangings on two of the walls. Alice ran to a deep embrasure, kneeled on cushions, looked out at the stars flying high among wind-driven clouds. She saw the Citadel! The thin moon shone down on its pallid dome, putting her uncomfortably in mind of the swellings round Felipo's tomb. They had been lit by the same moon that now confused shapes with shadows. Along the Palace roof Alice made out cornices and boulder-dotted slopes, chimney-stacks and spiky cedars, gullies and gutters; sprinkled through this panorama she saw tumbledown shanties, and fowls roosting in bushes or on the arms of statues in a row. It was strange, it was ominous in that cold light, it looked to be another sealed-off world, from which one could not get back. But what of that? She did not have to go there. It was something to look out on, through a window. And, like the places that she called home, it lay beneath the sky, and the moon shone on it.

Slowly her eye retreated from the chilly stillness of that scene; she turned to have a look at Possy's shop. It was a pleasant room, she thought, with its hangings and carpets and windows. It seemed to contain hardly any furniture—a table, a wardrobe. The fireplace was not large, just the size for an ordinary fire; of course, there was none lit now. In fact the room was rather disagreeably warm. And there was something else odd about it. Alice tried to focus her thoughts, but her brain was growing fractious. Then Edgar, standing beside her, said,

"Where is all the light and noise coming from?"

Alice listened. She heard a constant throb like the thunder of surf. A booming shuddered in its depths, and then unrolled a flotsam of cries. But no one was shouting. And the light: it was dull, intermittent: two tapers could never account for it.

"Look," said Edgar, "look at that wall! No, *that* one." He pointed. "With the hanging."

"I see it," Alice yawned.

"Well, it's not a wall at all. Look again. The tapestry's hanging by rings from a wire."

"O, you're right!" she exclaimed. The wire sagged in the middle from the weight of the hanging; its ends were fastened

142

to two mighty piers of stone. "There's no ceiling," she added dreamily. Indeed she could see none; only a chain swagging down from unguessable heights to catch a ring, set in one of the piers, with a monstrous iron hook.

Then the curtain parted in the middle. A reek of heated metal billowed in on coal-smoke, which unfolded to disclose Mr. Dizzy.

"Gruntings!" he called, his broad yellow face dividing in a grin. But Alice did not have to reply, for he walked straight across to the other two cats. Possy was leaning over a table, where the sheaf of drawings and notes was outspread; he was declaiming, while Zawailza poised attentively on the table's edge. Drowsily Alice admired the picture the three cats made, lit from one side by cold moonlight, from the other by the pulsing red glare. Zawailza in particular seemed to catch both lights and subdue them, so that the red one blent into the ruby shadow of the white . . . it was as if she were no cat at all but a lens changing the moon's candor to flame . . . Alice was nearly nodding when she felt her shoulder seized and shaken.

"Let's go," Edgar whispered, "they're waving us over. Wake up."

"I'm not asleep," she protested.

Zawailza motioned them to stand by her.

"Dizzy is come from the banquet," she declared to them shortly. "Possy and I return with him, by Equivair's command, to join our persons to the revels. We must not seem refractory, we must go to smile and collogue. I am to hear my beauty pledged by those I groundly hate. So we must lose you, now, to the outer world again, else will Equivair desire to detain you; he knows whose kin you are. But we will say we never encountered with you. He may search the Palace himself, if it so likes his new-minted magnificence. But we will show you, presently, the next way out of the Palace, whereby you may avoid all eyes. I am grieved so to part from you, bearcubs. It was my hope to make you some show of our devices, and to enlist you couriers to your Great Golden Bear."

"Ay, ay, but 'tis better so," said Possy earnestly. "Mistake me not, gentles, my faith in you is entire. But there will be those abroad in the city tonight (good fortune keep you from them!) that would if they caught you put you to the hard question. 'Twere better far for bears and cats that you know nothing. Avoid encounter, when y'are out; keep the shadows and the quiet streets, have your wits about you. I too am loath to despatch you on so hazardous a voyage, I would gladly secrete you somewhere about these quarters, but Equivair must return here in short space on certain business that we have, he'll bring spies who in their zealous bestirrings will hunt for you. Go to your uncle in the Citadel. Tell him, tell the Great Golden Bear . . . curse me, what shall they tell 'em?" he lamely ended, turning to Zawailza.

"Say no more than what you have seen and heard, while you have been among us," she answered firmly. "'Twill serve to raise a question, at the least, for the discerning hearer. Tell your story to the Great Golden Bear, to him above all; you will not fail of this, you will promise it, will you not?" Alice, held in that steady gaze, could not help but nod. "You do not know what all this should portend," Zawailza sighed, "but he will know, or so I hope. Some day we'll meet, and then, my Alice, I'll make a tale of it for you, and Edgar shall view the whole of Possy's shop. Stay," she added, speaking slowly, a new look in her eyes. "There's time yet for one displaying, if 'tis brief."

"My sweet," began Possy, eyes clouding with apprehension; but the silver cat cut him short.

"Nay, Possy, Equivair must stay *my* pleasure, these five minutes more. You, Dionisio, do you go fetch our guests some warm and wakeful drink from the neighbor room; they shall not be sent forth into danger all a-chill and half nodding." Mr. Dizzy rose, bowed, and sauntered through the curtained aperture. "Bethink you, Possy Damp Paws," she continued reproachfully, "our guests have seen nothing of our skill at making, bating the barren Treasury, and our hoard of all dead cats that ever were. Shall these show us truly to uncle Claudio and the golden hero? They shall know better of cats than so! Bring out, I prithee, some toy of your devising; bring out your Butterfly Hunter while we wait for Dizzy's return." And when Possy stood staring at her, as if in disbelief, "Hurry, friend," she urged him; "do you forget that Equivair awaits us?" He turned without a word and vanished behind the curtain.

Zawailza lazily rose, and opened the window behind her. "We will invite some other friends to join our sport," she said. Soon pale-winged butterflies came floating over the sill. "They are fresh from the silk," she observed. "I have seen their cloudy nests out yonder in the hawthorne brakes. Pretty things, are they not? Little they know of the wars that are toward in Bargeton."

Edgar and Alice stared sleepily at the butterflies as they drifted in quirky orbit about the yellow tapers on the table. Both young bears had despaired of understanding the mess they had got themselves into, though the word "wars" touched a nerve in Edgar, and caused him to shudder and straighten. Alice had fixed her thought on the drink Zawailza had promised; beyond that, her only idea was to carry out the mission the dancer had entrusted to her, and then to find her bed in Claudio's attic. Possy returned with a box. He set it down; "Ah! You have found him some prey," he said lightly, noticing the butterflies. "Come nearer, young friends, this hunter is no giant." He opened the box, withdrew something bright, and placed it before them on the table. Edgar and Alice leaned forward to get a better view.

It was a tiny golden cat, no bigger than Edgar's paw. It stood on its two hind legs, its tail curving up behind. The bears admired the perfect form of its head, and tensile whiskers, the soft pile of down on its cheeks and brow, the alert erectness of its ears. But the thing was not a doll. The rest of its body was open as filigree, and contained what seemed a miniature of the Throne's mechanics; the surface of the table beneath its feet shimmered gold and silver as the minuscule works caught the light of candle and of moon. Each limb had its complex action. Every toe was distinct. In its right forepaw it held, at the end of a fine brass pole, a long, white, silken net.

Possy seemed to stroke it behind its ears, and it leapt into life. It ran down the table, brandishing its net, stopped just before it reached the edge, skewed around, ran back again. After Possy had once more caressed it, the golden hunter appeared to see the butterflies, and its demeanor changed. The bears watched spellbound as it slowly stalked towards the taper. As it raised each leg and set it down, with excruciating deliberation, it was possible to observe the shuttle of rods, the winking of oiled cogs. The butterflies still flopped about. Then the hunter came to rest. For a second, before Edgar noticed the climbing net, he thought the automaton had run down. The net ascended as undetectably as the minute hand of a clock. Higher and higher it rose, but the insects, absorbed in the taper's flame, still noticed nothing. Then the white silk ballooned and sank, as the cat gave a curious twist of its arm; the wings scattered in desperate gyres. Zawailza burst out laughing; the golden hunter stood veiled to the knee in its own translucent net.

"He's not yet perfect," Possy ruefully confessed, scooping the automaton up and starting to pick the silk away from its fragile mechanism. Edgar could have sworn he saw the little thing twist in its maker's paw. "'Tis but a toy, a trifle, the work of an idle hour," the black cat muttered brusquely. But the quick words of the bears, and even more the look in their eyes, soon brought an answering glow to Possy's own, as he worked to free it from the net, and began explicating its action. He had pointed out no more than the mainspring, however, when Mr. Dizzy appeared through a rent in the hanging with a pair of steaming mugs.

"Ah! Here's a drink we much affect," said Possy jovially. "'Twill drive the vapors of sleep from out your brains, and speed you on your journey. We brew it from certain roasted berries. Pray, drink, drink, while 'tis yet hot, it loses its virtue a-cooling."

Alice held the dark liquid under her nose and inhaled its scent; at once her mother's kitchen was around her. She stared at Zawailza.

"Why, it's coffee!" she said.

FOURTEEN. **The Sally Port.**

"*L* ord Possy, why do you trust the Great Golden Bear, when it was the bears who put you in prison?" asked Edgar.

They were walking down a hall in darkness, arm-in-arm, Zawailza and Alice behind them, Mr. Dizzy farther back. Edgar could plainly hear his sister's scuffle and the murmuring of her voice and Zawailza's replies. They were on their way, the cats to join Equivair in the glade, the bears to their promised liberation from the Palace; Edgar, his curiosity rekindled by strong coffee, was now athrob with questions, and felt he must put at least one of them to Possy before they parted. He had hit on this one after passing over several others. The cat did not at once reply.

"He is your Felipo," he slowly began at last, "not in's office—I know you have no king, but freely suffer the government of aged fools, forgive my candor—but in his largeness of spirit is the Great Golden Bear very like Felipo. No other kind in Bargeton hath such a champion, no, nor the scant idea of one; bating the cats, and they the idea only. But the times call for heroes. Fortune prepares for us a tempest, rolled together from many passionate exhalations. Lusts blow freely out of many, young sir, hungry covetings, ambitions honest and foul. You must have felt some squalls of vengefulness since you have been in Bargeton. A storm gathers, the sea 'gins to roil. There must be found some oak to stand against this wind, and, flourishing, to break its blasts, or all

148

our lesser trees will be knocked flat. There must be found some boulder to divide the wave that's now a-building, before it can topple upon the shingle's lesser stones, and grind 'em down to sand. We cats do not own our strength; we have lost our Felipo. We strive, 'tis true, to reinvent him, but the storm stays not her blow till the boulder form, or till the oak reach his deep-rooted power; she strikes when occasion directs her host of several winds all the same way. That time comes soon, comes now; therefore I'd shield the nascent vigor of cats behind the champion of bears, in spite of quarrels betwixt us. But I thank the unruly tempest for this," he added more lightly, "that its fore-breezes have sent us two friends, driven to harbor by a catspaw of Fortune, as 'twere."

Zawailza's gruff laugh swelled in the darkness.

"Well turned to compliment, most courtly Possy," she drawled. "I see y'are in practise to meet with Equivair and deflect his barbs. But now, I would hear more of this hero from our friends. I have listened to all the tales, but I could never discover from them why so great a person aspires not to princely rank, but lives aloof like a philosopher. Can you resolve me this?"

Edgar waited, hoping his sister would answer. He was in fact ashamed by how little he knew of the Great Golden Bear. "And she's the one who saw him, after all," he told himself, still begrudging her that glimpse she had not shared with him. Presently he heard her, thoughtful.

"I don't know. We all have heard of him, but no one ever talks much about him. He has no family, no relations, no society. I don't know where he lives, except that it's not in any of our cities. He has nothing to do with our daily lives, but when there's trouble, he comes."

"Do you know," asked Zawailza, "of the teachings of the silver foxes? They say he is no bear, no mortal creature, but a god that appears at whiles, coming among us from some other world, a protean spirit that indifferently takes on the likeness of bear or fly, bird or fish."

"O, I don't believe that," said Alice rather scornfully. "When I saw him last night, he was a bear; I've never heard of him arriving anywhere as a *fish*. Wouldn't he be the Great Golden Fish if he did?"

"The foxes are ever quick to see a god," Possy remarked. "They worship the goose before they kill and eat it."

"Anyway," said Alice, "the Great Golden Bear had parents once, he was born, he wasn't always there, full-grown. My mother has a cousin who saw him as a cub, living in the woods. Among the farmers thereabouts he was famous as a mischief-maker and a bit of a thief, but also as a singer. There are bears," she went on, "who go wild, who can't stand to live with others and by their rules. Some are outcasts, some are hermits, some commit crimes. Some travel and travel. I have a friend in school whose aunt disappeared; they hear of her from the strangest places; they say she has lost all language. I think the Great Golden Bear might have been like that, but his life took a different turn."

"There be wines too heady for bottles," said Possy cryptically. "But now, young friends, I pray a wordless moment whilst I feel about me." Edgar felt the air close in around him. "Here's the door!" came Possy's jovial voice at length, from a few feet away. "Now I will unlock him and have him open— ungh! 'tis heavy—ungh! these hinges are—ungh! uncommonly obdurate—ungh! Belike they want oiling. Dizzy, come and lend a shoulder." Bone under bristle rubbed past Edgar's arm. Then came a volley of laboring grunts, and the shrieks of metal turning on metal. "Ha ha! 'Twill do, this opening's wide enough to let us pass," Possy panted. "Come towards my voice, bearcubs, once inside we may make a light, come in, in, all in. Is Alice in? You must betake yourselves a few paces down, to give me room to wrestle this rebel door. Make a sound, Dizzy, to guide 'em."

"Rooburgle-oogar," sang Mr. Dizzy. Edgar shuffled towards him, tripped, was caught by long, sinewy arms furred with abrasive stubble. "Whoa, pork-cipitous chitling," murmured the Clowncat in his ear. "Don't hurtle about like a hobbledehog nor a snouty lout. Light on the trotters does it."

A light flared behind Edgar's back; the broad, yellow, grinning mask of Dizzy's face bloomed suddenly inches from Edgar's nose, and he recoiled from it with a vigor that nearly sent him over backwards, as his heels hit the same snag that had caught his toes before.

"Sorry! I'm sorry," he called out to no one in particular.

"Step high, young bears, this floor is not a little rough through long disuse," said Possy, coming up with a pair of smoking torches, one of which he passed to Zawailza. "We are now, I'd have you know, in the passage whose full course, were it cleared of fallen rubble, would bring us seven leagues by secret ways to the seraglio of the Concatenate Kings. Felipo there maintained, 'tis held, seventy-seven of the fairest pantheresses that ever were, though none but his royal eye e'er feasted on their beauties. Time was, young bears, when guards in full feathered panoply stood along this way, so nearly spaced that each might whisper the news of royal approach to his next neighbor." Possy continued for some time to dilate upon this subject, but the vanished pomp of long-dead tyrants was not what Edgar and Alice wished to hear; their hearts were pounding, now, from the effort to breathe the tunnel air, acrid with torch-smoke. Their minds bent on escape from this ensepulture.

All at once they felt a draught of fresher air upon their right sides; it ruffled their fur deliciously. The party halted. Zawailza turned to them:

"The sundering of our ways is now at hand. Look you by what road you must leave us." She thrust out her torch to gutter in the draught; they saw a low, round arch in the wall, the mouth of a storm-drain, perhaps, hardly a passage for creatures of any size. They could not enter without bending nearly double.

"Strait it seems, no doubt, and low," said Possy, observing their hesitation, "and you will find it dwindles further ere it reaches its end; a sally port for the old King's guard, through which, in time of siege or other need they coursed at full speed though armed cap-a-pie . . . ."

"And so 'twill serve for young bears," Zawailza interrupted. "My lord Possy could fill a sennight of winter evenings with tales of the heroic gests of these most martial pards, and all the valor and nobility to which the hole gave passage; but we will excuse him for now. One day we five will find ourselves rejoined in easeful company; that day, my lord, we give you leave to draw the cork from out your frothy lore of heretofore, but now, a fast farewell. Do not neglect your purpose. Go quickly to the Citadel; speak to the Great Golden Bear."

"Ay, to him, there's the thing indeed. Follow the passage faithfully; though it wind and shrink, you will find it lead you sure and safe beyond the walls of these ancient precincts. Nor have you need to fear another meeting with our wild Clown-cattery, for Equivair himself detains them where they ask not much detaining, that's a-feasting. Farewell!"

"Follow the river!" said Zawailza.

"And stay away from the Thoog," added Dizzy. "They're even fonder of pigs than we are. Good-bye!"

Before either Edgar or Alice could think of a reply, the torches went out, and they were alone in the darkness again. They stood for a minute or two, waiting in case a cat-face should suddenly reappear or a cat-voice from nowhere rap out some fresh injunction, but there was nothing. They turned their faces to the draught, excited by the moving air but dreading the way ahead of them. Alice waited for her brother to say, "Well, let's get this over with. We're going to have to stoop here, though. I'll go first. You'd better stay right behind me, Alice."

"I'll stay right behind you, but don't go too fast."

"Keep a hold on my tail."

"All right, I'll hold on to your tail. Just don't go too fast."

"Well, I'm not going to take all night about it," snapped Edgar, who actually had not the least intention of going even so fast as he would normally walk; he was already thinking of hidden pitfalls. So they entered the tunnel. The floor was smooth and the way was straight, so that for many minutes they made good progress; moreover, they could feel the walls on either side and so make sure that no other avenues offered which in the darkness they might miss. They had the fresh air always on their faces, though Edgar had the best of it. The worst part was the stooping. Their necks and backs soon ached miserably, and it was not very long before Edgar suggested that they might go more comfortably on all fours;

there was no one there to see them. Alice agreed, though it meant she would have to loose her grip on her brother's tail. By this time they both felt fairly secure that the tunnel still matched Possy's description of it, and contained no horrible surprises; and Edgar was making enough noise in the grunting and sniffing line (each grunt and sniff magnified to operatic proportions by the tunnel) that Alice did not doubt she would know where he was.

Not long after they adopted this mode of progress, the passage constricted into a tube so narrow and low, it hardly allowed them to straighten their legs after each step taken. It was like squeezing one's body down a smooth stone pipe—a very disagreeable and, to Edgar's mind, unnerving experience; he was not fond of cramped spaces. What if they should find the tunnel's roof fallen and their way blocked? To have to crawl backwards as many yards as they had travelled, and then still to have the lightless labyrinth of the Palace's cellars to negotiate . . . it did not bear thinking of. But no sooner had he dismissed this thought than his mind began to dwell upon an even more sinister fancy: that the tunnel was somehow aware of himself and Alice, and was adjusting its proportions to impede their progress. Then the floor began to slope gently downwards, and a still more terrifying idea drove out the last. The tunnel would grow narrower, and at the same time steeper, till they were sliding through the blackness on their bellies to some dead-end underground. They would try to back up the slope (Edgar could already feel his sister's frantic squirmings and clawings, behind and on top of him), but the polished tube would give their claws no purchase. Nothing would remain but the long wait till the air went foul—or till the first runnel of water wet their fur—or the walls began to heat—or grew so cold . . . .

Absorbed in this fantasy, Edgar ran snout first into an obstruction and let out a wild yell. It drew an answering shriek from Alice, who had been distressing herself with similar thoughts.

"Edgar!" she shrilled, "What's wrong? What is the matter? Are you hurt? Tell me what is happening!"

"I've run into something—a wall," he answered. "I think—no, wait a minute." He felt the draught. It blew on his left cheek; he felt with his left forepaw. "O," he groaned in relief, "I've been so stupid. The tunnel turns a corner here, to the left. I was so busy thinking horrible things that I didn't notice the turn and walked straight into the wall. Come on, we're all right now, only we'd better move a bit more cautiously."

"I told you we ought to go slow."

"Remember, Possy said that the passage winds around a bit."

"I just hope it doesn't get any narrower."

It did not. Bends and corners, some of them quite acute, came fairly frequently now, but Edgar was on his guard for them, and navigated them successfully. There were no traps, no culs-de-sac, no pits opening into immeasurable gulfs, no bowls lined with knives. Edgar began to see and even to explain to his sister the defensive value of the tunnel's twists and turns, which offered so many points at which a few or even only one armed cat-soldier could arrest the advance of a party of assailants. Alice was used to having things of this sort explained to her in detail, whenever Edgar felt anxious about something else, and in fact she usually enjoyed it, since she would learn things she hadn't known, and have her mind taken off her own problems into the bargain. So she squeezed onward, half-attending to the lilt of her brother's disquisition on military architecture, when all at once his monologue cut off; she heard a little high-pitched whine of terror.

"Edgar!" she screamed again, but this time no answer came back. She called and called, for sheer relief of terror in shouting, inching her body forward as she called her brother's name. Then her paw, groping the floor in advance of the rest of her, met empty air beyond a clean-cut stone lip. Alice squirmed ahead to feel about; as she did so, one of her own panicky fantasies came true: she felt the floor beneath her tilt forward. She scrabbled frantically, but the whole interior of the tunnel was as smooth as polished marble, offering no smallest crevice for the points of her claws to catch on. She felt herself start to slide, screamed, shot down the slippery chute like an otter down a mudslide. It was a short descent, though steep. She had not even time to expel her latest breath when, after a long skid across a glassy floor, she came to rest.

Edgar, after he had slid to a stop just seconds earlier, lay panting and trying to understand. Presently he heard other huffing, how far away he could not tell.

"Alice!" he called, "Is that you? Are you all right?" His voice echoed strangely. For a moment there was no reply. Then Alice's voice came faintly, as if from a distance: "Yes, I . . . I think I'm not hurt. Where are you?"

"I'm a few feet ahead of you, down the tunnel," he answered, making a wild guess about the nature of the place they were in. "Just grope your way along to where I am."

"But I can't feel any walls, Edgar!"

Neither could he. Edgar put out his paws this way and that, but met with nothing. There was no longer any ceiling, either, that he could touch. He stood up.

"Alice, listen," he called. "I believe we've fallen into some kind of underground chamber." Even as he uttered this phrase, he wished that he had chosen another: it seemed too much like a nice way of not saying "tomb." He wanted badly to touch his sister, to feel the bulk of her against him; then, hearing in his mind Possy's confident instruction: "Alice, come towards the sound of my voice," Edgar echoed it. "I'll keep talking so that you can find me. Come forward *very slowly*. We don't know . . . AYIII!" he screamed, as sharp claws gripped his foot.

"It's only me," grumbled Alice, rising to her feet beside him. "I wasn't that far away." Edgar could not at once find words for a reply; then Alice forestalled him, calling out,

"Look over there! Where I'm pointing! Do you see a sort of blue square?"

Edgar was about to demand how, when he couldn't spot the tip of his own muzzle, she expected him to make out where she was pointing—when his eye was caught by a patch of deepest indigo, floating, hardly detached from the surrounding black.

"I see it," he said.

"I'll bet it's a door," she said. "Let's go see." And before he had time to articulate any one of the dozen sarcastic responses now disentangling themselves in his brain, she had let go her grip on his arm, and was gone.

"Alice!" he shouted, but even before her gay call came back to him—"Here I am! And it is a door!"—he had seen her silhouette against the patch of blue, and moved to follow it. As he approached, pinholes of white began to prick through the indigo against which his sister's outline was developing, and his heart leapt. He put his arms around her shoulders, she gripped him fiercely by the waist, and together they stood looking out at the bright night sky.

E dgar and Alice stood side by side on the threshold of the low stone doorway. Fleecy clouds, backlit by the moon, made silver continents in that sea of stars. They could smell water plants, damp earth, and the evening exhalations of the desert. Before them, stone steps marched down to the black, silently flowing river. Only a slapping against the bottommost stair betrayed the strong tug of the current.

Across the river lay the desert shore, mounded in shapes of black against the sky, except at one point. There, a little to their right, the forms of bushes and scrub stood out boldly, as orange lights winked through the tangled branches. The moon picked out, above them, a dozen, rising, curl-headed plumes. The young bears looked at them for a while. Neither doubted that they were seeing the watchfires of the Crimson Bears, who had arrived at last. But Alice felt a stirring of surprise in her tired brain at the sight of fire. "I didn't know they cooked their food," was how she would have put it into words, had anyone asked. But no one did, and together, in silence, the bears bent all their thought upon the problem of getting back to the Citadel and safety.

Edgar walked out from the doorway; the wall in which it was set ran parallel to the river as far as the eye could see, leaving only a few yards of cobblestoned quay between its blind mass and the Flood's embankment. Zawailza had told them to follow the river, but which way? For all that he could tell, this was a different city. After some hesitation and a fruitless search for landmarks, Edgar decided to be guided by the river's current and make to the right, where he thought he could descry a dull glow that might be the city center. Alice agreeing, they set out that way. For hundreds of yards they travelled beneath the unwindowed bulk of the Palace wall, so high that it utterly concealed whatever lay behind. When at last they reached the angle where the wall ran inland, they saw to their dismay that only the narrowest, darkest, muddiest of alleys ran between it and the next building, a solid structure with wide doors giving onto a rickety ramp. Evidently a warehouse; the alley looked not at all promising. Eager as they were to get away from the river and the fires on the opposite shore, Edgar and Alice had still had enough of holes, tunnels, and enclosed spaces generally. The quay growing wider, they elected to follow the Flood downstream till they could find some more open thoroughfare into the heart of the city, or at least some way into an inhabited district where they could hope for directions.

But as they trotted along the quay, this hope left them. There did not seem to be any streets leading back through the bunched masses of riverside warehouses to the city behind. Worse still, never a light showed itself in window or tavern-door. Except for the echoes of their own steps and whispers, all was shuttered, bolted, silent. The pavement grew uneven beneath their feet. Edgar startled himself and Alice by walking straight into a bush that grew waist-high from the buckled paving.

"Oof!" he said wryly, when he had recovered himself. "Not much business done in this part of town, from the look of things."

"Do you think we could be heading the wrong way?" asked Alice nervously; "*out* of Bargeton?"

"No," he replied, "we're going downriver now, as we should be."

"Are you *sure* we should be?"

"Yes. We walked upriver this morning; that is, north. There is no more of Bargeton downstream from the Citadel. Citadel Hill is the southernmost part of the city."

Alice was silent as she struggled with the thought of a place where Bargeton came to an end. She still couldn't see why all the buildings should grow increasingly dilapidated towards the city's heart, but she had no real rebuttal of her brother's reasoning; she took his paw again, and they went along. Soon they were struck by the increasing brightness of the pink glow in the sky.

"That's sure to be the Market Square," said Edgar. "They never stop trading there by day or night." And he went on to make bad jokes about the amount of light needed for shady transactions, a sure sign to Alice that her brother was uneasy about something. For a long time they walked. Then,

"Look," said Edgar, "the river bends to the right, up ahead. Once past that last warehouse, we should be able to see the Citadel."

The building at which he pointed was roofless and ruinous. Part of its topmost story had collapsed, and a sizable tree had rooted itself up there in the debris. It flourished its branches against the strange glow he had earlier remarked. This warehouse stood a little in advance of the line of buildings past which they had trudged. In front of it, the quay swung left into the river and came to an end in a spit of rocks and reeds, seemingly. The rosy shimmer was reflected in the water, and it shone through the tall house's glassless casements. They slowed as they came to the corner; rounding it, they halted. Bargeton entire was before them; Bargeton was casting the glow up against a ceiling of dense brown cloud.

They stood on the ragged point where the embankment veered sharp right and swung round to embrace the great crescent basin that harbored the shipping of citizens and strangers. At the far end of that enormous bight, beyond the point where the right bank returned from its long westward swing to run in harness again with the desert shore, southward together, there where the Flood once more collected its waters into strait channels, loomed the bald crown of Citadel Hill over city and basin. The moon struck it fairly, but the hill no longer gave back a white glare. Stained, instead, with shifting streaks of yellow, it seemed to waver, almost to sway.

"Edgar, what's wrong with the Citadel?" cried Alice. The one solid place in the city, the place where she had hoped to find safety and rest, was being taken from her. Must even the hills in Bargeton dance like Clowncats?

"There's nothing wrong with the Citadel," said Edgar morosely.

"Then why is it moving?"

"You're seeing it through smoke. The city is on fire."

Alice looked again, but she could see no flames. Certainly a dingy veil hoisted from the city, as though borne on an updraft. It tinged the distance with smeary saffron. Stars stuck in its folds; they were shaken about in that diaphanous waving. Overhead, a fat cloud, seared in flickering rose, slowly rolled over the city like a turning joint of meat. Looking along Bargeton's shore, far across the half-moon basin, Alice saw the great Market Square, deserted and dark.

Nearer at hand, the riverbank houses were cloven with crimson flarings that opened up vistas of facades washed in red. She moaned as doubt vanished. The hidden brush applying all that color was fire.

"Edgar, what shall we do?" she whispered. He straightened from his despondent slouch.

"Let's go on a bit," he said. "It doesn't seem to me that the fire has spread throughout the whole city. We might be able to find our way around it, maybe, if we stick to the shore. Let's look."

They moved forward slowly, following the quay. Beside them marched, still, a phalanx of gutted warehouses. By and by they found the embankment broken by another river, or rather a canal, that debouched into the Flood; they halted again. There was no bridge, the piles that once had upheld one still raised weedy white-caked heads. For a moment Edgar thought to swim across. It was not a wide stream. But each pile trailed such a fork of swirling, violent foam, he was forced to admit they could go no further south.

All the buildings on their side of the canal were as ancient and empty as any they had passed since leaving the Palace. On its far side a serried mass of ornate houses made an unbroken wall. It stretched along two fronts: one ran away from them inland along the canal's farther bank, the other curved with the Flood toward the Market Square. Here was the true commercial district of Bargeton; so much was clear at a glance. Barges by the hundred rocked at the quayside, while the quay itself was piled high with crates, barrels, and bales. The riverside buildings were broad and tall, and all were built to the same pattern, with floors for storage of goods below, then a wide roof planted out in willows, flowering cherries, and plumtrees, in whose fragrant midst, delicately screened from the world, there nestled elegant villas. Bullseye windows peeped through espaliered roses and over privet hedges; in every case, a mansion perching on a warehouse roof. Alice, looking up at these residences, fleetingly imagined how things would be for the pampered daughters of those houses, living among all things fine and rare in a rooftop kingdom, carrying on their light loves in miniature wildernesses, coming down laughing through all the stories packed with their fathers' goods, past the workers; every day . . . . The buildings were painted in bold geometrical patterns, or interweaving inscriptions that covered the whole facade. Gilt portals embossed with the house's device looked out on the water.

They saw this rich district by the illumination of a little cosmos of lamps and torches set all along the warehouse walls. Higher up, on the roofs, paper lanterns palely glowed among blossoming boughs, while within the villas every window showed a light, as if some fete were toward. And in those same windows shapes, coming and going, hastened from one to the next, as though each household were dancing a coranto through every room. Down on the quays the mad bustle of business continued in full spate. The waterside was alive with hurrying figures that darted out of the warehouse doors pushing carts and handtrucks and barrows. Some merely rushed in and out with their arms laden. Lashed bales lowered tensely from the upper windows, pulleys sang with the strain; ropes groaned; some snapped. In places bales were simply tossed out to burst where they landed. Meanwhile the cranes on the barges kept at their translation of bulging nets and platforms pyramided with crates; the holds took each load in a gulp. In many places creatures had formed a file from door to waterside; incredible burdens passed from hand to hand up the gangways. And all of this went on in uncanny silence, rarely broken by some sharp, urgent shout. Perhaps, Alice thought, the Crimson Bears had set the fire that had inspired all this emptying. Then was Bargeton conquered? Was it the sack of the city that had set all these creatures to flight, with what wealth they could carry?

An unexpected lull interrupted the hectic scramble of lading. In a minute the embankments were overrun by a milling crowd, five times larger than before. That these were not warehousemen or stevedores was plentifully evident, in the light of the flambeaux held aloft by servants, shedding gleams on looped braid and upon the winking galaxy of jewels nested in the fur and feathers of the ushered throng. These were the merchants and their families; Alice saw a few pampered daughters.

"Why have they come out? Where will they go?" she wondered aloud. Edgar pointed to the quayside; here, along the canal, in between the great trading barges, were moored a host of smaller, more graceful craft, built for pleasure, display, and elegant conveyance. Gold adorned high bow- and stern-pieces and snaked up the masts. As oars were run out, their blades and shafts glittered with further aureate tracery. Precious threads shimmered from silken tents amidships.

Into these craft the grandissimi swarmed. Footmen treading narrow planks hastily bundled trunks and chests aboard the galleys. As Edgar and Alice watched, one of these porters, a stout porcupine in garnet livery, missed his footing and toppled into the water. The massive box he let fall broke open to release a score of brocaded gowns that spread on the water like so many gorgeous lily-pads cut for imperial frogs. Only one voice on the quay raised a shrill cry of dismay, and it was soon hushed. The porcupine struggled to the bank. No one made the least effort to retrieve the gowns, which floated away on the swift current.

The loading of goods and creatures continued apace. The bears saw a slew of portraits handed across the inky water into a galley. A stream of candelabra followed. Now the quays themselves became bare, as one by one the boats, dangerously low in the water, cut loose from bollards and maneuvered into the stream, oars rising and dipping, hoarse voices calling competing strokes. Out into the river the frail galleys nosed to mingle with the broad-beamed barges. These too had slipped their hawsers and were drifting downstream, sails raised or rising. The surface of the half-moon basin soon was so densely dotted with craft that none could make any way, and panicky, cracked curses fired back and forth, carrying clearly to the bears.

Then two black barges, forced together by the pull of the current, caught between them a tiny yacht, its gilt poop wrought like the twisting tail of a cloud. A din of cracking and splitting drowned out the screams. When the heavy hulls parted, the water was littered with wreckage and bodies, some thrashing. Ropes were thrown from the sides of the barges. Those who could grab them were pulled up. Soon other vessels drifted in and blocked Alice's view.

Edgar had already turned from the chaos of jammed shipping to watch for signs of the fire's advance. He had not yet seen any flames. But the glow in the sky had intensified, the thick air smelt of burning and hot metal, and from time to time a cinder hissed in the canal.

"It's getting nearer," said Alice, half in question.

"Yes," he admitted. "You can hear it."

She listened, but for such cracklings as logs on andirons make. It took her a while to hear the deep murmur, which did not so much sound as shake the air. But when she had heard it, every nerve in her body commanded her to leave. Only fools wait to look fire in the face. She should run away.

"Edgar, let's go back."

"Not yet," he pleaded. "I want to see this. There's the whole width of the canal and no wind to speak of. We'll be fine."

She did not demur. She found that she too wanted to watch the conflagration come on, not just infer its presence from effects. She wanted—but it was not really she!—to see flames take the warehouses, their tidy, sentimental gardens, all those nice homes. So in defiance of her own will to bolt she stood by Edgar, held his hand, and looked to the opposite bank.

The quay was deserted now, strewn with abandoned goods. Still all the torches burned in their high brackets, making the brave facades flicker. Nothing else stirred all down the waterfront.

"Maybe it's moving another way," said Edgar.

As he spoke, a square tower suddenly jumped into view. Strangely lit from beneath, it cast a shadow onto the low-roiling ceiling of smoke. The next minute the entire tower bloomed, its outline hid in a fiery mantle; a second tower, grey and round, stood up from the summit of the first, balanced like a ropy column, then swelled into the spark-flashing canopy. The roar of flames boomed in their ears but did not drown an outcry from the river. Like a floating carpet, the crush of vessels had now drawn opposite the Market Square. As Edgar and Alice watched, a swarm of sparks from the shore struck the lead boats, and another wail rang across the basin. The sparks clung to yards, rigging, hulls. Sails changed substance to shuddering rose from triangular, moonstruck white.

"O, the cowards!" cried Edgar. "They are shooting with flaming arrows!"

"The cowards!" echoed Alice fiercely. "But who are they, Edgar? Crimson Bears?"

"I don't know. I don't understand it. How could they have got into the city?"

"But who else could it be?"

"I don't know." Edgar did not feel ready to voice his idea, that Equivair's cats had seized their revenge.

"What are we going to do now?" moaned his sister. "Where will we go, if the Crimson Bears hold Bargeton?"

But her question was lost as the burning tower collapsed. The air shook with its fall; a fountain of flame spat embers into the water. Alice's desire to see the warehouses burn had left her, but she was forced to watch.

Eaten through from behind, the warehouses gave themselves over to riot. Crimson revellers jigged past the tiers of windows, then launched outward in showers of exploding glass. They landed on costly bales, on tuns. As these broached and ruptured, the bears saw strange sights. The tuns' liquors grew intoxicated with the drinkers and gabbled excitedly in tongues of blue and green. Yardage bellied and writhed with the fiery masquers. Chaste linens, caught against those bodies, put on new raiment. Twisting silks, jostled in the dance by crimson madcaps, leapt, fell, wriggled black on the pavement, and lay still. A gallant sat on a crate, nearly spent from the reel he'd just danced with a bale of brocades. The crate puffed smoke through its seams, flew apart. Spitting globules spouted, then flew to the water, spinning corkscrews of white smoke that lanced the bears' nostrils with a spicy smell.

The gusting heat fanned their fur as building after building took fire. The deafening roar burst and rumbled. Alice pushed her face against her brother's shoulder. Edgar held her and wondered what to do. Zawailza's message must be gotten to the Great Golden Bear. It was time to set about it.

He shifted his gaze from the fire to survey the dark route along the canal. The dirty buildings blushed as the fire swelled and relented. On the wall of one of these stone husks, a shape emerged with each erubescence. It was taller than Edgar and longer than tall. He could not see what cast such a shadow. Then a pervasive flaring took another warehouse, its garden and villa. The torches in their mounts blent into the greater light. In that enduring glare the shadow stood out stark in crocodile jaws, humped hogback, lashings of tail. Alice, waking to her brother's fear, pulled her face out of his fur and looked where he was looking. She missed the terrible shadow but saw at once what cast it, small and low on the edge of the quay, looking at her with gold-flecked eyes. The Slizz had found them.

SIXTEEN. The Bidding of the Slizz.

*A*s the beast came loping, Alice dropped to her knees to embrace it, caressing its head and softly cuffing it by turns. Edgar dazedly stared at the Slizz. How had it found them? There was no time to puzzle about it. A surge of heat from across the canal caused them to turn to see a warehouse sag and buckle with a roar; then where it had stood was only fire. Gledes shot from the wreckage. Swooping across the water, they burst against the stone embankment in sprays.

"If one of those finds a way through a window on this side," Edgar shouted, numbering the slots, "we'll have to take to the water. Alice, let's go away from here! Bring the Slizz."

"Which way?" screamed Alice above the booming. Edgar cast one last glance along the canal, and his will quite failed him. It was too far to run. The heat would cook them, or the flaming rain burn holes in them.

"Back!" he yelled, and pulled his sister to her feet. They started running the way they had come, toward the grassy spit and the bend in the river, till Alice, looking over her shoulder, pulled up short.

"The Slizz!"

The Slizz stood mournfully on the spot they had abandoned, gazing after them, its monster-shadow once again projected in fire-rimmed black. The bears called to it, whistled, stamped, and pleaded; the beast would not budge. When Edgar took a few steps toward it, it retreated. A rain of soot and ash was falling all about them now, and sparks cometted past their heads. Edgar was scorched by one on his forearm. Another lit on the back of his neck, and Alice ran to beat at the smoldering fur. They made a last dash at the Slizz, one from each side, but he evaded their concerted grasp in a wriggle and came to rest a few yards further down, staring at them over his shoulder.

"Leave it!" cried Edgar in his sister's ear. "There's no more time to waste!" Once again he pulled her after him, and they stumbled down the embankment toward the corner warehouse. Rooted above its ragged cornice, the tree rocked in the hot blast, shaking a thousand bronze leaves. They rounded the corner into shadow and still air. Cool stars re-appeared in the sky, the river flowed black as before. But they ran hard a dozen yards more, till a new sight arrested them.

A half a mile upriver a bridge had grown across the Flood. None had been there an hour before. It was built upon boats. Bobbing torches crossed from desert to city, with hundreds more to follow waiting clustered on the shore, lighting the conical bulk, the spoilage-hues of Thoog! As one swayed forward onto the rocking bridge, its crooked snout read plainly against torchflare. And there, roped together, a flock of long-legged avox staggered, their tails catching the red light and switching like incandescent fans, as they waited to be driven across the bridge.

Edgar and Alice backed cautiously through the shadows and around the corner. The Slizz was waiting for them. They no longer questioned whether they should follow it. There was no other choice. Their revulsion from the Thoog was greater far than their fear of fire.

Now on the far side of the canal hung a curtain of flaring smoke, of smoke-tasselled flame, veiling all that stood there.

Edgar and Alice could hardly breathe for the fumes, see for the cinders, or hear, for the unbroken thunder, the throaty yarks that the Slizz began to utter now, without which, for a long bad time, they would not have known where to go and would have been burned or hurried blind into the water. But they eventually got free of the smoke. Smarting from small burns, they gagged at the stink of their scorched fur as they stumbled after the Slizz. Straight along the embankment it trotted, toward some interior district of the city, and they followed. Alice was as good as asleep. Edgar, holding her upright and steering her dragging steps, was not much better. He kept his eyes on the jogging haunches of the Slizz. They began to pass a district already swept by fire, a zone of roofless, blackened shells. Here and there flames still licked the charred edges of things. In due course a street crossed the embankment, spanned the canal with a single-arched bridge, and plunged into the wasted zone. At the crossroads stood a fountain. The Slizz gripped the rim of the basin, raised itself, and drank. Edgar brought Alice there. He splashed her face, scooped water to her lips. Then he bent and plunged his whole head in. A little revived, he shook his whiskers and looked about him, first searching the street on the far side of the bridge.

Gutted buildings, still steaming, lined the broad way, and a pall of smoke hung there. Beyond the corner where the street at last bent, the fire was red still and lit some handsome porticoes. Then a cluster of lithe, cursive shadows appeared, crouching and dodging among the debris. They darted up the avenue, then vanished abruptly. Edgar could not make out their kind; not Clowncats.

Before he could think twice about them, another shape was there, between the smoldering houses, a dim giant's shape, a great bear. It was out of scale. It could hardly have fit through any of the ruined porticoes; it could easily have looked in at a second-story window. It was unthinkably big and had stepped into the city street from outside the pale of Nature, yet it was a bear—a terrible, but not a monstrous shape. Would it kill him, if he met it, or know him, adopt his purpose and his errand, carry him on its shoulder to the Citadel? He could not tell its color; he saw both red and gold, but it was reflecting a burning. The shape, as he wondered about it, jerked into shadow so quickly, leaving the street so dead and empty, that he couldn't feel sure he had seen anything at all.

The shock knocked him awake, all the same. He must not give in to fatigue and fancy. It would not do. And was it going to do for them to trail through a burning city after a silly beast of the fields? He must not think a guide had been appointed them. Creatures must find their own way. Fortuitously the Slizz had brought them by the route that Edgar himself, had he been sufficiently alert at the time, would certainly have chosen. They were skirting the fire, as they must. Eventually they would find another bridge across the canal, and a street leading south. If the fire had not reached so far, they would take that street. Otherwise they would follow the water to the next bridge and next south-leading street. Sooner or later they must pass beyond the blaze's spread. Then they would turn and go south. They could not miss the Citadel then.

But the canal and the embankment took several sharp bends to the right, so that soon they found themselves walking north! With every bend Edgar felt his sister grow heavier on his arm. He was nonetheless determined to get over the canal. By the time the next bridge came into sight, they had left the fire behind them. On the opposite bank of the canal were wooden tenements with roofed staircases climbing their walls. Edgar breathed a goaty air. Surely, the Tapestry Works were somewhere hereabouts; now the Tapestry Works are a government enterprise, and an official, if one could be found, would owe duty to Claudio. But the first thing was to get across the canal.

The bridge was that sort of drawbridge that fishes up a span of wooden decking with counterweighted poles. Its static half, a demi-arch of stone, loomed over the water. The drawbridge was up, hoisted, luckily, from their side. He had only to undo a thick line from a cleat, and the deck would marry its span with the tongue of stone. He lowered Alice onto a bench, then with fumbling fingers attacked the umbilicus of hemp.

Cessation of motion and the easing of pain in her muscles drew Alice a little way out of her doze. She opened her eyes on a very dim world. There was her brother with his back to her, and there by her feet the Slizz, and Bargeton still all about her. Her fur stank of smoke; she remembered a fire.

The Slizz did not look happy either. As she sleepily studied it, she grew conscious of something new in its mien.

"What is it," she softly said. The Slizz's eyes met hers, and sent her thoughts reeling. "What?" she gasped. Standing, clawed feet splayed upon the cobbles, it bent over her. Her hand was enfolded by a hand like leather laid over steel; it pulled her to her feet. Where was the languageless beast? The olive wool fell in locks over its temples and curled around its nape. The delicate nares lightly flared.

The Slizz was staring, and then pointing, lifting a single shaggy talon-tipped digit, along the canal, away from the bridge. It looked at her to see if she had understood, and she suddenly wished for more coffee. The Slizz had not let go of her hand. It was leading her to Edgar. Together, paw in claw, they stood behind his rounded back as he swore at the cleat and the difficult knot. He was beginning to ask himself whether he ought not to gnaw through the cable with his teeth, when a chilly hand rested on his shoulder. The knot began to loosen. As the beast began its racket Edgar shrugged, but the chilly hand stayed. The yarking was uttered in a peculiar series of sounds: a click, a moan, a hum. Its hoarseness had vanished. Click, moan, hum, very fast: click, moan, hum. *C-oo-mm*.

The rope tore free of the cleat, and the drawbridge sank. It slammed on the stone. Edgar stared at the Slizz, but the beast was looking past him. Alice, with the Slizz's word still in her ear, saw its eyes grow filmy, its pale tongue loll, as it dropped to all fours and hiccuped with beastly fear.

Running feet beat on the deck. Edgar swung around, and a squad of bodies hurtled at him and caught him by the arms, clawed hands locking there, and jerked him off the bridge, spun him, and ran him down a street where hanks of fleece dangled dimly golden over every doorway, where upper stories extruded so far that in many places they met and made bridges over tunnels where running feet drummed and breaths rasped around his panting, till he was being driven dead at a wall that closed off the end of the street, a wall of majestic blocks; but at the last moment he was turned left through a puddle of lamplight and run into a house, the last on that side. Still at a run he was shoved down a narrow hall in the midst of jostling backs, napes, and elbows, all stubbly. A fishform lamp swam quickly over his head. He heard a scrabble of claws on iron and wood. Then was tossed into blackness, and a door slammed.

SEVENTEEN

The Goldsmith's Shop.

*E*dgar lay sprawling on smooth stone and carpet. If he could only make sure that Alice was in there with him, and not hurt, then all that remained would be to drag himself wholly onto the carpet and sleep. Tomorrow would be soon enough to consider his disastrous error. But before he could even speak his sister's name, the silence was broken by a clatter and a wheezing grunt.

"Found it, Colonel," breathed a husky voice, not a bear's. "Not just where I thought it was. I tripped over someone, I think, sir."

The calm voice replied from directly overhead, as though the speaker were straddling Edgar's body.

"Make a light, Dvanko, and then we can see what we've got."

A tinder-box rasped; a droplet hung in the blackness, grew to a flame. The candle was righted, a glass chimney set over it. At first nothing showed but the edge of a table and a long face with worried eyes set high on its brow, but then the flame spat. The face grew a naked torso, cinctured with straps of dark leather.

"Hold it up, Corporal!" commanded the voice from above, impatiently. Edgar still could not see the speaker. The other did as he was bid. A sector of white wall came into view, and a heavy-barred door; on the floor, at the limit of the candle's rays, lay the Slizz, its muzzle buried between its forepaws. "Faugh," said the same voice in quiet disgust, "how did *that* get in here? Give me the candle, Corporal. I want to take a look at our prisoners. Here, I'll come and get it." Edgar ducked as a claw-footed leg grazed his head. When he looked again, two creatures stood at the table. The second, like the first, was hairless and girt with dark straps, but the eyes glowing near the crown of its long skull were darker, harder; the slender body bulged with muscle. Where the one slouched and gaped, the other stood erect. With legs slightly apart and one fist on his hip, he held the lamp aloft. His searching eye left the Slizz and lit on Edgar, who blinked; then it moved right, to where Alice sat on the floor, trembling.

"So," came the quiet voice, "it is the young bears we were told of. A brown one, and a russet one. Master Claudio," he pronounced the name with firm contempt, "will have to jump through our hoops before he sees his young relatives again."

"These two is kin to Claudio?"

"His nephew, Dvanko, and his niece; so I am informed."

"Gor! What a piece of luck we run into 'em."

"No luck at all, Dvanko, but a sign. We are favored in what we do. Our work tonight, for all that you did not like it, was well done, you see: here we collect our first prize, far sooner than even I had hoped. So much for all your doubts and fears, Corporal Dvanko. You will do well to put them from you altogether. Our course is right. Our cause is justified. You may see it here, in the presence of these prisoners in this house."

"Yes, sir, I see it."

"Continue to hold that vision, and you may, if you acquit yourself with unwavering confidence, see the rank of sergeant again."

"O, sir, I will, it grieved me bad to complain before, I was fairly busted for it; I swear I won't do so no more."

"Who are you?" Edgar, racked by fear and frustration, could not regulate his voice; the question came out in a hoarse bark. "What are you?" he could not help adding.

"*What* are we? Claudio's kin, and not know what we are? Really, the ignorance of mammals defies belief."

"We're not from this city," said Alice boldly. "We come from the City of Bears."

"So? You are in Bargeton now. You wander the night like a pair of spies . . . strange spies, though, that do not even know who you are spying on. We are Ceruk, Claudio's niece. Surely, even in the City of Bears, you have heard of the Ceruk?"

"O yes," she replied, "we have. Some live there—I've seen them, but—but they had wool on their bodies—and they wore clothes."

"Yes," he answered drily, "and they love gold, and are really no better than Slizz who have acquired speaking tricks. Is it not so?"

"Well, they . . . are of the same kind as the Slizz."

"Faugh," he said again. An angry blush muddied the amber of his skin. "You are extraordinarily stupid, even for a mammal, if you suppose that I, and this soldier here—"Dvanko straightened and closed his mouth—"can be related to such a thing as *that*." He pointed to the crouching Slizz. "Look at it, creeping and cowering! How dirty it is! You bears have a job, to wash all the dung from its shearings. Your cattle, are they not, these beasts? And do we look like cattle?" He certainly did not. Edgar could not help admiring his martial but athletic stance.

"I'm sorry," said Alice, a little chastened but still defiant. "The Ceruk in the City of Bears have a fleece and aren't dirty at all and . . . and they are very civil creatures."

"Say *servile*, rather," retorted the Ceruk.

"Y'see, miss," put in Dvanko, "it's true the Ceruk all grows wool on their bodies like Slizz; but we shave it off, don't y'see. Because we're not going to be thought of as being like them Slizz. And that's why we're called the Shaven Ceruk. On account of the shaving."

"Be silent, Corporal Dvanko. We owe no explanations to bears. But so that you will never attribute to me the fear of being known, you may tell your uncle, when you next see him, that Colonel Gribo took you prisoner. And now, if you hope to rejoin Claudio, study compliance well. Arrogance will not serve your turn, so just school yourselves out of it. Corporal, get rid of this disgusting beast." Gribo kicked at the Slizz. But when Dvanko went to shoo it away, his waving arms stilled suddenly, and he crouched down beside it.

"Beggin' your pardon, Colonel," said the corporal, "but this here Slizz—this here disgustin' beast—I've had a look at it, and it is not unknown to me, sir."

"Not unknown?"

"Yes, sir. Have a look. It's *him*, sir. I mean, it's *it*. The one. You know, sir. The very one as got this trouble started. It's Master Xenko's Slizz, sir."

"Are you sure?" Gribo queried with genuine surprise. "But how do you know?"

"O, I'm sure of it, sir. His cook, Master Xenko's cook, Mistress Ardannen, sir, she's my aunt, you know, sir, so as a littl'un I was right in the thick of it, all that hoopla, and he—and it—this here vile Slizz—well, that's him, sir. It."

"Really? Another sign! The strands of our fate are all winding up together here; let the catastrophe come! I know how this drama ends. Well, well, then we'll leave the vermin here, I think, to keep these good young bears company."

"Excuse me again, sir, but—leave 'em here? Hadn't we better pack 'em all down cellar?"

"Why? They'll keep very well here."

"But this here's Master Xenko's shop, sir! He does all his work here, and his trade, too; keeps samples of his wares for display in this room. Will it be, well, quite safe?"

"Why not? They're hardly likely to steal anything, being under lock and key themselves. And Xenko, I fancy, may relish a nice morning chat. If he gets a shock from the sight of that dung, then perhaps it may whet his purpose in our cause. But I ought, no doubt, to set a guard over his gold. You, Dvanko, will stay here with these prisoners, who will be under your care till Xenko comes. It will be the first step of redemption for your recent cowardice."

"Yes, sir."

"Make sure, Corporal, that you do not fall asleep."

"No, sir, I won't."

"Then I will bid you good-night. I have business in the Palace. I must go see what that bumbler Equivair is about. They will be happy to hear of this capture! So, Dvanko." He paused on the threshold and passed his hand lingeringly across his crown. "One more thing. Tomorrow you will shave the regiment. First thing after morning exercise. Have your razors sharp."

"Yes, sir. Always keep a keen edge on my razors, sir."

The door closed and Gribo was gone. Dvanko, holding the candle-lamp, puffed out his cheeks, ran his palm over his own bald pate, crossed his eyes, and let out a plosive sigh.

"I could use a shave myself," he said reflectively; then he seemed to remember his prisoners. "All right, you bears," he barked, "hop up on that chest, and don't stir off it till you're told. There, behind you, the big one. You too, chum, you hop

179

up there as well," he said to the Slizz, who rose and guided Edgar and Alice into the shadows. The chest was enormous. Alice could rest her chin on its lid without stooping; Edgar had to boost her up. A moment ensued when he and the Slizz both stood with their forepaws on the edge, ready to mount; they exchanged a glance; then the Slizz bounded gracefully, leaving Edgar to scramble up as well as he could. There was a rug, soft and deep, across the lid. Edgar settled near Alice, who nestled up, and the Slizz curled beneath their feet. An extraordinary happiness lit their minds as their muscles unwound. Alice thought that if one were to bring her a bit of a snack, now—a slice of cool melon, say, with a fat wedge of cheese—she would die of sheer pleasure.

Meanwhile Edgar's mind sank towards oblivion, hesitating above its black surface. Awake for so long, he could not dive at once. Soon, though, he felt Alice's slow breath by his side. Had he been dozing? He had been reviewing the scenes he had passed through that day, but which one he had got to, he could not quite recall. He raised his head to a curious sight. Dvanko passed the chest with a half-dozen candles, all lit, clamped in his long jaws. Rolling an eye at the sleepers as he marched down the room, he stuffed the sticks into holders. Six small islands emerged from the ocean. Some change in Edgar's breathing, some catch in his throat, must have awakened Alice, for she too now sat up and looked out on the treasure-house.

Apart from the furniture, made of plain, dark wood, every object in the room was of unadorned gold. Bowls in every size, cups and flasks, dishes, trays, frames for pictures and mirrors, inkstands, sandcellars, snuffboxes, peppermills: all were of gold, and so massive and severe in form the eye weighed them. Little art had gone into their fashioning. Few curves deviated from the circle's, few angles from the square's. Cups and bowls all were inverted domes, vases and candlesticks all squat pillars. Glassfronted cases along the walls displayed tiers of heavy merchandise. Alice, half-dreaming, began to imagine the house she would build on Citadel Hill, and its garden. Edgar mused on restoring the fortunes of Concatenopolis. In their visions of wealth, neither saw the objects that actually stood before them. None of these golden objects would ever inhabit a room of theirs, for they seemed neither useful nor beautiful. To Edgar, it was as though a number of shapes had been chosen—partly to suggest consumption of victuals, candles, flowers, pepper—but really to lock in place quantities of the pure metal. So he felt no qualms at melting it down again, coining it, spending it. But these fantasies made their legs and arms feel as soft and heavy as twisted ropes of gold; their heads slumped as their thoughts rolled like marbles in a wide golden bowl; so brother and sister fell back on the rug, sound asleep.

Once more Alice awoke in the night. It was a puffing and scraping that roused her; but the slow horror of waking dissolved at the spectacle her eyes met. The six candles stood on the floor around a tall mirror, but the amazing thing, a sparkling cloud, hovered between mirror and candles. Lavender-white, it winked at her with all the tints of the rainbow while continually changing shape, and grunting. When the long razor-blade emerged from a foaming lump, Alice understood. Then she giggled: Dvanko, lathered from head to foot, bent, his back to the mirror, head down between his knees; he was shaving his buttocks. She watched this homely operation for a few minutes, till sleep overtook her again.

EIGHTEEN. **Slizz and Ceruk.**

*A*lice fought her waking hard. Sleep had removed her from adventures, and she resisted, for as long as she could, coming back to a world of dangers and detours. She opened her eyes. The darkness of the room broke up into various glooms in which dim golden glows were abroad. She thought she could make out some faint gray lines, tinged yellow or blue, far away down the room. Dvanko and his candles were nowhere to be seen. What had wakened her? Some part of her mind held the memory of a repeated noise, a quiet tapping. Now she heard it again, the quick ringing of metal on metal; she twisted around to see.

An oil lamp burned low in the middle of a table. Its light made a small pool. Nearby an inverted golden bowl, poised on a column, was turned by a bespectacled Slizz. He was plainly but richly dressed, and as he sat at the table, turning the bowl, he struck it with a small hammer. This Slizz wore a wine-red sugarloaf hat with a brim turned like a sea-boot's. The gold spectacles sat high on his muzzle. He had rolled back his wide, azure-damasked sleeves to give his agile fore-paws more play. Yet wisps of fine, mossy wool sprouted under his cap, and on his arms. Behind the eyeglasses peered familiar eyes that contemplated the bowl with the same look Alice had watched her own Slizz bestow on a plump mushroom. The effect was ludicrous. It was like the woodcut illustration to a nonsense rhyme, where fleas wear waistcoats and gaiters.

Alice raised herself on her elbow in order to see better, and at once the great eyes, bulging through the lenses, had fixed her.

Then she remembered: of course, it was a Ceruk. This was the goldsmith, who owned all these treasures, the master of the house, and her jailer. She even remembered his name, Xenko. Was he waiting for her to speak? Though detained there by force, she felt like an intruder. If she spoke, no doubt the Ceruk would answer; and at this thought she felt her will weaken. So she lay there in the vague, vacant stare, like a Slizz's, but exaggerated to chaotic diffuseness.

The goldsmith dropped his eyes and fell once more to tapping. Alice shook her brother awake. He started, yawned, gaped at the new personage, gaped at Alice, shook his head, and blinked. Alice silently mouthed "Ceruk" several times; Edgar regarded her as though she were mad.

"How our shame finds us out, such indeed is fatality." The thin, dry voice crept from behind the workbench. Alice would hardly believe the goldsmith had spoken, so little expression showed on his face. But each phrase was accented by a tap at the gold. "It knows where we live, does our shame, *tap*, no one better; it visits us at its will, *tap*, in spite of years of toil, *tap*. All our labors to make amends goes for nought, we made our mistake, *tap*. Our shame is born, *tap-tap*. Nothing we do thereafter can keep it away from us: through locked doors it finds us, it enters as it pleases, it blights our lives over and over again, *tap-tap*. It takes possession like an heir, indeed it is our child, *tap*. Shame is our only son, and gets everything, everything, *tap-tap-tap-tap*. But you see, Master Bear, and you, Miss Bear, pray excuse me if I do not rise to salute you, *tap*, I must keep on with my work. You see, though my shame comes back to me, I do not embrace it, *tap*. I do not make it welcome, *tap-tap*, why should I? That is too much to ask. I may not cast it out of my house, *tap*, how could I do that, no no, *tap-tap*; one's shame is not so easily dealt with. It would only come back again, *tap*. So I sit at my bench, eyes lowered before my guests, and tap-tap at my work, *tap-tap-tap*."

And then, before Alice could even begin to think of replying, the Ceruk uttered a shriek of rage, flung his hammer down, and came racing around the end of his work-table as if he meant to launch himself at the coffer and pummel them. The two bears sat bolt upright, the Slizz edged its way in between them; but the Ceruk halted, and then gracefully executed a balletic bow.

"Please to make yourselves at home in my home," he said. "Would you like some gold?"

"Thank you, we have no use for your gold," said Edgar very stiffly. "As you must know, we are here as your prisoners. I don't know why. We have done nothing to you. We mean you no harm."

"Ah, no harm, says you. That's as it may be, young Master Bear," the Ceruk replied. "You have brought my shame back to my house; you cannot deny it."

"I don't know what you mean. We ourselves were brought here by force. If we are embarrassing you, you'd better talk to your Colonel Gribo about it."

"Ah, my Colonel Gribo."

"So now, please let us go."

"I am Xenko, at your service," the Ceruk responded with the utmost blandness. He performed another elaborate reverence, and then stood in silence, his forepaws folded in his sleeves, staring very hard not at Alice or her brother, but at the Slizz nestled between them. It gazed back with its usual unreadable expression, head resting upon crossed forepaws.

"Then won't you let us go, Master Xenko? Our uncle Claudio will surely show his gratitude to you," said Alice pleadingly. But the Ceruk seemed not to have heard her. He stood rapt in contemplation of the Slizz, who bore it meekly. Alice could not tell if wonder, distrust, or a strangely ironic benevolence held the upper hand in the goldsmith's countenance. After the conversational hiatus had grown to a distressing length, the Ceruk at last spoke; his voice was once more dry and distant.

"You see how civil they are, these delightful young bears, our noble masters. How well they have been brought up! They had no fools for father and mother. And how sweet for me, now, fallen into the decrepitude of age, and fit for but few of the tasks that can guarantee my livelihood, how sweet, how decent, if I could only run, throw the doors wide, call and clap, and then, when all were gathered, bow and say, 'This is my household! These are my sons!'" He stooped and shrugged; then turned slowly, as if bent by years of troubles, and shuffled back to his table. Laboriously he worked himself into his seat, brisk enough though he'd been in the leaving of it. Picking up the hammer, he gave the bowl a few languid taps, and as the golden ringing died away, murmured, "*This* is my son."

Who was his son? For several seconds neither Edgar nor Alice could find any meaning in his words. They waited for the goldsmith either to acknowledge clearly their desire to depart or to resume his own work, which they were ready to take as permission to leave. But he did neither one. After several seconds it became uncomfortably evident that he was awaiting a response to his declaration. His hand rested on the hammer where he had despondently laid it, and he slouched anxiously, one ear cocked. Suddenly Edgar and Alice became aware that the Slizz was also attending the event. Its flanks quivered, though it crouched still, head on paws. And then the truth of the situation struck them both at the same moment, and they struggled to form an answer that would fill the silence. But they could do nothing for several long moments except look from the father to the son. As Xenko's slouch grew more anxious and pronounced, he fell into the very pose of their own Slizz. Alice wonderingly compared the long muzzles, the unblinking eyes. Yet one wore a cap and spectacles, toyed with delicate tools, and spoke trippingly. What she had taken for absence of mind in her pet's features now took on the character of absent-mindedness, not her uncle's scholarly kind, but rather an absorption in things not visible. She studied their eyes: large, round, bird-hypnotizing eyes, neither gentle nor cruel. Xenko continued silent. She looked from the artisan to the beast. The family resemblance was complete. But Alice thought that it was as though she had gone with her father to visit one of his friends, and that wellborn bear had leaned over his fishpond, and introduced one of the carp as his wife.

Of course it was rude of them to let such a silence prolong itself, still more to gawk as they did; but Xenko possessed himself in his attitude of grief with a certain self-conscious flair, as though he were pleased by the discomposure his case had caused the bears, and didn't mind drawing it out a bit. But neither Edgar nor Alice was brooding on Xenko. All their thought was for the Slizz and the word it had spoken in crisis. Once more questions began to flood Edgar's brain. Alice was no less bewildered, but she felt the moment's pressure more keenly. They must say something, say it now; to continue in silence would be insulting, and they were in this Ceruk's power. So she stammered, "What is your . . . your son's name, sir, please?"

"So polite. You are really too kind to ask," sighed the Ceruk.

"You must remember, sir, that we have travelled a long way with your son, but never known how to call him; and he could not tell us."

"No, no, how could he? He is Slizz, Miss Bear. He is a brute, and cannot speak to you. My son and a brute," he moaned.

"But has he no name? Did you never give him a name when he was little?"

"Ah, when he was little. Ah, well, that is another story. Perhaps a name was prepared for him then, before he hatched, and inscribed in gilt characters on his shell. Perhaps it was my father's own. But, miss, he is Slizz. My son, but Slizz. Do Slizz have names? I fear not, indeed, no more than do—" he groped in the air—"than do . . . weevils, or . . . or chickens! Unless, of course, their herdsbear should call them 'Floppy Ears' or 'Stumpy Tail' or 'Old Smelly'; or after someone he thought it resembled, his wife, perhaps, or some local grandee. These are the sorts of name that Slizz are given. I fear you would need to inquire of his pastor to discover how he was called, if indeed he was ever singled out for notice."

There followed another pause, during which Alice tried to think of what to say to all this, when the Ceruk unexpectedly resumed. "But since you are so condescending as to ask, I will tell you that the name by which he would have been called, had he been as his brothers and sisters, and not moved his mother and myself to folly and grief, was Ganno. My father's name, as I may have hinted." He stopped. Alice laid her paw lightly on the Slizz's spine.

"But how do you know to give your children a masculine or a feminine name while they are still in the egg?" Edgar asked.

"O, we candle the eggs four days after their mother drops them," Xenko replied. "The Cerokin—that's the males—generally have their tails by then; the Cerugai, or daughters, get them later on. How delightful of you," he added, "to show interest in us and our ways."

"Ganno," murmured Alice, now stroking the Slizz, who rolled his eyes back up at her, but otherwise remained still. She measured her next words carefully: "And has Ganno never spoken a word at all?"

"Why, my dear young lady, what a question, if you will pardon me. Had he spoken a word, he would have spoken several thousand; in short, he would be Ceruk, and all of the pain that this family has suffered would have been averted. Why, you yourself have travelled with him, if I understood you correctly. Had he a word to speak, I am sure that he would have spoken it to you, out of the warm feelings that naturally attach to two such amiable and genteel young masters. Do I understand—you will excuse my curiosity, a father's inquisitiveness, nothing more—am I correct in thinking that you are his owners, at present?"

Edgar then explained the circumstances under which the Slizz had become a member of their party.

"I see; I see," Xenko went on, in tones of injury swelling to anger. "Ah, wretch! What, vagabond? Fled from his owner that paid good money for his worthless fleece! Imposed himself upon these fine young bears, that's bad enough, but to foist his stinking carcass on the President of the Bargeton Senate! So! There is to be no end to our disgrace. Not while he lives, and creeps around on his brute's four legs, I can see that very plainly. Witless wretch! To run away from his kind master! Too good, is he, to mingle with the others of his silly kind, that he must come bringing shame on ours? What, once again a runaway? Once again, the cur? And then to lead these gentlefolks to my door, bless them!

"I rail and scold, but it does no good," the Ceruk coolly pronounced, and, turning his hammer around, he drove its spike through the crown of the golden bowl. "What can change the past? It is dead, dead and buried, if only it wouldn't keep popping up again on my doorstep, you black-guard! He cannot understand me, to attempt his correction is fruitless. I might as profitably admonish my hatrack! But a hatrack behaves. You hang a hat on it; it keeps the hat till you want it again. Why cannot he stay in the fields, drat him! It is my father's heart, you see, that betrays me into berating him like a son and Ceruk, but ha ha! He cannot understand! It is just noise to him."

Alice, glancing at the expression in the Slizz's eyes, was very far from sure that this was so.

"I have only my folly to blame. Doubtless so. Ceruk, you see, are not warm-blooded, not warm-hearted. We are not like you generous bears. Do not be deceived by our abundant wool. We are reptiles. In exercising sympathy, I did not follow the example of my hatrack, ha ha! Shall I confess to you my error? I did not give him up at once. Do you under-stand? He hatched—and I kept him. His mother's heart was

intelligible, I must inform you how the Ceruk bear their young; a matter poorly understood. I will pass to you the explanation given me, in his shop at Bargeton, by Master Xenko, chief instigator of the late troubles in that city.

That I choose such a source may seem strange. Who does not revile the projects of Xenko? I was his enemy, and, at the time I speak of, his prisoner. Yet however abhorrent his solutions, Xenko's grasp of the problem was absolute. He saw, as no other Ceruk of his day saw, the issue central to *Katsurogommax*, whose great champion he was; its few productions all paid for with his gold. Nor was his response to the play confined to that fanatical passion, those acts of sedition, that have marked him down a villain; Xenko is the author of a fragmentary tragedy that touches nearer to the quick of the matter even than *Katsurogommax*, its model. Called *Kosilezi-voromon*, it relates, in twenty sequent episodes and one unnumbered, the story of his own household, and Xenko himself is its protagonist. One might expect a self-justifying, self-aggrandizing tone to this work, but there is nothing of the sort. "Young Xenko" is shown as quite criminally naive in his handling of the Problem of Kind, the issue of *Katsurogommax*, the same that arises each time the Ceruk go to breed a new generation. The exposition of that problem is the matter of the extrasequential scene, entitled "The Explaining Episode." In it "Old Xenko," at work in his shop, speaks with two young bears, his hostages, who have with them a Slizz; he reveals to them that the Slizz is his son. Then he proceeds to inform their ignorance how Nature permits such an anomaly as a creature father to a beast. This episode, then, makes an ideal gloss upon *Katsurogommax*; it, and my own memory of the occasion upon which it is based, are the sources for the exposition that follows. The reader may find further interest in "The Explaining Episode," in that it lays out the very origins of all the civil wars at Bargeton.

The Ceruk, then, being reptiles, are oviparous. The new-laid eggs are planted in fine white sand, where they lie for twenty-one days. On the fourth day the shells are held to a candle; where a tail-bud is seen to sprout, that embryo is known for a male, is blessed, is given a name which the father inscribes on the shell in gold letters. Then the eggs are returned to the sand. Concentric rings are raked around each, three for the females, nine for the males, seventeen around the whole bed. This boundary even the parents may not transgress. From Naming to Hatching the house is kept quiet, the nursery silent, except for a fountain. Anxiously tended braziers warm the sand. Each day the mother effaces the outer-most ring of the seventeen; the last is wiped from the sand in the presence of the entire household—several families, scores of individuals—and of delegates from the other households of the Ceruglio.

They arrive armed with gifts and with compliments to witness the Hatching. The compliments, written out on strips, they paste to the door of the house as they enter. They crowd into the nursery, whose margin has been swept to receive them; in silence they crane to see the first stirring in the sand-bed, to catch the first muffled crepitation. All family quarrels, all commercial rivalries, are forgotten on that day, for it would be injudicious to cross a house blessed with a Hatching. Why this is so is succinctly stated in the notorious "low speech" of *Katsurogommax*. Ziramanko is the speaker. He is the grandfather of the Ceruga whose ten eggs, all overspread with golden names, are about to hatch; he gloatingly surveys the crowd and notes the presence of many old enemies.

Ha! Tread lightly, you who throng the narrow space
Around the sand, for here's a fearful clutch of eggs
To beat you back, to jostle past you in the press,
To wedge between your longest-nursed affairs and you!
Ten eggs! Ten sons! Ten brothers raised to handle gold,
Ten wits and twenty arms, one undivided mind,
One single purpose, to extend the fortunes of their house.
And if their loins are true, and if they choose good wives,
What acreage of ocean sand will they not pat
To steady shells by wives well-shaped, by them well-filled?
Till now our steps went halting, this is a mighty leap
Out of the mud, a long vault toward the city!
The rutted lane we walk, Ceruk, has smoothed, has broadened;
Now ten abreast we march. Fill in behind us as you can!

(XXIX: 1037-50)

What a change from the inexorable regularity of stress and cesura in *Hakashibais*, or from the densely layered figures of *Wae-voromon*, or from the cloud-hopping diction of *Ssubanja-matterax*! The hopes of the Ceruk, in their long struggle to be born as a kind, are here laid intolerably naked before an audience accustomed to see its aspirations clothed in the scarlet and gold of an imaginary future grandeur; in this one speech *Katsurogommax* stretches out its neck upon the block. And indeed, at the first performance forty years ago in the Isles, when Master Ptoyko damned it from the Critics' Box, he had no more to do than to allude to the pair of hypermetric lines, and then sit down. From that day to this it has never been staged, except at Bargeton. But the moles printed it, and it has been widely read.

The secret joy that Ziramanko utters is offset by fear no less intense, a special dread to which *Katsurogommax* does not give voice only because it will be realized in action. Xenko explained it thus to me:

"The truth is, Ceruk do not always bear Ceruk. Come, that must sound odd. If Ceruk do not always bear Ceruk, what the deuce *do* they bear? Codfish? No, young mistress, not codfish. Not owls, not little dogs. Our shame does not extend so far, though far enough, far enough indeed. The horrid truth, the ground for our fears on Hatching Day, is that out of an egg dropped by even the purest-blooded of Cerugai, there sometimes creeps a dull-eyed, slack-jawed little Slizz. Perhaps just one. Perhaps two. No mistaking them for Ceruk. But surely not all? Not *all* Slizz? Ha! That would indeed be the final disaster, would it not?"

Of course this is the outcome in *Katsurogommax*. At this point in "The Explaining Episode," "Old Xenko" makes the reference, then delivers himself of a critique that his original hearers were spared:

> The Hatching of the Ten! How somber, how sublime!
> I feel again that lull, that awful silence, fall
> Before the thunder-clap of madness rocks the house,
> And Ziramanko dies, cackling hexameters
> Of bitter augury; long before knives are drawn,
> And blood is shed upon white sand, before all this,
> I hear the feeble chirrups of ten tongueless Slizz,
> Fresh-broken from the egg, most coldly give the lie
> To all our boasting chronicles. The heavy hush,
> Wherein their cheeps resound, denies that history
> To be, whose lines our pompous plays pretend to trace.
> Affecting! Yet, young bears, this danger is not real.
> No no, so fell a Hatching never has there been,
> Nor ever will there be; the truth is otherwise;
> Our greatest hazard comes in quite another guise.
>
> (2809-23)

195

If only one of the Hatching is Slizz, it must be removed from the rest at once, for the legendary adhesion that binds brothers and sisters of the same brood grows into being in the very first hour, whilst each weaves, blindly and silently, into the squirming heap and noses the rest. If this bond should join "healthy" children to a Slizz, there is a probability that none will ever speak. For this reason a Ceruga adept in the detection of Slizz stands by at every Hatching, to carry off the throwback at its first appearance. She is the Silezzia; for five days she nurses her charge in a sealed apartment, then sells it to a Slizzherd bear. The rest of the brood never hear of it, never miss it.

The hazardous case to which "Old Xenko" makes allusion is that in which the mother is tempted to defy the laws and keep the single "diseased" child. Here in "The Explaining Episode," "Mistress Bear" is made to cry:

> To keep a Slizz! With love to nurture a disease!
> To damn her brood to silence and stupidity!
> Why, such a mother must be mad!
>
> (2828-30)

and "Old Xenko" replies, "Ay, she was mad." He goes on to personate a mother so tempted, and to speak her thoughts as she watches the old Silezzia reach forward with her long crook:

> Poor little beast! Is it so different from the rest?
> Have I not borne it as I bore the other five,
> Surrounding each alike, through many patient days,
> With careful housing of fine, pearly shell? Have I
> Not patted sand around and over this one egg,
> To keep it warm, to keep it steady as the rest?
> And did I know, as snouts came butting bravely out,

That this was not the same? And did I ever pray
That it might fail and languish, dying in the shell?
Or did I hope for all to break into the light,
Into the air, into the world, into my love?
And now this one alone, must I surrender it
To the uncanny crone? She'll carry him away.
In five days' time, while I sit in the nursery,
Ringed round by all my children but that one, she'll come,
She'll carry in a short, black purse, which, curtseying,
She'll drop into my lap; then silent she'll withdraw.
No, no! There must be room, room in so large a world
And various, for the weak to know a mother's love!

(2834-52)

At this point the fragmentary "Explaining Episode" ends. Xenko assigned it no number; but it seems certain that he meant it to stand at the head of his manuscript, for the events of the play unfold from the hypothesis, suggested in the last-quoted speech, that such a "mad mother" might carry out her design. That is to say, the events are presented by "Old Xenko" to the two "young bears" as if they were such an hypothetical case; in reality, they correspond quite exactly to the true history of his own household. All of the characters are based on real creatures (except, of course, for "The Conscience of the Race" who harangues "Young Xenko" in Episode XX); the "mad mother" was in life Onkannen, a name that needs no introduction from me.

But a case could be made that "The Explaining Episode" should follow Episode XX, since the events described in *Kosilezi-voromon* carry "Xenko's" career forward to the time of the two young bears' arrival in his house. In either case the drama's end is not written, being such as Xenko could never have foreseen. It is a part of history; and the completed work, retitled *Xenokotashi*, will stand as the only chronicle of real events in the entire canon of the Ceruk drama. That full version, including a meticulous redaction of *Kosilezi-voromon*, is now being prepared by the very last hand that Xenko would have expected to round off his labors; since it will not appear soon, I here beg the reader's indulgence of a brief synopsis of Xenko's fragment, by comparison with which the salient features of *Katsurogommax* may the more clearly appear.

Kosilezi-voromon begins with the struggle of the "mad mother," resolute to keep her single throwback child, with the father, "Young Xenko," who stands upon the Law. She prevails. The Slizz is to be raised as a son of the family, albeit separately. The following episodes detail the consequences: the Silezzia, balked in her office, spreads scandal in the Ceruglio; neighbors cut off relations with the family; tradesmen and servants grow impudent. The father is censured on Exchange, and the house's credit is affected. The mother exhausts herself between two nurseries, while the Slizz, for all her pains to teach it language, continues Slizz. At last "Young Xenko," pressed by his brothers, insists that it must be disposed of, and after frightful conflict the mother gives in. The Slizz makes its first appearance in Episode VI, a harrowing scene in which the father must force his way into his own kitchen and pull the little beast, dressed in a night-gown and clutching the spoon with which it has been trained to eat its porridge, away from the mother, whose last flaring of resistance is seconded by the cook, a surly Ceruga. The Slizz is handed to the broker who has purchased it and who will sell it into the flocks of the bears; there ensues a short burst of cut-and-parry between Broker and Cook:

B: Pray take the spoon away. What needs it with a spoon?
C: Why, porridge is too hot to sup without a spoon.

B: This gown it must not wear. Its fleece must fairly show.
C: This gown he wears to bed, as other children do.
B: But this is not a child! 'Tis Slizz, and no Ceruk.
C: 'Tis pity, then, he's taught to think himself Ceruk.
B: In pasture are no beds, no porridge, hot or cold.
C: Ay, ay, he has been well prepared for pasture life.

(VI: 1260-7)

The Cook's choice of pronouns shows her sympathies, but the ironies of this passage cut both ways.

The Broker carries off the Slizz. Episode VI culminates in the mother's madness, played out in the nursery before all her terrified children. She is confined to her room by force. The next few episodes depict the very gradual improvement of the situation, as "Young Xenko" takes on the roles both of father and of mother. He stills the children's memories, leads them to speech, teaches them their first letters. Slowly business and social relations are resumed. A minor crisis arises in Episode IX, as the children make their first friends and learn why they were formerly shunned. They torment both parents with questions at the very first meal when the mother is permitted to rejoin her family, and demand to know the truth about their "little brute brother." The mother flees back to her chamber, the enraged father metes out harsh punishment, and all the work's to do again. At last, by Episode XI, thanks to "Young Xenko's" patient cares, the family is once again reunited.

The catastrophe must be told in its author's own voice: not the words of *Kosilezi-voromon*, but those he used to me as I sat listening in his shop, my hand on the back of the very Slizz around whom this whole long storm has grown.[*]

* Xenko's synopsis corresponds to the action in Episodes XII-XIX.

"Two years pass. One fine day, Slizz, dissatisfied with pasture living on account of lack of spoons and beds, runs away from herd, finds own way back home. Arrives at dinnertime. Trots in, climbs on chair, grasps spoon; looks around as much as to say, Where's mine? Children in uproar: Our lost brother is come back! Daughters gather around, pet beast, feed it. Sons race to tell mother. Result predictable. Faced by pleas from mad mother and wild children, father again capitulates. Pleads nevertheless for secrecy. Reminds family in strongest possible terms of likely consequences, should Slizz's presence be known: ostracism, poverty, prison. Yes, yes, all swear, yes, papa, O yes. Beast discovered *the very next day*. Follows children to school, sits at desk, holding spoon. Entire family promptly cut. Father's brothers withdraw from family business, set up rival house.

"Now father and children unite to plead with mother: let the Slizz go back to the fields! New energy in mad mother, however. Makes impassioned speeches, first to family, next to former friends, at last to strangers in street, to whom Slizz, spoon wantonly displayed. Response at first derisory. Mad mother continues her rounds, gets up in public to defend rights of untongued offspring, feeble euphemism for Slizz. Community begins to be impressed in spite of itself, her fervor is so great. But children meanwhile sullen, angry. Banish Slizz from nursery. Mad mother preaches; they will not hear. Suddenly, smallest daughter loses power of speech, never to be regained. Begins to walk on all fours. Children confront parents. Mad mother, rapt in crusade, continues adamant. Children declare that mother cares only for Slizz now; they will all be Slizz. Drop to floor forthwith, race yarking around the room. Distracted father then promises children to make away with Slizz. Secretly summons Slizzherd, pays gold that he can ill afford to have Slizz removed as far as may be, kept under close guard. Abduction accomplished at night. Mad mother misses Slizz in morning; ghastly scene. At last largest son, lest mother destroy self, reveals father's action. Mother leaves without a word. Gone two months. Three more children grow silent. Servants give notice, all but cook. Father incessantly followed, abused by mother's disciples: What have you done with her? Mad mother returns, near-dead of exposure, carrying Slizz; locks self and beast in chamber. Desperate father leaves to carry out trivial transaction, all that general hostility has left him. Returns to find all children gone. Frantic inquiries. Result: own brothers invaded house, stole children *for their own good*. Long, costly lawsuit. Mad mother appears in court; uses up last reserves of strength in address to bear magistrates, Claudio presiding.* Speech begins calmly. Full of moving sentiments. Frequent quotation from tragedies. One justice seen to shed tear. But oration degenerates, at finish, into

* The late President Claudio of the Bargeton Senate. The reader must understand that the whole body of law governing the relations of Slizz to Ceruk was framed by the bears, the issue having arisen within the Commonwealth of Bears when the First Ceruk, Okko, spoke his first word. Xenko's case was tried in the Strangers' Court, the venue for all litigation involving non-bears; the galleries were packed not only with Ceruk but with creatures of all kinds, eager to see how the bears would deal with this challenge to their laws. Claudio must have given a remarkable performance that day. At all events, he impressed himself into the literature of two kinds, stepping straight from his dais into the Clowncat Comedy, where "the Claudio" is still a stock character (the figure, as one Cat has punningly put it, of "overbearing authority"); likewise declaiming magniloquent sentence in Episode XIX of *Kosilezi-voromon.*

TWENTY. Some Fruitful Meditations.

"*A*nd that is how the story runs," Xenko grimly concluded. Edgar's eyes were wet; Alice was silently but unashamedly weeping. Both were stroking the Slizz's back now, and could feel its flanks trembling. Then Alice caught a gleam of light reflected from Xenko's eyeglasses as he squinted across at them. "Ah," he cried, "I see this little tragic supposition has moved you. Permit me, therefore, to set your minds at ease, as far as I may. It might be, that the misfortunes of that ill-used, unhappy father were the occasion for him of some fruitful meditations." He laid one paw on the edge of his work-table and thrust the other into the bosom of his robe; his voice swelled, and his lenses reflected wheeling gold, like the gears in Possy's butterfly hunter; they flashed with rage and calculation.

"O, it will seem strange to you, what that father did then, at the end of his solitary years of thoughtful nights. The mother, the mad mother, she gave him his cue. What, so criminal an example? He recalled, as he sat at this table and worked,"—here Xenko rapped his fist on the surface beside him—"how she found words to challenge the law. But her principles were corrupt, you see I anticipate your proper, your decent reproach. However, that the law *is* bad, the father of my tale now agreed. He saw it was bad, but why was it? Not in that it forces us to surrender our offspring. He had come to see that its worst particular was, rather, that it binds

203

us, however distantly, to the stupid, squalid Slizz. This law, which is imposed on our kind by yours, young bears, is none of our own making, and it upholds the humiliating bond between city and pasture. Thither by law we send our tongue-less sports. Thence we receive, each year, a dozen mud-spattered Slizz who have learned to stammer a poor sentence or two. And by this perpetual shame we are kept down! Ceruk are rich, skilled, cultured, yet do not take their place in the world, on account of the Slizz. You will grant that a connection so degrading must be broken, and will be by any with strength. What other kind, capable of speech, skilled in craft and trade, participant members of a polity, would endure enforced kinship to cattle? Bears do not do so, young masters. Thoog do not. Even the degenerate Clowncats, our neighbors, do not suffer such indignity, but create their misery by free election. Then Ceruk must not either. This is the message which that father now brought to ears opened by his wife to reform. He took to the streets as she had done, accosted former acquaintances, seized the hem of their hastening robes, spoke. Many listened.

"But some said to him: 'We are not an old people. Few centuries have passed since the first Ceruk grew brain and tongue. No family can count more than ten generations from the pasture. Let Time make two races of us when it will. Nature will cause our emancipation when she and we are both ready.'

"But why must we wait? And there are greater fools than these, *lunatics* I should call them, the disciples of the dead mad mother. They say Ceruk and Slizz are not two. They would have us adopt, teach, interbreed . . . . But they are shunned, they are shunned, you need not fear them. The

Shaven Ceruk, who answer to me, keep them out of the streets and serve whisperers rightly for their *unclean* imaginings. Offal that they are, they use the mother's name, they call themselves only by her name . . . ."

Xenko's voice trailed away peevishly. He stood for a moment, his delicate fingers groping the table for a tool, or a weapon. Then he turned and hobbled to his bench, hoisted himself once again, and set to work on his spoiled bowl. His body became more bent as he worked, his eyes grew dull; his hands alone active turning the bowl, wielding the hammer, shaping the gold into glowing orbicularity with a rain of quick, tapping blows.

TWENTY-ONE. **The March of the Crimson Bears.**

A lice had her arm around the Slizz; she glanced down shyly at his face, but saw no pain there. She recalled all those hours when she had prattled away, reciting poetry, naming trees and flowers, explaining her family, and saw the Slizz's face as it was then, when she'd first studied it for response. Now, as though for the first time, she perceived its settled melancholy. All along the way she had discounted it, knowing how apt she was to lend her own moods to the features of pets. The lugubrious Slizz had been rather fetching. Her favorite dolls had all had sad faces.

Edgar was still sitting stiff and abstracted. He was amazed by what he had heard. Bargeton's Ceruk community had split on account of their Slizz, the very same that had made its entrance as a soggy rug on a toppled tree! And somehow, it seemed, this schism, conjoined with the cats' grievances, had brought war to the city. This, this was the moment for the Crimson Bears' invasion! The clock of their occult history had ticked for generations; and now it struck the exploding hour. But what fatality, Edgar wondered, had brought him and his sister now, just now, to Bargeton?

Finding no answer, his thought began to drift back to their present situation. As he watched the goldsmith turn and tap at the bowl, Edgar grew aware of another rhythm in the air.

The Slizz's back tensed. Alice looked up, puzzled. For a minute they sat as the tremors increased and Xenko still tapped. At length he too raised his head and laid down his hammer. By this time the glass in the cabinets was rattling.

"Can you hear anything?" Xenko asked in alarm. "I almost fancy that there is some sort of noise in the street, but my hearing is not what it was. I rather think," he said, rising from the bench, "that I should take a quick look out and see what is making this clatter."

"The Crimson Bears," murmured Alice unhappily to Edgar; but the Ceruk caught her low words despite his infirmity.

"Aha, quite so. The Crimson Bears! Let us hope you are wrong. But I dare say you're not. You had better stay here. Perhaps, you know," Xenko said a trifle eagerly, "perhaps they are looking for *you*. Young bears of consequence. You had better stay hid. I will deny you, never fear. But no, no!" He clutched his brow and started to hurry in circles. "What if they break in? Perhaps they want to despoil me! O, those villainous Crimson Bears!" He looked wildly around. "I shall lock you in! It will be safe. If I do not return alive, it is all yours, young bears, for I have no son!" He flourished both arms in hysterical largesse, ran to the door, pulled a key from a pocket. The concussions grew louder; the heavy feet tramped in formation.

"Mum's the word! Not a peep!" hissed Xenko, then popped over the threshold and was gone.

Alice gave a low moan and buried her face in Ganno's soft wool. The Slizz licked her ear, then gently squirmed his way free, jumped down, landed nimbly on his hind paws, and stood erect. He seized Alice's paw; "Come," he said magically, in his whispering croak. Edgar and Alice scrambled from the chest and followed as he loped down the room. The next instant they were by a window, while the Slizz's forepaws stretched to the catches. Then he pushed one of the leaves a very little ajar.

Even as he did so, a voice just outside the house barked:

"Stay in line, soldier, *stay* in line there. For heaven's sake, don't you boys even know how to walk in a straight line yet? O what a lot of babies! I'm going to have to say a word to your mummies! Toddlers could march straighter than you louts."

Edgar and Alice easily recognized the petulant, half-jeering voice, which seemed to cry through a windy hiss, as the Thoog commander's from the Market Square. It was the last voice that Edgar expected to hear; as for Alice, she drew out the little wooden bear from the bag at her waist. She was about to put it back when she noticed Ganno staring at it; she offered it to him. As his fingers closed around it, she felt glad. For a moment he studied the toy.

Then, crowded to the thin slot, the three stood, head on head, looking out. The morning was not far advanced; the street lay in luminous shadow. When their eyes had adjusted to the muted light, they distinguished a narrow arc of streetscape. Directly across from them a house door stood open. The pavement still shook with the pounding, but no marchers appeared. Edgar even ventured to push the shutter farther open, to gain a vista broad enough to include the Thoog they had heard. Instead, a file of gigantic figures met his eye. He forced himself to regard the huge totemic heads bobbing towards him, each behind each in semi-eclipse. The leader's shoulders, as broad as Edgar himself was high, crowned the swellings of his breasts and gorbelly. A leg like a wharf-piling swung forward; the massive block of its foot stamped, and all the windows rattled; then the great frame lurched forward. Its arms hung so straight by its sides, they seemed elbowless; and all over its body innumerable sheaves of crimson fur tapered like inverted flames or dagger-blades tempered in blood. Edgar stared. He had never seen any creature whose fur was of so perfectly uniform a hue. Nor had he ever seen bears so large, until the night before. But he did not recognize the vivid prowler among burning houses in any of these unlimber striders. They looked extinguished and walked like dead things; Edgar wanted to duck and hide, as their faces advanced.

"Column right—*march*!" called the wheeze of the Thoog. "You know your right foot, don't you? Well, good! In that case, can we speed things up a little? Everybody inside on the double!"

For a moment Edgar panicked at the idea that they would come marching straight into Xenko's house. But, of course, *right* meant the house opposite; so the stolid leader, drawing near the window, veered, swinging his bulk so sharply that he tilted, one leg sweeping the air. He seemed about to topple, but regained his trim at the last possible moment, and lumbered through the door. The second in the file performed the same maneuver, listing to the verge of imbalance, then righting himself with a crash as his foot hit the ground; and so the next, and the next. Edgar had a good view of their faces as they made the turn: utterly expressionless, each lacked expression in just the same way. Yet their features were not identical. He got it: it was the eyes, how they seemed not to notice anything. Could they see? Did they know where they were? Come from the farthest edge of the world, perhaps they found Bargeton too peculiar to look at. Perhaps they walked so stiffly from strain. Edgar tried to imagine such cramped rage as would make one's arms hang so poker-like. Or perhaps they were drug-eaters, or formidable mystics. Their souls, in some far garden world, would not feel for what their bodies attacked. Finally Edgar asked himself why the Crimson Bears had chosen the Ceruk quarter, the house opposite Xenko's. And why was a Thoog giving orders? And how did he dare to mock them?

Puzzling over these questions, Edgar grew restless. "Here's some real news at last!" he said to himself. "The Thoog in league with the Crimson Bears! I wish I could get to the Citadel, just to see Julio's face. But how can I, when I don't know the way?" And then, the Citadel might have already surrendered; even now, muffled Thoog might be spurring their draggle-plumed fowl through the inner gardens, trailing a fetor along the walks. And other giants could be crowding into Claudio's study, mashing the pasture-carpets, clumsily knocking the starred coffers. Could they be receiving, so soon, his uncle's capitulation? "That wall should be thick enough to keep them out," Edgar decided, and then added, "Also, there's the Great Golden Bear."

Now the street was deserted. The Slizz pulled the shutter to; then, cautiously, he opened the other leaf, and they all turned to look out. This new view offered their squinting eyes only a mottled ocher wall, which closed off the end of the street. Except for a knob of tarnished metal, the wall lacked any distinguishing features. But Edgar had not time to study what purpose the protrusion might serve before an uncreaturely thing occluded it, a high-stepping mass of sunset-stormcloud color, staggering on two legs abristle with white hairs: an avox.

The rider was having some difficulty controlling his bird. The long, saurian snout turned sharply this way and that. The Thoog heaved his swaddled bulk about in the saddle with a violence so great that the bird, its blind head bobbing and weaving around its knees, danced a few sidewise steps. But one more torsion turned it round; then the Thoog laboriously dismounted. The bird continued to lash its head; its stubby wings quaked so that their jewelled fronds waved gorgeously. The Thoog looped the reins round the knob on the wall. With this gesture, the avox fell to pecking violently at the cobblestones, as if in hope that one might crack to expose some succulent treat. The Thoog waddled away. Edgar was about to pull the shutter to, but the Slizz laid a paw on his arm; then a loud hiss echoed in the narrow street.

"General Skaling!" called a tremulous voice. "Sir! What news!"

"What? Who *is* that?" answered the Thoog, piping like an organ with a vast, leaky bellows. "Step outside, why don't you. I can't tell who you are. Why, it's Xenko!"

"Sir, it is," said the goldsmith's voice, steadier now. "General Skaling, I have—"

"Well, good morning to you, Master Xenko," the Thoog interrupted. "And it is a lovely day, isn't it. Especially after all that ruckus last night. Lord, what a hurly-burly that was!"

"Yes, sir. Please, General Skaling—"

"Did you watch my little review just now? I'd be glad to hear what you thought of it."

"Is it the marching bears you mean?" asked Xenko stiffly.

"Yes . . . good to see those big boobies on their feet, wasn't it? *I* thought they did a splendid job. Of course, they still could use a little practice, but for a first shot they seemed to get the hang of it about as well as you could hope. These streets are rather rough work for tyros in the marching business."

"It is high time they found their legs here, sir, high time, after all the expense they have put us to! If indeed it is not already too late."

"O, no, it's not too late. At least *I* don't think so. You have to be reasonable, Xenko. In my experience, a little patience pays high dividends when you're on campaign. Well, anyway, I'm pleased. That new fellow of Equivair's seems to know his job. I was starting to have my doubts about those cats, you know. They aren't very well organized, are they?"

"No, general, not very well. Not organized at all."

"Well, that's what I thought. Not too efficient. I was starting to wonder if it was worth the effort to carry them in this business, but now, well, this changes things, I guess. And I'm glad. It's best when everyone pulls their weight, don't you agree? And say, Master Xenko, while we're handing out bouquets, I owe a few to *you*. Those little boys of yours, those Shaven Ceruk, what a *fine* crew they are. Lord, how they work, and smart? Well, really, I can't say enough about how dedicated those little fellows are. Game to the core. Well, isn't it nice we met like this. I'm pleased as punch to be able to let you know how I feel about those Shaven Ceruk; but to tell you the truth, Master Xenko, I'm not quite as much at leisure as I would like, right now, to chew the fat with you, and so on."

"But, General Skaling, is there no news?"

"O, there's *news*, all right," said the Thoog in a teasing tone. "Good news and bad news—aren't wars just the most complicated thing?—but I'm afraid it's all going to have to wait a few hours. You'll hear about it at our meeting. You've been notified, haven't you? Two hours from now, in the Feast Hall. Everyone, and I mean *everyone*, will be there, and we'll just hash it all out at that time. But I can give you this much, Master Xenko, to mull over inside that hat of yours: we've got the bears cooped up on Citadel Hill, and the rest of the city is ours. The only problem is, there's someone in there with them. Can you guess who it is?" He paused, and then declared roguishly: "The Great—Golden—Bear. Now wouldn't that put knots in your wool? So we've got to do something fast. And between you and me and the avox," his voice sank to a confiding whisper that screaked like an out-of-tune fiddle, "tonight's the night, Master Xenko. Think about it. Now I really have to go."

"Sir!" cried the old Ceruk, "please wait! I too have news, good news."

"O, really?" said Skaling.

"It cannot be shouted in the streets, General Skaling."

"Well, it must really be hot. Come on and whisper it to me, then."

A silence, broken only by the avox' pecking, settled on the street. If any whispering took place, Edgar heard none of it. But he did not really need to eavesdrop; Xenko's news, he felt sure, was about him and Alice. They were hostages of a confederacy that now appeared to include—why, almost everyone they had met in Bargeton! The Thoog commander was in it; Equivair and the rebel cats were all in it; the Shaven Ceruk, certainly; and Xenko was near to its heart. And now, Edgar realized bitterly, the Crimson Bears, who took orders from Skaling, were the unlikely servants of this unlikely league. What did they all want? Did they *all* hate the bears?

Beyond this burst of knowledge his mind took but one more step, as he saw how small a part coincidence had played in the converging events. Design there had certainly been: Skaling and Equivair, Gribo, Xenko, and the Crimson Bears' chiefs had concocted the evolving plan.

Now Ganno pulled him away from the window; Alice followed. They passed the chest on which they had slept, passed Xenko's work-table, and travelled all the way down the room towards a door. As Ganno worked the stiff bolt, Edgar stared at his fleecy back. Only now did what he heard about the Slizz begin to make sense.

"His name is Ganno," he began, then stopped; shook his head. "Xenko is his father. He threw Ganno out of the house for being a Slizz, but he isn't. Then how did he come to be in that flock near the City of Bears? Why did he run away with us? We brought Ganno all the way to the Citadel, and then he disappeared in Claudio's study. But Alice says that when she woke up in the middle of the night, he was lying on her side of the bed. That was when she got up and saw the Great Golden Bear in the garden—and next morning we learned that Possy Damp Paws had escaped from the Citadel prisons."

The Slizz threw the bolt. The door stood ajar; Ganno was beckoning him through. Edgar hung back, amazed and unsure, but Alice had already forged ahead.

"O where is he taking us now?"

TWENTY-TWO

Ardannen's Kitchen.

*T*he smell of baking awaft in the corridor drove all questions from Alice's mind; it was time for breakfast. Gribo had called them prisoners, Xenko guests, but whichever they were, they had to be fed, Alice reasoned; she stepped past Ganno and her hesitating brother into the passage. It was not so dark once you were inside. She saw light ahead and moved towards it; very soon they had come to the head of a steep flight of stairs. At the bottom a hallway, set with tiny high windows, led off left and right. Cool daylight, poured down between houses and through panes thick with grime, made a heaven of this humble rear-corridor for her. Now Edgar was thumping down the stairs. Alice did not wait for her companions but turned left, whence the aromatic gusts.

Through an open door she looked into a low-ceilinged room, a kitchen after her heart; its oven silently glared. Within the hearth a pot swung from an iron jack and plumed vapor with a preoccupied burble. Six arched windows let in the pale morning, and savor of rosemary mingled with bread-smell. Outside, a kitchen garden, steep and dim, rippled with four-petalled hearts-ease on the maculate roughcast. Inside, Alice recognized the same dark, polished cupboards that had lined Xenko's study; but here, instead of golden mugs and bowls, plates and candlesticks, there was blue and white crockery. And at the table that occupied the room a fat

215

Ceruga was athletically punching and kneading an immense slab of dough. She was dressed in a loose gown of corn-colored cotton, roped at what should have been her waist; some azure stuff, wrapped like a turban, hung down her back to the floor.

"Yes! What is it now?" she barked, without looking up. "O, it's you." Gentler: "Well, don't dawdle in the doorway. Come sit down and eat!" Alice meekly walked to the end of the table and climbed onto a bench. Three bowls, three mugs, and three spoons had already been set. Edgar slid in by her side, and Ganno hoisted himself up next to Edgar. Alice watched as the Slizz slowly picked up his spoon. Holding it carefully before him, he stared at the Ceruga, who gave the dough a last brief but vigorous beating, dropped it in an explosion of flour, and exclaimed, "There! That settles your business, Mister Ball of Bread!" Then she bustled around the farther end of the table, hurried to the door, put her head out, heaved the door shut, and, turning, stood for a moment, her hands on her hips.

"So! It *is* you," she growled. Running up, she flung herself upon Ganno, kissing him smackingly several times on the head. Then she swept over to the fire, got the pot, and ladled generous portions. Hungrily they sniffed: it was a kind of porridge, that was clear. Comparing notes later, Edgar and Alice agreed that it contained raisins, anise, and a sort of tart, lemony banana; Edgar thought it had nuts. The foundation could not easily be told, but they made it out at last to be cake, so that the dish was really more a bread-pudding than porridge properly so-called. They did not mind. The old Ceruga gave them a pitcher of thick buffalo cream, one of the delicacies for which Bargeton is famous. Alice had looked forward to tasting some; now, as she poured it liberally over her porridge, she felt for the first time since Claudio's like a visitor rather than an intruder. With each spoonful, her anxieties fell away.

As she concentrated on her bowl, she heard the Ceruga lunging around the kitchen in the performance of a host of small tasks. But Alice looked up when a bellow of indignation burst from nearby.

"O, so that's your game is it, Mister Sticky Drawer?"

The Ceruga was facing a cupboard from which a drawer crookedly projected. "Well, then, won't you like it when you're broke up for kindling?" She knocked it shut, crying, "Get in with ye!" while the utensils rattled and crashed. "Eat up, babies, eat it while it's good," she commanded, and Alice obediently spooned porridge into her mouth. "Ay, that's the ticket," the cook approved. "Shovel it in, Miss Bulky Bear, you've a ways to go before you're as fat as your uncle."

Did everyone know who they were? Alice worked her spoon a little faster till the fat Ceruga turned away. Several times, before the bowl was emptied, she heard loud apostrophes to various articles:

"Who's this a-bubbling at me? Why, cry you mercy, Lady Saucepan, I didn't know your ladyship at first. But you knew me, says you. Knew me by my great fat belly, is it? Well, if that ain't like your sauce! Ha ha ha! But, says you, if I didn't like your sauce, I shouldn't have my belly! ha ha ha ha! Come now, here's Sir Spoony to settle our quarrel. Mmmm, he says that your ladyship wants what I've too much of. What's that, says you. Body, says he! Ha ha ha ha! Now, Sir Spoony, you've proven yourself a stirring gallant among the *ladles*, come help milady to a nice *flour*-y compliment!"

In between these skirmishes the Ceruga would urge the three breakfasters on to greater conquests, laying out fresh fields of battle in blue-and-white platters. She stood back with the air of a captain who, having pointed out the enemy, looks to see how his men will perform their duty. Alice marched to the assault; this was her sort of warfare. Edgar likewise did no shame to bears. As for Ganno, Alice paused a long second between spoonfuls. The Ceruga had erected around his bowl a veritable palisade of pastry. As she plied her own spoon, Alice pondered this affectionate largesse. But the cook did not limit her demonstrations to the setting out of delicacies. She petted and fussed over Ganno without remission, finding excuses to sweep by and pinch or kiss him, or pull at his ears. Then she'd exclaim, "O mischief, will ye look at them tangled ears, and don't ye never get near a comb? What, weaving your wool while it's growing, are you, to save everyone trouble?" Then, winking at Alice, she'd leap to quell some insurgency among the pots and pans with a cry of "Have at you, Signior Sifter!"

This had gone on for a while when the door burst open, and Xenko dashed in.

"Ardannen! Ardannen! Thoog take her, where is she when I want her?" He was halfway across the room, still waving his arms and seeing nothing, when her edged voice arrested his career.

"Here I am, master, just where I should be. The week's bread is just put into the oven."

"Why, Ardannen, there you are at last," the goldsmith breathed, quite surprised. "At your baking, are you? And so," he sighed, "I suppose you have seen nothing?"

"Nothing of what?" she snapped.

"Ah, yes, what indeed! Come, mistress, do not play the innocent. I think you know what I mean."

"Indeed I do not," the cook retorted, flinging open a nether grate that released such a blast of heat, Xenko skipped backwards.

"I mean *that one*!" he hoarsely wailed. "He is back, I have seen him. He has run away again! Ardannen, tell me where he is! I shall be angry if you do not. I know he always comes to you, mistress, who in defiance of my orders feed him! Stop poking that fire, you stupid Ceruga! I must know where he is! I will not have him here. You have seen him, I know. He had a couple of young bears in tow, rather important ones too. I must answer to General Skaling for them. Now tell me where they're hiding, and don't bother to lie, for I've searched every room but this kitchen!"

"Lower your voice, master, you'll spoil the baking," Ardannen said drily. "They're sitting just over there, having their breakfast, good as gold."

Xenko spun around. When he found his voice, it was level, unflustered, but his eyes watered heavily.

"Forgive me for not seeing you at first, I am a little . . . my eyes are not what they once were. I am glad you were able to find the kitchen. Have you met my cook? She is—you will find this interesting—Ardannen is the last member of my original household—the only one to stay with me through these long years. She is the faithful old Ceruga of my story. You remember! The servant who carried the news of the mad mother's death." Ardannen winced. "She was with me before that and since. Remarkable loyalty. You were wise to come down here. You could find no safer place in all Bargeton, just now. I am afraid that the city is badly unsettled. There's been

219

a monstrous fire. I've just been chatting with an acquaintance, you may know his name: General Skaling, of the Thoog. He was leading a patrol through the quarter; says the Crimson Bears are at large, the streets highly unsafe. You had better stay here till all has blown over and we can see how things stand. Ardannen will look after you."

Xenko laid a trusting arm across her shoulders, but the Ceruga shrugged it off. She busied herself at the oven. Xenko stood smiling upon Edgar and Alice as though he expected to be thanked for his benign hospitality. Was he really unaware, Alice wondered, of how Gribo had dragged them there? She glanced sidelong at Edgar, who was staring into his bowl with indignant disgust.

Then Xenko's eye fell upon Ganno, and he started as if he had only that moment noticed the Slizz.

"What is this now," he slowly began. "What, you glutton, you defy me still with your spoon? The bane of his family, his mother's young death, the disaster of the father that spawned him! Yet he flaunts his wretched spoon as though that would make him Ceruk! Down, you dirty beast! Shoo! Shoo! Ardannen, this is your doing! Out of this kitchen! These, the fruits of your weak-minded fondness, you who have encouraged him. Xenko isn't blind! But I will not have it! Where's the broom? I want no part of him. Do you hear?"

"Leave it alone, master," Ardannen said evenly, elbowing past him with a loaf hot from the oven. She pushed the swelling brown crust so near his face, he had to jump back to avoid being singed. "Ain't you got no other business to attend to? I'll mind things here, same as I ever done, when there was none but me to do it."

"See that he leaves, then," Xenko said sternly, retreating towards the door. "When I return, Ardannen, I expect to find this contamination gone from my kitchen. Look to it, Ardannen! And, Ardannen," he added, standing in the doorway, "I expect my guests will still be resting comfortably, *here*, when I come back. Very likely Lord Skaling will be with me, and he will be very angry if my guests are not *here* to receive him. Even you, Ardannen, would not care, I fancy, for Lord Skaling's displeasure. So, you are warned, mistress." Ardannen muttered something inaudible and slammed a crock down on the table so that the three breakfasters' bowls and mugs jumped. "It is your safety I have most at heart, Claudio's nephew and niece," continued Xenko from the threshold. Then, gesturing with furious finality at Ganno, he pulled the door closed. They heard the rattle of a key in the lock and a metallic *snap*. Then, after a pause, the same sounds replayed, the door opened, and the goldsmith's red cap wormed in.

"I expect you heard me just now," he said, "lock the door. Such gently nurtured young bears, so sensitively organized as to nerves, I have no wish to alarm you; but wars, you know, are such . . . such complicated things. Ardannen will look after you. You must make yourselves entirely free of my larder, young bears. O, I wish there were some gold down here too," he added. "I would like you to have some of my gold!"

"You've a pot of gilding in the cool-pantry," the cook remarked blandly.

"Why, quite so. So I have indeed. Thank you for reminding me! If you feel an urge to gild something, you must yield to it at once. Perhaps you would like to gild your spoons? Spoons! Ardannen!" he suddenly screamed. "That . . . that fleecy ordure! I ordered you to drive him away! My dear young bears, I will say good-bye, now, and . . . and lock the door again."

And once more vanishing, he did so, and did not reappear.

TWENTY-THREE. **A New Resolve.**

*I*n the silence that followed Xenko's departure, Alice stared
around the kitchen, hoping to catch someone's eye and
obtain an explanation. But Ardannen relentlessly busied herself about her baking, Edgar stared morosely into his bowl,
and Ganno spooned porridge into his mouth. Finally Alice
touched her brother's shoulder.

"We're really in trouble, right?" she quavered. "I mean,
we're really his prisoners, aren't we?"

"Yes," Edgar said heavily, "and Gribo's and Skaling's and
Equivair's. Not to mention the Crimson Bears. Don't you
see?" he spoke to his sister's anguished look. "Weren't you
listening, when Xenko and the Thoog were talking in the
street? They're all in this together."

"No," said Alice, although she had not missed a word; she
wanted Edgar to spell everything out.

"Well, if you had listened," he said, "you would have heard
Skaling refer to the cats as allies. You would have heard him
talk about a meeting they're going to have, which Xenko will
also be at; and Equivair is somehow mixed up with the
Crimson Bears, who were marching at Skaling's command.
Didn't you hear that part at least, Alice? The Thoog are
supposed to be terrified of the Crimson Bears, Julio said they
were hurrying to take shelter from the Crimson Bears. He
was trying to convince Claudio to accept their offer to help
defend the city. Don't you remember what I told you about
all that?"

"Yes," whispered Alice. "So the Thoog were lying?'

"It certainly looks like it; unless they've had a mighty change of heart," said Edgar sarcastically. "And the Shaven Ceruk, who captured us, answer to Xenko. He told us so himself! Didn't you hear Lord Skaling compliment Xenko on how well his boys had done? They're all in it together. It doesn't leave us much room. That's where we stand," he ended grimly.

"Xenko don't have no boys but one," Ardannen's voice bellowed across the kitchen, "and he ain't no Shaven Ceruk! They's no boys the old fool is playing with. Eat yer mush!" she barked at Ganno, who obediently worked his spoon double-time. "And don't you pay your father no mind. His wits turned way back. You've ten times more than he's got left, voice or no voice. So," she turned to Edgar and Alice and cleared away their bowls, "he told you his sad, sad story, did he?" Violently she cut them off two wedges of melon. "Thought he might have. It's his only one to tell. And ain't he built it up into an amiable tragedy, with himself as the hero, the mutt! Poor, put-upon Xenko what stuck himself with a loony missus! 'The mad mother'! I heard him, right here in my kitchen, and not the first time neither. Onkannen mad! Not her. At least she had an eye to see. The mama, that's who we're talking of, your lovely mama," she kissed the Slizz noisily as she bustled past with a broom, "same as Ganno and me remembers, what time he slips back on the sly. I do all the talking, but I know what he's thinking. Why, Thoog take the old windbag!" she burst out afresh, emptying a dustpan full of imaginary dirt, "anyone can tell that this one has a brain. His mama, Onkannen, she knew it, soon as he was properly out of the shell. Have to be a blind old fool not to. But Xenko's sort don't want children. His sort want *sons*. Wager he told you about the poor little business he put together after the family busted up."

"Yes, he did," said Alice.

"Why, Timothy Tightwad! How *do* you do!" she shouted while greasing a pan. "He's the richest goldsmith in all the Ceruglio! Makes the rest of them look like Clowncats. And *that's* why his Thoog lord friend dropped word about the meeting, I'll be bound. Why, Xenko's floated the whole show! Who else would pay for them fancy bears? I know, I got ears. Ain't never said nothing about it, but nobody comes down here to ask. So now you know, anyways. Sick of it all, that's what I am. Pack of google-heads what comes around here these days, and I have to cook for 'em, carry around the pipes and the tea."

"The Shaven Ceruk?" Alice hazarded.

"Ay, them and other fools. Them bullying shaky-brains!" Ardannen muttered angrily, and hurled a dishrag across the room. "Never seen anything like them prating piddle-artists in all my born days. You seen 'em?" she exploded. "You see what they done? They shaved their wool off!" she bellowed at the ceiling. "Shaved off all their lovely wool! And what's the great uplifting purpose of that, Mister Mad Mother?" she continued, evidently apostrophizing Xenko in his absence. "What does it get us, being bald as a baboon's bottom? Every inch shaved off, from tail to crown. Walk around naked as eggs, not a stitch on 'em but a load of straps; you never saw such a ugly sight as them thimblewits. Say it's all to show that we're reptiles not mammals, because mammals are the one with hair. Say it's to show kinship with the Thoog. Slizz have hair, say they, Ceruk should show their hide. But you know what they really look like, after they've shaved? Anyone that was ever out in the pastures in summer

224

could tell 'em. Son of one of my sisters, little Dvanko, he joined up, the oaf, and I told him. What you want to shave your nice wool off for, numskull? says I. Makes you look like a Slizz just fresh from the Slizzherd's shears. Dvanko didn't like that. He's the one that shaves the lot of them. What d'ye think you're going to do when wintertime comes, eh? I asks him. Well, he starts in with a line of malarkey that'd make a monkey sick. All about how we're reptiles you know auntie, and reptiles are cold-blooded you know auntie, not like mammals like bears, so from now on we're going to be naked, because that's what it means to be free, because our blood goes hot and cold according to the weather and the time of day and is it fall or is it spring, so why should wonderful we forswear the drama of continual change what we can partic-ipate in with our very own gorgeous bodies, it is our birth-right, auntie. Long way to say we don't want to be Slizz no more. O, so anyway, *I* knew where all the claptrap was coming from," and she jabbed with her thumb at the ceiling, "so I didn't say nothing more but how I thought he looked a right goof walking about with no clothes on and no wool, and he comes right back at me and asks me, thinking to floor me, you see, Auntie, are we bears? Not me, says I, and I ain't going to *bear* any more of your imbesilly Thoogwash. Ha ha ha ha!" she roared, gleefully juggling three turnips and an onion at the recollection of this triumph. "Made him mad too!" The next moment she was across the kitchen again, rummaging for something in a drawer. They could hear her chuckles through the crashing of unwanted utensils being shoved out of the way.

Her violent mirth seemed to clear the air. Edgar was sitting straighter; Alice noted the look of intent concentra-tion that came and went on his face.

"What is it, Edgar?" she asked.

"O, I was just thinking," he said. "About that meeting—the one that Skaling mentioned. If we could get out of here . . . if we could somehow overhear what they said . . . . 'Tonight's the night,' Skaling said."

"The night for what?" asked Alice.

"He said the bears, our kind of bears, were all shut up in the Citadel. He must be planning an attack."

"And if we could hear his plans, we could warn Claudio?"

"Yes. But we'd have to get to the Citadel first. And we're locked up in here."

"And we don't know where the meeting is going to be held," prompted Alice, who thought her brother's idea completely foolhardy.

"The Feast Hall, Lord Skaling said. Do you know where the Feast Hall is, Ardannen?"

"Not I. No such place in the Ceruglio."

"What is the Ceruglio?" asked Alice, who had never quite grasped the meaning of the word when Xenko had used it.

"Why, this is. All this part of the city. Where the Ceruk live, we call it the Ceruglio. From the Wall to the canal."

"What is that wall?" asked Edgar.

"Why, that's the old Palace of the Clowncats. Clowncats used to be much bigger and smarter, they say. Very clever at building things in the old days. Had kings and everything. Never know it to look at them now, poor starving rascals. One of their kings built hisself a big palace, and that wall's one end of it. Whole thing must be *huge*."

"Then that's probably where the Feast Hall is," Alice remarked, insouciant. "Felipo could never have done without a Feast Hall." But when she found Edgar looking back at her with an abstracted stare, she regretted having spoken. "Edgar!" she gasped.

"You know," he said, "I'm sure you're right. That's just where the meeting will be. Alice, you're a genius!"

"No, I'm not," she replied unhappily. "But it doesn't matter, because we couldn't go back there, and anyway, we're locked in."

"I'll bet there's a way out," said Edgar at once. "Isn't there, Ardannen?"

"Well, since yer asking me," said the Ceruga, "I know of about six ways out for a nimble couple of young 'uns like you, though maybe," she added reflectively, "you're a bit bulky for one or two of 'em. But you won't need to squeeze yourselves. Come here with me."

They got up and followed her to the door, watching while she set a broad hand on the door-handle. "Okus-pokus," she intoned, rolling her shaggy brows, then pressed; the door opened. She burst into laughter. Edgar could disguise his joy no more than Alice her discomfiture.

"It's five year and more since I stopped telling the master he'd have to get that lock replaced. 'Yes yes,' he says, 'yes yes, but we never got no cause to lock up the kitchen, Ardannen,' he says. 'What's to steal in a kitchen?' You can go right out by the way you come in."

"Edgar," said Alice firmly, desperation lending her cunning, "I've just had a better idea. Instead of hunting around in the Palace for this Feast Hall, and getting ourselves lost or caught by Thoog or Crimson Bears, why don't we wait here till the meeting has started? And then run to the Citadel and tell Claudio and the Great Golden Bear what we know?"

"Which isn't much."

"But the streets will be clear! We could get through—everyone will be at the meeting."

"Making their plans for attacking the Citadel; those plans are what we've got to find out, or else we'll just be sitting in the Citadel with everyone else, wondering what's going to happen. Anyway, what good will it do for Claudio and the Great Golden Bear to learn that their enemies are meeting, that the Citadel is going to be attacked? They can guess that for themselves! What they need to know is when, and especially how. If we could tell them that. . . . "

"But how are you going to find the Feast Hall, Edgar? You don't know your way around inside the Palace. You don't even know how to get inside it. What are you going to do, climb the wall?" Seeing that he said nothing but frowned, Alice pressed her advantage. "And don't you suppose the meeting will be guarded? They're not going to let us just walk in and eavesdrop, then trot on out to warn our friends."

"There has to be a way," he muttered. "Possy would help us."

"But we have absolutely no idea where to find Possy," Alice riposted. Edgar said nothing, but turned away. For a triumphant second she thought he was merely avoiding her eye—he had always been slow to acknowledge these forensic victories of hers—but then, when he did not turn back, she followed his gaze, grown ominously steady, to its object, which was Ganno; and then she knew all was lost. The Slizz still sat at his place, leaning on one elbow, wearing a most inscrutably knowing smile, and tapping gently on the table-top with his spoon.

"Ganno knows where to find Possy," exulted Edgar.

"Ganno! Do you?" Alice wailed.

Ganno's eyes then began to bulge alarmingly, while his throat rippled and swelled as though he were trying to swallow an apple whole; at last his mouth opened and disgorged, like a cross between a hoot and a belch, the strangled syllable, "Yes!"

A loud crash resounded through the room. Ardannen was standing in the middle of the kitchen, brought to a full halt for the first time since they had entered. A large blue-and-white tureen lay in shards around her feet; she was shaking, her hands were clasping and unclasping. "You can talk, then," she said, her voice grown hoarse and tremulous. "O, Onkannen. What, grown a tongue, have you? After all these years? Ain't you going to say no more to me?"

"Come," gulped Ganno.

Ardannen's whole body quivered. She ran her long tongue around the rim of her mouth, she reached up to tug with her fingers at the wool growing from the sides of her muzzle. The quivering increased; Alice was beginning to fear that the old cook would fall into a fit, when Ardannen suddenly opened her jaws and let out a bellow of laughter. She laughed and laughed till she had to sit down, a free, clear laugh without the edge of anger they had heard before.

"Yes, and Come, is it?" she said then, wiping her eyes. "Why, them's two excellent words to begin a vocabulary with. Come on and stand up here, you sly dog!" He went over to her chair; then, in a second, she first caught him around the waist and lifted him off the floor in the heat of her hugging, next swept him off in a wild waltz. The old cook billowed in surges around the room, and Ganno, nimbly pirouetting, had his work cut out to pilot her clear of disaster; Edgar and Alice, seeing the Slizz so confident and graceful a partner, felt their own brains go around in a dizzying twirl of changing ideas; the wayward pots and pans on the walls, the crockery on the shelves, the utensils in the drawers, all this mutinous kitchen-plebs winked and swung, jarred and rattled in tune with their despot's license, as she and her cavalier whirled past. The waltz quickened, turned in upon its center; the couple re-volved, faster and faster, through tighter and tighter whorls, till Ganno stood still, and by calculated touches kept Ardannen spinning like a top, her arms outspread, her upraised face a blur. At last he stood off a little; the Ceruga slowed, wobbled, caught at the Slizz as she toppled, and together they dropped out of sight beyond the table's far end. Edgar and Alice jumped up and ran to see that she was not hurt.

"Whoo!" hooted Ardannen, stretched out at full length on her back with her head beneath the table, and fondling Ganno's ears that draped across her belly, "I ain't done noth-ing like that since I was a slender young Ceruga, and my sister wed the yellowest Ceruk in Bargeton! Kids all come out sort of greeny-yellow too. Maybe that's why little Dvanko went and shaved hisself. Hoo! Come on, boy, help me up. You lot had better look slippy if you mean to find that Feast Hall."

"O," said Alice, upset; and then paused while Edgar and Ganno together heaved Ardannen upright. "But, Ardannen," she went on, "what about Xenko? What will become of you if he comes back with the Thoog and we're not here? We can't leave you to face them all alone!"

"That's right," said Edgar, also looking worried.

"Ah, don't worry about me," Ardannen replied, adjusting her headdress in the mirror of a bright-visaged skillet, and smoothing down the folds of her robe. She flicked the skillet's burnished middle, and it returned a loud, resentful *bong*; "Hoity-toity," she sniffed, turning away.

"Ardannen, why don't you come with us?" Alice urged again. "That way we'll all take our chances together. Ganno, speak to her—tell her to come!"

"Yes. Come!"

"O!" bellowed Ardannen, grabbing Ganno again and squeezing him fiercely. "Yes, and Come, again, is it? O Pickles, but I wish yer ma could've been here today to hear you say them words. But you go on without me, darlings. You've need of speed, and I'm fair winded with all that loopy twirling. 'Sides, I'm too fat to squeeze through some of the cracks *he*'ll lead you through. No no, babies, off with you now, and never mind me. I've my baking to do, and a hundred other chores here in my kitchen. O crabs and dumplings, my dreams are coming true! Yes, says he, and Come! O Yes, let 'em come! They'll find me here. And if even the scaliest Thoog that ever wheezed tries tricks on me in my own kitchen," she concluded grimly, "he'll find a kind of greeting that'll heat his chilly blood. Get along with ye, now, quick— your road begins here."

She held open the door, and hugged them each in turn as they passed by her. "Allus a pleasure talking to *you*, sir," she archly declared to Ganno, and when she had released him all disheveled from her embrace, she added, "Come back and have another little chat some time, won't ye?" When they were already a fair way down the dim back corridor, Ardannen hissed loudly after them, "You can go where you like in the house, 'slong as you don't make no noise; *he*'s in his shop." Then she closed the door, or all but closed it; as Alice turned to climb the stairs, she heard the echo of a rumbling chuckle.

*T*he staircase took them to Xenko's shop. Alice had led
Edgar down it earlier; now Ganno was leading him up
it again. The goldsmith's tap and mumble sounded clearly through the door. Even halfway up, Edgar was weary,
as weary as he'd been the preceding night. His resolution
drained away, a fog wrapped around his brain. Ganno hovered in front of him, taking them somewhere again. A crack
opened on the right, and the creature stepped into it. Edgar
peered: a second flight, which he had not noticed on the
way down, branched obliquely. He squinted at the nimble
haunches and flourishing dark tail. Then Alice nudged him
from behind. Edgar pumped his legs again. Riser and tread,
riser and tread; where was it they were going? To spy on
Thoog and Crimson Bears? Audacity had come easily in
Ardannen's kitchen. He wished he had listened to Alice.

At the top Edgar wiped a cobweb from his nose and
searched the long, dim hallway for a window. Impossible to
tell to what height they had climbed. Corridor led into
corridor, with never a casement but hundreds of doors. What
lay behind them? The Slizz never looked left or right. Edgar
could not help but wonder which of the rooms they were
passing had served as setting for Xenko's tragic life. Those
betrayals and suicides were working on Edgar. Able to shake
one episode only to have another rise in its place, he grew so
thoroughly unstrung that, at a movement in the moldy mat-

ting, he started, tripped, and fell. But the chirp that whistled angrily under his ear had him back on his feet very quickly. From then on, he resolved to give more attention to his footing and less to his fears; even so, the Ceruk civil wars would not leave him.

Alice, who had twice trod on his heel, now did it again; he turned on her.

"Can't you walk a little faster?" she cried. Hearing her wretchedness, Edgar summoned up a show of fortitude.

"Cheer up, Alice, we're on our way."

"On our way to get locked up or eaten," she grumbled, but her voice brightened as she vented a little misery in complaints. "How far do we have to go, Edgar? Are we still in Xenko's house?"

How could they not be? "So I assume," he returned, "judging from the circumstance that we have not left it."

"Pretty big house."

"Yes," he agreed, "it is big, isn't it. But, you know, Xenko spoke of six to eight children at a hatching—and I don't know how many broods a Ceruga mother expects to hatch, but still . . . over several generations you could wind up with a big family. And then there are marriages. The Ceruk probably add whole floors and wings as they're needed."

"O," said Alice. "So," she added, after a reflective pause, "where are they all?"

The question brought Edgar back to his former train of thought. He was about to unburden himself to his sister, when he saw Ganno standing some yards down the passage beside an open door. He disclosed a serried phalanx of garments. The Slizz dove into the closet; for a moment nothing remained but his tail, flagging them after. Edgar thrust through, his nose atingle, and emerged into a long chamber. At its far end a slender Ceruga in a peignoir sat oiling and arranging her tresses. He suppressed a sneeze and hurried after Ganno; if the Ceruga saw the Slizz and two bears skipping through her room, she gave no sign of it.

Then on Ganno led them, still at a brisk pace, through a kitchen quite like Ardannen's, but empty except for a simmering pot. And farther still, they crossed yet a third kitchen where a Ceruga nurse was irritably laying out bowls for six noisy young Ceruk; this endless domestic interior began to seem a world in itself, from which burnt, war-torn Bargeton was as remote as the City of Bears.

"How many kitchens does Xenko have?" Alice whispered. "And where is Ganno taking us?"

"I have no idea," shrugged Edgar. "Perhaps he thinks Possy is lurking in some Ceruk laundry. Or, it could be that one of these doors will open right onto the Feast Hall." That silenced Alice. As they left the third kitchen, Edgar glanced up the flue, another possible thoroughfare; its perfect freedom from soot was not lost on him.

But soon they departed the warren. Ganno threw open a door, and Edgar, pained by sunlight, saw the corridor shrink to a rickety walkway that wandered across rooftops and between chimney-stacks. It had no railing at all. Slits winked where the walk leaned and twisted. Edgar's last thought, before he stepped gingerly out, was how little Alice was going to like this; she hated heights. But as the planks were not wide enough for two, there was nothing to be done. He kept on after the Slizz, wishing they did not have to rush so. In the bright morning Edgar stood level with the sun, just clearing the rooftops of Bargeton. There was no pall of smoke; the wind must have swept it away. Now the air was clear and very still. Launching himself from plank to plank, Edgar was conscious that the Citadel must be visible somewhere on the horizon, but he couldn't spare a glance. Instead, he glimpsed ravines steeped in shadow, bedding spread out to air, and ranks of chimney-pots with nests stuffed among them. He crawled above these homely declivities on sagging decking.

But though their guide frequently paused to urge them on to greater haste, Alice lagged behind. Finally, she refused to go on without help. Not trusting bridges that jumped from one roof to another, from which one viewed gardens and lanes, she announced that she would proceed no further. Edgar did not like this flimsy planking either, and told her with the least reason in the world that if it could support one of them, it could surely hold two. Why Alice, who ordinarily caught the lapses in his logic, should have found this convincing, Edgar would never know; but soon he was steering her by shoulder and elbow, almost shoving her over, while waiting every moment for the first splintering rip. He was anxious and busy enough not to care for the sunshine, till the twilight of a covered bridge swallowed them.

With the sky behind, Edgar plunged again into chambers and antechambers, closets, pantries, and attics, Alice in tow, hastening in Ganno's wake. He pulled his sister over floors tiled and matted, floors carpeted, flagstoned, wide-planked, strewn with rushes. He scurried across one entire pavement of mirror-glass, and his alarming reflection, all foot and thick leg, clapped sole to his sole.

Ganno led them a last furious sprint that spilled them into sunlight, but once again Edgar could not take much pleasure in it. He approached as near as he dared to the tilting platform's edge and looked into a court. Six flights, botched together from unwanted lumber, drooped crazily out of sight; he could not tell whether they actually reached to the sunless floor. Sooty houses backed the court on three sides, but the fourth wall towered as high above their heads as it sank below their feet. "Well," he breathed softly, not looking at Ganno and Alice, "it may be that I'll find Possy after all!" Above the slate shadows, the Wall glowed with light. But from the plain, smooth masonry a tail, carved in high relief, lashed its length across six monumental blocks, and flicked a tuft like a giant pinecone. Not two feet removed from that tuft, just below the eaves of one of the houses, a pair of scrawny geraniums brightened a window ledge.

Edgar had only a second to take all this in, for Ganno was already loping down the stairs. Now Edgar had to step even more cautiously, for many of the treads were missing or unsound. It was the bridges all over again. He held Alice by the arm, easing her down, murmuring encouragements and directions, the most frequent, "Open your eyes!"

The last flight, at least, afforded a railing that seemed firm. As Edgar picked his way down this final bight, the musty tinge of the court grew too strong to ignore. Its source was not far to seek: directly across from the base of the stair and built against the great Wall itself was a refuse-bin, grey wood eight feet high. A ladder rested against it and warped lids with black handles kept the sun out; the sloping roof did for rain. When, as Edgar neared the bottom stair, one of these lids began to lift of its own agency, he pulled Alice down and peered through the slatted railing.

It was perhaps then, safely seated at last, that Alice, for the first time since beginning this harrowing journey, fully opened her eyes. Till that moment she had simply stumbled terror-stricken after Edgar, only hoping to be allowed to regain solid ground. She was about to set foot there; but as the hatch opened wider, she despaired of an easy peace. Her heart whacked against her ribs as a tightly furled pink umbrella thrust into view. It paused, seemed to survey the scene; then, hopping to one side so as to wedge the hatch ajar, it planted its handle and ferrule. A black feather emerged and briskly swept the rim clean. Then into the light, like a skate mounting through shallow water, a wine-colored disc undulated. Alice recognized a hat, but could not see who wore it. The creaturely procession continued with bodice and sleeves of embroidered canary silk, hauling up a pink sash that swelled to a panniered skirt, glittering stripes. As the brilliant ensemble balanced on the slope of the trash-bin, Alice began to guess. When it flounced gracefully onto the first rung, reached to retrieve its umbrella, then lightly descended, she was almost certain. Once down, the finery paused to adjust itself; and when the broad hat removed for brushing, there was Zawailza's sleek head. Alice turned to her brother triumphantly; and this so annoyed him, after all the to-do of getting her across, that he scowled, motioning her to be still.

But before he could decide if it would be safe to greet Zawailza, a door slammed nearby. The silver dancer slipped quickly around the corner of the bin, into the shaded angle it made with the Wall. A moment later a stout Ceruga came shuffling across the courtyard, lugging a barrel of ordure; and behind her, as if towed at the end of a rope, slouched a young Ceruk, freshly shaven from crown to tail-tip, a splash of lather still unwiped behind one ear. With windy sighs and shoulder-heavings, he enacted a most dolorous long-suffering, though in fact he carried only one small box. As the Ceruga reached the foot of the ladder, he set it down.

"What the dinkus d'ye suppose yer doing with that box?" she snapped, not even turning around. "Bring't on over here, drat ye." She started up the ladder with practised tread, still hefting the can.

"Aw, Ma, can't you let me go? The big council's just about to start," whined the Shaven Ceruk. "Corporal Dvanko'll skin me if I'm not in my place when the inspection begins."

"Corporal Dvanko!" the Ceruga exclaimed with the greatest contempt, spitting onto the floor. "As he's already had yer wool, it don't matter none to me if he has yer lousy bald skin as well. You and your precious Corporal of Chuffinses! Get that box over here, and never mind your precious Dvanko. Corporal Crud and General Junk is all the corporals and generals we follow in *this* house. And anyways," she concluded, balancing her barrel on the top rung as she threw open a hatch, "I seen that fool Dvanko help his auntie hang out the wash, not three days ago I seen um."

"Wasn't no war on three days ago," grumbled the Ceruk, as he dragged the box a few inches nearer the ladder.

"War! War be doodled!" jeered his mother. "Trash still got to be took out, war or no." And with this sentiment, she up-ended her can over the hole, releasing a smoking deluge. Then she grappled the box which her son held up to her, overturned it as well, and shiny metal bits cascaded into the bin. "Now!" she ordered, backing down the ladder, "take this un back to that closet, and fill her up again, and hump her back out here." But, arriving at the ladder's foot, she found he had vanished. For a long moment, bosom heaving, she cursed her son under her breath; then, seizing both barrel and box, dragged them after her into the house.

As soon as she had vanished, swearing, through a door that Edgar could not see, Zawailza was at the top of the ladder.

238

"Possy!" she called through the hatchway, in a low, urgent voice, "Dizzy! Ay me, what filth! Come forth, sirs, and breathe."

A pair of ringing coughs echoed inside the bin; then, to Edgar's joy, Dizzy and Possy hauled themselves out of the hole. Both cats, liberally powdered with grey ash, left a smoky trail in the air as they descended the ladder, still coughing.

"Nay, nay!" drawled Zawailza, dancing away from them. "Avoid, till y'are somewhat cleaner, Clowncats! Now truly," she added, as they set to beating at one another's clothes, "here is a mime I must teach my players: *The Duello of the Dust Kittens*. Lord Skaling and Master Xenko, seeing you so floured, will think to wear you both for wigs, sirs. Make haste, make haste, or she of the house will return with fresh bombard of dust!"

"Conshrew the cronibarbative old reptile!" growled Mr. Dizzy. "What a time to dump the hearth-sweepings!"

"Indeed, it is a curst hag," Possy replied, between coughs, "and her trash none of the finest; but prithee, Chief, my back: some dirt yet clings above my tail, I fear."

He twisted himself half around to see, while Dizzy cuffed at his spine. Edgar, glad as he was to see Possy, and anxious to put his request and claim the cats' aid, still could not bring himself to rise from behind the railing and declare his presence. His sister's impatience, for once, did not move him. Partly he was abashed at having failed to carry Zawailza's message to the Great Golden Bear, but partly it was just curiosity: in the daylight Dizzy, and especially Possy, whom Edgar had met before only beneath the moon or by fire, looked very different. Both, he saw, had changed their clothes, but it was not simply this, for so had Zawailza, who appeared quite the same. Still herself, her carriage languidly graceful in spite of the volume of fabric she upheld, amidst its garden glare her drowsy-eyed, laughing strength did not suffer diminishing. The two males had both put on much plainer, almost military gear, short buff jerkins and grey leggings. Although Edgar had always thought Possy the larger of the two, now he saw it was not so. Out of his black robe, the artificer's figure seemed slight. So delicately boned as to be almost ungainly, the thin body made his head too large. Dizzy's rangy limbs and barrel shape, now stripped of his Hooburgaloo motley, allowed his broad skull and flat grin greater emphasis, and made him, if uglier, still far more imposing than Possy. Edgar involuntarily compared the yellow cat to Gribo: neither one made a secret of his force. But where the Shaven Ceruk had arrogantly commanded, Dizzy seemed to follow Possy, and even, half-humorously, to serve him. He squatted now to dust Possy's back, and licked his own paw to wipe clean the other's fur, while Possy examined some small object he held.

"Yet I malign good Dame Dump!" he exclaimed. "Costive old hag that she is, her latter voiding hath dropped into my hand what I shall know how to use. A little labor shall fit this cotter-pin into the action of his neck, Zawailza, and then bating ill fortune, he will be perfected. 'Twas worth the shower of ash deposited on our heads by that volcanic huswife, well worth!"

"Hist, sirs," said Zawailza suddenly. "I smell bears nearby." The three cats stiffened and peered around.

"Bears, Zawailza?" very softly inquired Possy at length. "Bears in this place?"

"I smell 'em too," asserted Dizzy. "In fact," he added in a louder voice, as he stared straight toward Edgar, "I would call the aroma quite cons*pig*uous."

Now Edgar knew that he must show himself; slowly he stood. Ganno, beside him, also got to his feet, while Alice shot up and ran down the last steps to Zawailza.

"What! My Alice!" the silver cat gaily cried, embracing her. "I did not think to encounter so soon again with you, nor of all place here, in Lion's-Tail Court."

Edgar saw a look of surprise and trouble cross Possy's face. Dizzy continued to grin.

"Ganno, my friend! And young Edgar too!" exclaimed the black cat. "By Felipo's toes, how come you here? And why?"

"We came to find you, Possy," Edgar replied. "Ganno brought us."

"Ganno brought you! Ay, to be sure! And by queer ways, I'll warrant. What, mad wag, up to your jests, are you, roaring boy? Come here and embrace me, both." And when Edgar had received his hearty hug, and seen Ganno taken in the black cat's arms and roughly tousled, Possy admonished the Slizz, "Now, sirrah, Possy Damp Paws is a Shaven Ceruk if he knows how you guessed where to find him."

"That is no wonderful conundrum," Zawailza said. "I told him. I said we should be hereabouts, if he had news to bring, what time the morning sun should sweep night from the Lion's Tail." She pointed up the Wall; Edgar saw the house's shadow had not cleared the great carved tail by more than a quarter-hour. "Yet that Ganno should restore our friends to us, I did not know; I had hoped them secure in the Citadel. But Alice has told me how it was: the fire stopped them, and then they were taken by Shaven Ceruk, indeed, by Gribo's own self, and lodged for the night—mark you, this, sirs—at Xenko's house, who made them his prisoners."

"Xenko's! His prisoners!" Possy, bewildered, murmured.

"Yes," replied Edgar, "and we saw General Skaling and the Crimson Bears; and then Ganno brought us here."

"With the connivance of the good Ardannen," Zawailza added.

"So," said Possy, "I see you are resourceful travellers and not such simple bearcubs as I thought you. But now tell me, pray, on what errand Sir Ganno brings you to me?"

"Well," began Edgar, summoning his courage, "I overheard General Skaling tell Xenko about a meeting, to be held this morning in the Feast Hall, and . . . I thought it might be a useful thing if I, if we, could, could listen, somehow, and then . . . . Skaling implied that the Citadel would be attacked . . . tonight . . . so I thought . . . ." As he spoke, doubts assailed him. What if these cats also were Skaling's confederates? Possy looked grave.

"I divine," he pronounced, when Edgar's voice had trailed off into silence. "You would make report of the Thoog's plans to your uncle in the Citadel. By my tail, you are bold, Master Edgar, to contemplate so perilous espials. Dizzy, what think you?"

"O," said the yellow cat, "I never doubted my Gruntusculo's intrepiggity."

"Nay, but his design?"

"We shall not debate it here," Zawailza said firmly. "Old Mistress Midden will shortly return with brimming barrel and must not find us. Possy, ye have what ye came to seek? Then let us go where we may be secret. My Alice, follow me."

"Where are we going?" asked Alice anxiously; the thought of another rooftop journey appalled her.

"No great way, my love," laughed Zawailza. "Just into the trash-bin." And she danced up the ladder.

TWENTY-FIVE

Inside the Trash Bin.

*A*lice, standing by the ladder, watched Zawailza ascend in one smooth billow of silks, as if borne upwards on a petticoat-cloud, and wished she herself might some day own such grace. While she lived in the City of Bears, she had never seen poise as anything but empty-headed artfulness, and had scorned it. In Zawailza it was language, one of many the silver cat knew, and an avenue into her complexity of temperament. Next, Edgar climbed the rungs with a stodgy maladresse that would have made Alice laugh, had she not realized she would look just as awkward; she held back, therefore, till Possy and Dizzy had mounted. The black cat was as courtly as one could be on a ladder, seeming to think of anything but what he was doing. As she took her turn, Alice wondered why he and Dizzy had changed their finery for such drab gear.

Dizzy lifted her down inside the bin. He stretched out long, yellow arms, caught her by the waist, and gently lowered her; as she rubbed down past him, she smelt smoke and sweat on his fur; his breath blew sour in her face. Then Alice was standing in dust to her knees. She looked about the bin's roomy interior, surveying trash that had been sorted by kinds: bottles laid in pyramids as at a wine-merchant's, paper folded and corded, and in one corner a small mound of metal. Then the hatch slammed shut, and she was in the dark again. The Ceruk would not have taken these pains with their discardings; she remembered the Throne. Now Dizzy took her paw and led her on without speaking. After ten paces, Alice grew puzzled. From the courtyard the trash-bin had not looked so deep. A few more steps, and there was stone beneath her feet; she heard an echo to her breathing.

Then a hollow *boom* sounded behind her. Through a frame, beyond whose edge all was black, she saw a cataract of sparkling dust; a rain of objects mounted where she had so lately stood. The Ceruga had returned; the fuming cascade she unleashed poured into the bin as if to fill it with thunder and bright haze; but Dizzy pulled Alice forward again, and she followed, hurrying, through this passage that must pierce the Wall, once more into the Palace and the maze of its ways; she expelled a long sigh. For all she knew, they would be in the Feast Hall directly. Skaling, Xenko, and Equivair were there; Gribo and the Crimson Bears too. As she named them, she read their visages afresh, the weakness long enforced, appetites unappeased. O, she wanted to run away! Edgar had been right, and his plan the sole one. She understood that those hungers could and would break the Citadel, never counting the cost. So there was no going back to Claudio's. To lurk and listen where she and Edgar would, if caught, certainly die, was the only choice left them. But they were inexperienced, small! They had travelled too far.

Alice lost all reckoning of how far she'd been towed by Dizzy's grip. She sensed the clammy weight of stonework all around her. Airs colder and colder clung to her fur. At last, after a turn to the left and a high step, she was let to halt and her wrist released. Finding herself trembling, she attached the strong, calm face of Zawailza. *She* would not drown!

Alice watched a flame quietly arise in the darkness, and a minute later a tripod brazier appeared. Ganno was feeding it kindling. Possy and Zawailza lingered by, as though listening to the damp sticks' whistle. Dizzy was nowhere to be seen. Alice looked at her brother, who had come up beside Possy. In the firelight, Edgar's eyes seemed pinched together. Possy's black head lost all contour in the surrounding shadow, but his searching eyes shone blue. Zawailza yawned.

Fed by the Slizz, the fire burned more bright. Stone barrel-vaulting came into view. Now Dizzy emerged with six stools, which he placed around the brazier; everyone took a seat. Alice found herself between her brother and the Chief Hooburgaloo; Zawailza sat opposite, with Ganno beside her, bolt upright, legs spread and tail rigid. The cats began to talk; they debated Edgar's plan to spy on the meeting. Alice did not attend to what they said. When they reached a decision, she doubtless would hear of it. Meanwhile she studied the room. It was not too large for the feeble brazier's glow to show every corner. For furniture, it had only an immensely large press of black wood or iron, whose door hung a little ajar. On another wall, which seemed bare at first, she picked out an illegible scrawl and a skeletal figure sketched with the same chalk: it seemed to be a lion in mid-spring. Below its exaggerated talons something rude and white struggled. She squinted, but still could not make it out. There was nothing more to look at, unless one counted the two doors with iron studs to her right and left. They were closed.

"What is this room?" Alice wondered aloud.

Possy paused in mid-flourish. "Why, a guard-room, which Felipo built. Alas, he did not too carefully regard his loyal sentries' comfort. In these precincts they kept their duteous vigil and commanded the approach to the Feasting Hall, which lies through this door. Ay, and that puts me in mind, we must most festinately take that way ere our presence be missed, for Skaling's council must have commenced by this. It were ill to be thought laggards."

"They hold us so already," replied the dancer. "Do you suppose Equivair has over-praised us? 'Twere only decorum to tarry now. Your Skaling will but be the more pleased to win confirmation of his prejudice, holding all cats as nought and ourselves something worse. Therein lies our safety! It better boots us to bring these young bears into our thoughts, so that they may the more surely trust us for their friends."

"O, of great and momentous matter, that should now be unfolded to the intellectual beams of these our guests, there is no small quantity," Possy began importantly, "but in such little space! For soon, saving my lady's wisdom, we three cats at least must present ourselves in Felipo's feasting-hall, to hear report of what is toward in Bargeton. We must know what gains the Thoog have taken, how stands the present state of the bears, what rack by that insatiate conflagration wreaked, and other intelligence as shall appear. These several lessons, when we are more perfect in 'em, shall instruct us how to govern our course through periculous waters, where dangers lie like shoals, or raspy reefs, too treacherously submerged. It is a seeming-limpid element that doth conceal them from the unwitting voyagers. Yet now our ship's company is conjoined, as I may say, and in good time, and Fortune blows still a breeze to our purpose, if we but use despatch in weighing anchor, and, flinging overboard all dead weight of useless verbiage and thoughts unprofitable, clap on all sail, as 'twere (my figure, gentle bears, you have perceived it, is nautical), and mend our course by the light of those fixed stars of sure intelligence freely shared, and—"

"And to that end of swift, plain speech," Zawailza broke in, "Captain Possy yields the helm and office of spokescat to his much-indulged Zawailza, knowing his gallant self something too fond of similes and tropes." Possy rose and bowed as only a Clowncat can. "Now, our Alice and Edgar, I have watched, the while my lord spoke of our common enterprise, and I have seen questions darting like swallows and soaring out the windows of your eyes."

"Ah," growled Possy, "how zealously the frank Zawailza eschews to use figures!"

"Hush, hush, censorious Possy! Friends, your questions."

"Well," said Edgar at once, "I still don't understand why the cats and the Ceruk and the Thoog and the Crimson Bears should meet together at all. What is it they want? And you three . . . ." Edgar's voice trailed away in hesitation.

"Ay, what would you know of us?" inquired Possy.

"Why, Edgar would learn," affirmed the dancer, "what end it is that we, who are none of Equivair's creatures but round haters of the Thoog, propose to ourselves by making three to meet with such foul knaves. This question is more than just, and our reply long owing. Now Zawailza shall tell you how this has come to pass."

Alice settled to listen, watching the cat's strong face form a new mask. Her full lids, nearly closed, allowed only the slenderest gold to flicker; and as her features relaxed to immobility, her whole life passed into her voice. Supple and low-pitched, her sentences stepped lightly from her hardly moving lips.

"You have already heard, from Xenko's very mouth, who best could tell it, the first partition of that history which claims all present Bargeton for its field: it is no other tale than of your guide's birth and beginnings, the much-enduring Ganno."

Up to this point, Ganno had not stirred; now he rose and stretched. Alice wondered if he would leave. That he should not care to hear, twice in three hours, the hideous story his father had told, would not amaze anyone. But he remained. His arms hung by his sides while, like a traitor arraigned, he waited for Zawailza to continue.

"This sorry fable," she resumed; at once Ganno drooped with lavish sorrow, as though melting in ardor of grief. "This sorry fable was generally told in the city even as it unwound; and Clowncat mothers held their puling kits the tighter as they heard it rehearsed." Here Ganno quickly changed from an anguished mother to several kittens in turn. Their puling was no less tremendous for its silence. Zawailza allowed him due space for his dumbshow, then went on. For a while it continued just as Xenko had told it that morning. At first Alice attended the cat's compact phrasings with pleasure; but soon she stopped separating the words from the spectacle. Zawailza's telling and Ganno's mime married: each phrase wrapped itself about the Slizz like a costume, and threw him into the role. Epithets and adverbs turned characters on a stage already crowded with impersonations: Xenko and Onkannen with all of their brood, Ardannen, as well as various neighbors, types of the Ceruglio, not to mention Ganno's own infant self. Between furious renderings, Alice watched the Slizz become still as stone. While Zawailza was speaking, he stood erect, arms limp by his sides, studying the floor; but as soon as she paused, fresh convulsions.

Then came the moment when Xenko was "torn" between the received customs of his kind and his wife's rebellious bidding. Alice really doubted whether Ganno could remain in one piece. When the other children were said to suffer, he shrunk, his wool growing matted, dishevelled, his eyes starting out of his head. He agonized in five or six different places. And when Zawailza announced the infant Ganno's exile "to dwell with the uncivil flock," he presented a large flock of Slizz for whom "uncivil" was too mild a word. Alice found herself laughing with the others; yet the story was no less bitter than at its first telling, and she wept as she roared.

Zawailza, Possy, and Dizzy had been kittens at the time of this history. While their elders traced out the implications of the affair, they followed each turn of the drama with horrified sympathy. "Yet young or old, noble or clown, our hearts all were enflamed against what manner soever of unjust ordinance, created by bears for the government of Bargeton, and weighing on Ceruk and Cat alike. For Cat and Ceruk were as children in the bears' eyes, and still are deemed unfit to rule themselves," Zawailza commented. She then related how, on the day of the trial, when Xenko and Onkannen had sued before Claudio in the Strangers' Court for the return of their speakable children, both Clowncats and Ceruk had filled the streets around the courthouse, mingling and talking as they had never done before. (Ganno here enacted a conversation between a stiff Ceruk, who kept clutching at his hem to save it from muddy tread, and a goggle-eyed Clowncat who poured himself in loose-jointed condolence all about his interlocutor's person; Alice's laughter choked on shame: this, she saw, was how her own kind viewed the two races.) "You know the outcome of the plea. The bear-magistrates, guided by your uncle, stood by the old Laws of Hatching. They ruled Onkannen mad, and incompetent for a mother. Her death

to drive himself forth again, as mischievous a clown, in respect of nose-thumbing and cartwheels, as could be wished.

In the portion of Zawailza's narrative that followed, they learned how the movement for self-rule fell into the hands of extremists. Ganno's accompaniment then shifted to another key, as Equivair stepped forward at the head of a party of decayed Concatenate aristocracy. Decrying the wrong done to Possy, he usurped his place. This new leader of the reformists then declared his intention to restore the full glory and sway of Felipo's empire. The moody arrogance with which Ganno personated Equivair, swaggering back and forth, ignoring Mr. Dizzy to death, but considering Zawailza lasciviously from under half-closed lids, was vivid enough. But when it came time for Xenko to re-enter and preach his doctrine—the total separation of Ceruk from Slizz, though it cost the latter their lives—then Ganno flung himself into the role with an energy nothing less than maniacal. He rendered his father's emergence from years of solitary brooding by climbing into the black press, then stepping out transformed: head thrown back, eyes staring at visions that seemed to shape themselves beyond the ceiling, every tuft of wool projecting in furious rigidity. For his father's harangues, the son raised clenched fists, opening wide a mouth shaped to form and hurl invective; he rocked from side to side, lashing his tail.

"Kind, kind, and nothing but kind was all his speech; ranting ever incontinent on this same theme of purity of breed," Zawailza sighed. Ganno as Xenko unctuously blessed the order of the Shaven Ceruk, and enthusiastically wielded invisible shears about the person of Gribo, whose part he also took. He swelled his chest and struck statuesque poses precisely as the shaven commander had done the night before in Xenko's shop.

Then Possy was freed from prison. Claudio stood by with folded arms, nose in the air, as the black cat sauntered away. Possy had been received with seeming honor by Equivair, who hoped to attach his numerous followers; but at meetings where Xenko and Gribo spoke for the Ceruk, the black cat sat silent. It was at one of these meetings that Xenko and Gribo proposed an alliance with the Thoog. And Ganno, before Alice's eyes, became a little Lord Skaling, swelling his posteriors where he squatted, and baring his teeth in a razor-long smile.

"For it was Xenko's creed, not less than Gribo's, that Ceruk must take their place among reptiles and purge the woolly Slizz from their blood; and to make that purpose known did Gribo have himself shaved. He and his comrades trusted that their cousin-reptiles, the Thoog, would lend their help to so worthy an endeavor; but also for gold which Xenko would offer them." But at this point Possy and Dizzy had hotly demurred. This alliance, in itself odious, would also bring open war; a peaceful solution might yet be found! They soon realized, however, that open war was exactly what Gribo and Equivair wanted, while Xenko was for at least as much show as would spur the Senate to negotiation. In fact the Thoog's support had already been bespoken; Lord Skaling himself came to join the Ceruk and the Cats one evening at Xenko's house. When Possy and Dizzy had protested, they were expelled from the room, "and indeed, 'twas but a pretext to be rid of them; for Equivair had found means whereby to claim the sole leadership of the Clowncattery." This means, a lineal descendant of Felipo himself, was an aged cat named

Flibitto, whom Equivair now advanced to great dignity as Pretender to the Crown. At the same time, he himself took on the burdensome office of Vizier. In public he still feigned respect for the Chief Hooburgaloo, as Alice had seen at the banquet; but in private he set Dizzy altogether aside, and let fall references to a certain upstart. "So Equivair took command. And now this poor Flibitto must live in stiff state, his only joy forbidden, which is to hunt mice; for his Vizier holds, 'twould not sort with his imperial dignity."

Ganno had not stood idle during this exposition. Gribo's lust for war and Xenko's trimming, Possy's hot demurrals, his and Dizzy's expulsion, Equivair's new ministerial dignity, had all been played with such plastic distensions, compressions, and screwings of features, that the Slizz himself had all but vanished. The final pathetic vignette showed Flibitto, constrained to be royal, sitting in patient misery while mouse after invisible mouse chased right by his feet.

"It is now a year since we were excluded from Equivair's councils," Zawailza continued. She described how they three had gone to Onkannen's disciples in the Ceruglio but had found them too deadly afraid to act; the Shaven Ceruk had lately been through the quarter. So they could only watch and wait. Possy had returned to his workshop, while Dizzy and Zawailza had gathered whatever news; there wasn't much.

The turning point had come with Ganno's reappearance. The Slizz had returned several times to Bargeton in the years since his mother's death. Each time he had put himself in Xenko's way, allowing himself to be found in the kitchen with Ardannen. At length the goldsmith grew used to the sight of him, making it an occasion for renewal of fervor and embroidery of the text that he preached; so Ganno gained freedom of the quarter, playing ever the Slizz. But at this last return, he had sought out Zawailza, and demonstrated to her his true nature, and his willingness to serve. "There is none that knows the city nor its secret roads so well; not Possy so surely kens the Palace's ways," she said. And so, some months gone by, Ganno led the three cats to where they overheard the conspirators' deliberations, and learned of the Crimson Bears. Possy had gone to the Citadel at once. He had tried to get an audience with Claudio, in order to disclose the plot, for it had advanced beyond his power to quash it. The Citadel gates had not opened. The black cat renewed his attempts; but the Bargeton Senate had just begun to hear of the Crimson Bears from the bandicoot laundress. Bemused at first, when Skaling commenced his embassies, they had certainly no time for cats. At this point Zawailza's account moved onto ground that Alice already knew a little about. She looked to Edgar and saw him nodding confirmation.

"O, 'twas a pretty scheme," Possy exploded, "and concoct between Skaling and Equivair, the impress of whose malice convolute it plainly shows. For first," he went on, "Skaling feigns to the bears immoderate terror, and begs rather than offers that all Thoogry be admitted to the city, thinking that way to alarm the bears the more. For the Thoog, you know, own a universal name for fell soldiers, thus their own fear must argue an opponent ferocious indeed. Certain bloody stories of these crimson troopers Skaling next recounts, till he perceives the bearish illustrissimi doubtful betwixt their firm resolve to keep the much mistrusted Thoog from out their city, and their waxing fears of hideous pillage; and at whose hands? Why, those of bears—creatures of their own kind! O that's the stroke indeed! To come to bears with tales of murderous bears, O witty villain!"

"Still stubborn Claudio temporized with the Thoog," Zawailza resumed, laying her paw on Possy's arm to calm him, "the while he bethought himself, how ill it were to face this threat from without the walls, when not all within them gladly nor easily suffered his authority. It came to his slow mind that one rowdy malcontent was ever a-beating at his door, these latter days, a hot-head cat, no other than he that erstwhile graced his cells, black Possy Damp Paws. Of this renegade, at least, he would make him sure. The next time the caitiff shows, peremptory calling to be let in, your canny uncle admits him, but rather than hear him, despatches him jump to the jails. Then rubs me the old bear his paws, and thinks himself quit of one danger."

There Possy had languished, spreading his body into the most extravagantly doleful postures, if Ganno's mime were true. Possy himself laughed freely at it; Alice, also laughing, studied the black cat's face. She was surprised at the despondency that underlay his mercurial sparkle. Like a bad taste met in a spoonful of Clowncat *olla podrida*, it struck her, the bitter-burnt savor of melancholy. Looking to Ganno, she saw a witty amalgam of Possy's two sides, saw in those lavish droopings and head-clutchings an ebulliency of despair: ridiculous enough as the Slizz played it, but true. Alice suddenly understood. The black cat's two natures did not contradict each other: he relished defeat. He balanced the architecture of his spirit above certain collapse, drawing strength from the knowledge of doom. Finally he must give way, but until the hour he proposed to himself, he would expend all his power in keeping the brilliant structure intact. This was their leader, then, Alice thought. And Edgar's faith in Possy was utterly complete; he would follow him anywhere. Should she find words for her fears, Edgar never would hear them.

Dizzy had not joined in the laughter at Ganno's antics. Alice turned to steal a glance at him, and found her eye caught by his; she quickly looked away. The broad face with its grin, the steady green eyes regarding her coolly, had seen what she knew. What had she seen? Nothing fixed, nothing stable. In Dizzy's brain she apprehended a dance inelegant, even grotesque, that caught up many low appetites into its fluid figures; but it was merry, and the oblivion towards which it whirled was that of utter satiety. She could feel the pulse in the lean barrel-body beside her, she remembered how strong were the arms that set her down in the trash; gently they had done it. Dizzy liked her. She had gladly joined his dance. And she, did she feel more liking for him than fear? The yellow cat was a powerful motor, for good ends or bad. Possy would need him, but could the courtly savant rule the clown? Of course, one could not reckon without Zawailza. Alice, looking to the silver dancer, met her smile.

The story had gone on, while these thoughts engrossed her. She had missed what was said, but did not care much. Possy now had risen to his feet.

"We must presently make speedy determination of what our friends are to do. 'Twere tempting fortune, Zawailza, to tarry longer."

"But wait!" cried Edgar. "The Crimson Bears! Please, one last question. Who are the Crimson Bears?"

The black cat paused, his mouth open; he seemed about to guffaw. Hammering knocks filled the guardroom instead. Alice faced the far door with the rest. When the pounding ceased, she heard a high, plaintive voice, muffled by wood and iron:

"Break the door down, Sergeant, if they won't let us in."

TWENTY-SIX

Skaling, Skabny, Spurlak.

*D*izzy's arms wrapped around Alice's waist, lifted her; the room turned; she was hurtling toward the black press. She was deep inside it, standing with her back against wood. "Now I am in a closet in a guardroom in a trash-bin," she reflected. Edgar came scrambling up too. The floor of the press was raised a few feet; that was why Dizzy's legs seemed cut off at the hips. He looked like a hand-puppet. His arms worked stiffly as he hoisted the struggling bundle of her brother, and his face was as set as a mask.

"I'm sure I heard someone in there," continued the voice from outside. "Let's go, Sergeant, stop fiddling with that lock! Through the wood, use your claws! You're not afraid of splinters, are you?"

Wood screeched and ripped. Ganno, who was still outside the press, turned to Possy and loudly sniffed.

"Nay, make haste," the black cat begged, "what matter if the press be something malodorous? Now is no time to stand on niceties, good Ganno!"

"Stay, Possy," Zawailza's voice replied; Alice could no longer see her. "'Tis you have forgot how keen are the Thoog's noses; they'll sniff our friends out sure."

"Ay, me!" he wailed, "it is most true! O, why did I linger? They'll whiff that bears were here, find 'em or no! If Skaling learns that we had conference with bears, we are no better than dead cats!"

257

"What wiles, Chief, can you put on now?" Zawailza's calm voice demanded. As Alice watched, the Clowncat turned to face the Slizz. Against the brazier's glow their silhouettes made shadow-puppets rimmed in flame. Dizzy made Ganno a bow, which Ganno returned.

"Son of Stinko," said Dizzy sweetly, "what makes the world's worst smell?" Ganno raised his arms in a gesture of admiration. He threw back his head. The cat reached out and seized the Slizz by the throat. For a second they struggled while Alice gaped. Dizzy's hand came free, Ganno staggered back. The Clowncat opened his fist to reveal a large hank of wool torn out from Ganno's breast. The room re-echoed with the din of rending wood. Dizzy ran to the brazier; he dropped the wool on the fire. When the first coil of smoke reached Alice's nose, she understood the Clowncat's stratagem: no other smell could hope to assert itself above that terrific reek. Ganno climbed into the press.

"Aren't you through that door yet, Sergeant?" exclaimed the Thoog's voice. "My, but you're making heavy work of it." And then, in an altered tone: "Shokken's knees, what is that *awful* smell? What are they *doing* in there? Step it up, Sergeant, or I'll fly your tail from the Citadel's highest tower tomorrow." More groaning and splitting; Dizzy pushed close the door of the press. Alice was back in the dark, squeezed between her brother and Ganno. Slow to fade was her last sight of Dizzy's grin. The tricky light had greased his features with lime and violet.

She heard the continuing tearing of wood. She heard a strange little laugh, out in the guardroom; she thought it was Zawailza's. She started to tremble. Doors did not keep bad things out where houses bled together, where streets spanned rooftops and bored through closets. How big was the press? She swelled to fill the whole volume of it, then shrank to the size of a dust-ball adrift on its floor. She touched her nose with her paw but felt nothing.

Where was the Citadel? And all the spread of streets, river, desert seen from Claudio's? In the darkness, an image came to mind—a red-walled city on the banks of a blue stream. It seemed very small. It was as though she viewed it from hilltop and from sky, simultaneously, like a picture-map in an old book. Against the desert, crimson forms arabesqued. Then the picture surged with other colors which lost all shape as they unlocked. These eddying hues made new things clear. The fire broke out again, in shaggy olive flames. The Flood flowed backward and forward, mixing a lustreless Thoog-brown. A stone weighed on Alice's stomach, her arms and legs were cold. The Citadel turned on her with Dizzy's motley grin; Alice heaved herself over Ganno's legs, crawled a short way, and was sick. "Alice!" hissed Edgar. She waited a moment. Things grew a little steadier.

"It's the smoke," she croaked. "I think I'm all right."

In truth she felt miserable, but at least she knew why. She nestled back into her spot; both Edgar and Ganno put their arms around her. Outside in the guardroom the cats were singing! The song was a loud and merry one. Alice heard Zawailza's contralto weave its clear lilt through the sonorous growlings of Possy and Dizzy. Meanwhile the door was still breaking. The song and the smashing went on together for another stanza before a final ripping salvo ended the madrigal. A short silence fell. Then General Skaling's voice opened from near at hand. Alice pressed up against Edgar and buried her face in his neck, but she could not help hearing.

"Well! I thought I might find you three. You have been enjoying yourselves, now, haven't you? I wish I'd got here earlier, to join in the fun!" he taunted. "Still, I'm just a bit surprised to find you partying, when our meeting was supposed to have begun an hour ago. Maybe you lost track of the time. Well, now that we're here, why don't you offer me and Lieutenant Skabny a drink? You all know Skabny, don't you? My aide-de-camp. Skabny, this is Captain Possy, you know him, of course, and this is Chief Dizzio, and this lady is the famous comedienne, Zoolooza, now did I get that right? Well, how about that drink? But I don't see any bottles!"

Possy's reply was strangely loud; Alice wondered to hear his slurring and oddly placed emphases.

"My lord general, we have no wine imbibed," he said. "What cause engenders our present mirth is here diffused through the chamber; you may soon, and welcome, partake through the vents of your own most renownedly delicate noses."

"What?" said Skaling in a strained voice that failed to conceal some alarm. "Skabny, what's he saying? What about my nose, for Shokken's sake?"

"Sir, I think he means to imply that the . . . that that strong smell in the room—you commented on it earlier, sir—I *think* he means to say that whatever they were burning has some sort of an *effect* on them, sir, and . . . and may have on us as well."

"What?" said Skaling, much louder. "WHAT?" he bleated. "You think that this damn-awful stink . . . ? Skabny, go open that other door, please, at once. I want this room aired out! Why, it smells like scorched Slizz-wool!"

"Aye, General, and so 'tis," Possy affably remarked. "It works miraculously on the brain, and brings on most rare visions. But a few whiffs, and the mind is a garden of delight. Your lordship may shortly feel its effects, I hope, and then we may all be merry together."

"Withal," came Zawailza's throaty drawl, "it moves us, my lord, to amorous sport."

"Well, Miss Wazooza," Skaling's voice was now as cold as ancient buried ice, "I'm sorry to say that whatever urges this . . . substance arouses in you, it has no effect whatsoever on us Thoog. Skabny!"

"Yes, General!" Skabny was all alacrity. "What shall I do, sir?"

"Have you got that door open yet?"

"Yes, my lord, it's open."

"Well, good. Now come on over here, please. Captain Possy and Chief Dizzio," he went on in a tone meant to temper sternness with kindness, "I must ask you, please, to get to the Feast Hall at your best speed. You have held up the meeting for a full hour, and, in my opinion, frankly, that's just inappropriate. Quite candidly, I must tell you that I find your behavior here in questionable taste. Now, I'm sorry if I seem a bit outspoken, but you have to remember that it took a lot of people a lot of time to make sure you were included at all, as I'm sure you're all aware. Equivair was dead against it. Xenko and I had a tough job to convince him. Now what about *our* feelings? You see, you haven't ever stopped to consider the position you put Xenko and myself into, coming in hours late, and hardly, *hardly* in a frame of mind to do serious business. Do you see what I'm saying? The fact is, you three still have to prove yourselves, not to me, of course, but to Equivair, say, and Gribo as well. Gribo's a real professional. You really don't want to be counted on the wrong side at this stage of the game, now do you? I don't want to preach a sermon, but this makes a poor beginning. Now does all this make sense to you? Can you understand my point of view in all of this?"

The cats must have silently bowed, for Skaling continued in mollified tones, "Well, fine. Now I'm going to ask you to wait a moment, while I perform a disagreeable duty. Sergeant Spurlak, step forward, please. Why are you holding your claw that way, Sergeant?"

"Talon broke off, sir. Right at the base. Caught it on some metal in the door, sir."

"O, I see. Well, that's pretty serious. Now, Sergeant. I'm a little embarrassed to be standing here in front of these cats, who are allies of ours, after you made such a hash of that door. Now don't you agree you made a real hash of it? Five minutes to get through one door! And look at the mess you made! Splinters all over the place. I really can't say I think you did a very soldierly job of it. Can you see what I'm getting at, at all, Sergeant Spurlak?"

"Yes, my lord, I . . . I think I do, but . . . damn thing was full of metal bits, sir."

"O, now, Sergeant, let's remember where we are, and not start making silly excuses in front of our hosts and allies. We don't want them to get the idea that we Thoog are the sort of creature that tries to, uh, wriggle out of the consequences of our actions, and so forth, do we? No. Why, everyone fouls up sometimes, Sergeant. Hold out your claw, if you will. The wounded one. Lieutenant Skabny."

"At your orders, my lord."

"Would you be so good as to hold Sergeant Spurlak's wrist, there, to steady it, and so on. Thank you. Let's see the broken talon, Sergeant. O dear, that's ugly. I don't like to see a mess like that on one of my soldiers. Take it off at the knuckle, Skabny, if you'll be so kind."

Alice heard a sickening crunch, followed by a moan of pain choked back.

"Thank you, Lieutenant. You can spit that out in the corner, over there. Now, Sergeant, we don't want that stump to go septic on you. I think it would be a good idea for you to just push it into that fire, if our friends wouldn't mind making a little room for you, and then hold it there a second or two. Brace him, Lieutenant! That's good, that's right. Another second, Sergeant! Hygiene demands a little patience. There. Now it's all clean, and you won't have to worry about it. You just go and get that bound up, and make sure the wrapping is clean! Sergeant, I didn't dismiss you yet. I'll let you go in a second, but there's just one thing. Sergeant, a Thoog soldier depends a great deal on his weapons, doesn't he? Now what are a Thoog's weapons, Sergeant Spurlak?"

"Teeth and talons, sir," said the Sergeant faintly.

"Well, exactly. How many talons does a Thoog have?"

"Eight, sir."

"That's right. But you, Sergeant, you only have seven now. That means that when it comes to fighting, you're going to be just a little less effective than the next trooper, doesn't it? Yes. You're not going to be able to replace that talon either, are you, Sergeant? No. What is the first rule a Thoog soldier must obey?"

"To keep his teeth and talons sharp, sir."

"Why, that's right. You always have to take good care of your weapons; that's the first rule you teach to your own men. Now, how well would you say you've obeyed that rule yourself?"

"Not . . . very well, sir. I've been a little . . . careless."

"Well, I'm glad you've seen that for yourself. I just hope you understand that all these rules aren't just a bunch of fiddle-faddle that I make up to keep you busy. You need *all* your talons in a battle. But you know that, I'm sure. Well, I don't think we need to keep you any longer, Sergeant. You'll take good care of that claw, now won't you?"

"Yes, sir."

"Because we need every Thoog we've got now, you see. A good clean bandage, but be careful not to wrap it up too tight! All right, Sergeant, you're dismissed. Feel better!"

There was a longish silence while Spurlak withdrew; Alice felt her gorge rising again, and swallowed hard.

"It wasn't a very good idea to raise him to Sergeant," Skaling remarked at length. "But everyone has to have their chance. Make sure that he's posted someplace suitable, Skabny, will you please. The last thing we need is cripples cluttering up the regiment."

"Sir," said Skabny, "may I say, I thought you handled him beautifully? You never even once raised your voice to him."

"O well, it wasn't so *hard*. After all, I wasn't the one sticking my finger in the fire, was I! Ha ha ha! You'd have heard me raise my voice then, all right. Ha ha ha ha ha! But seriously, Skabny, it never hurts to speak politely to the men, and, you know, to keep the tone a little light. I know that commanders are supposed to bark their orders, and so forth; but I really don't see that that gets you anywhere. They *have* to obey your orders, after all. So why not just speak gently to them, and then, *you* know, show some concern for their well-being? I always make a point of wishing them good luck before I send them into battle. It doesn't cost anything; and it makes them feel better. Like when I said that to whatsis-name, Spurlak. You see, I knew he must be not too happy about getting chewed out in front of strangers and all that. Did you notice how I told him to feel better?"

"General, I did."

"Well, that's an example of the sort of thing I'm talking about. You could tell it meant something to him. Well, I don't think we need to detain our friends any longer. Why don't the three of you trot along to the Feast Hall, if your heads are clearer, and Skabny and I will be along in just a few minutes. We'll see you in there!"

Much as Alice longed for silence, the lull that descended was worse than the speaking. Why didn't the Thoog leave? She could hear their heavy scuffle outside. Zawailza had gone; now Alice sensed, in the hollow of her heart, how many strangers' histories stood like walls between her and the places she knew. Even Edgar, caught up in his new sense of purpose, was adding a layer to separate her from home. How could she find a way back? Ganno knew all the doors and ways, but his guiding had only brought them deeper into Bargeton. And now she was shut in the press, and Thoog were sniffing about right outside it.

"Smell anything, Lieutenant?" wheezed Skaling. Skabny's reply came from inches away.

"No, General, nothing but Slizz-wool." Alice could very easily smell the Thoog, however, the same sweet mustiness that had fouled her fur by the booth in the Market Square. "There's a sort of cupboard here, sir. Perhaps I should poke around inside it?" Edgar's and Ganno's ribcages, swollen with inheld breath, pressed up against her own stiff sides; but what had been that reluctance in Skabny's voice? Why did he hesitate, why did he need to ask? The press was the only hiding-place in the room, if they were looking for eavesdroppers. With unwilled acumen Alice read his tone: the Thoog was afraid that he might touch something unclean! Filth is what clings to, or drops from, the bodies of others, while one's own body makes a fond shell against the world. Bargeton had taught her this lesson very well; she might never recognize her own scent again.

Skaling ignored his subordinate's query; he pursued his own train of thought out loud, his windy voice querulous with disgust; O, Dizzy's ruse had been knowingly calculated!

"Damn it, Skabny, I simply cannot make head or tail of this whole business. I know these particular cats are the worst of the bunch, but don't they have any feelings of decency at all? Can't they take anything seriously? I don't like to have to make sweeping characterizations, everyone has their own way of doing things, and I'm the last person to pretend that my way is always the best—but the way they carry on, well, with all the good will in the world, I can't help finding it absolutely disgusting."

"Sir, they're mammals, don't forget that," Skabny soothingly returned. "No different from bears, really; the way they're all brought up, why, it's sordid."

"Well, I know that," said Skaling heavily. "That's what I keep coming back to. But you'd think they'd wise up, when they see all the jams this sort of behavior gets them into. Well, I can't say how glad I am that we won't have to deal with them forever. If we let them, they'll foul our nests as well as their own. I really think they'll be happier when we sever the connection."

"We'll make a much cleaner place of Bargeton with just the Ceruk," his aide agreed. "At least they're reptiles."

"It's interesting you should say that," Skaling mused. "I've been giving the Ceruk some thought too. Of course, they are reptiles, as you say, though that wool is a little odd, to say the least. I've often wondered: when they shave it off, don't they think it's going to grow back? Anyway, I'm not too easy in my mind about them. They're such volatile little fellows, aren't they? Look at that Xenko and all his rant and bluster. You see, as a kind they're not really mature. They have no traditions at all, except for their gold and that silly little theatre of theirs. Now, are we really doing them a favor by including them in this new regime? Have they got the character to pull their weight? And another thing, it makes me nervous to see how excited they get about this Slizz business. Frankly, that strikes me as a real mess, and one that I'd just hate to see Thoog get mixed up in. Between you and me and the cupboard, Skabny, I'd be far happier if they'd just pack themselves off somewhere, and grow up on their own."

"I suppose," said Skabny thoughtfully, "that when it's all over, if we don't want them to stay, there won't be a great deal they can do about it."

"O, well, you know, I don't think that Thoog should necessarily go flexing our muscles, just because we're the heavyweights of this operation. There's got to be some principle involved, or you just come off like a pack of bullies. At any rate, it's something to keep in mind. One thing at a time."

"Yes, sir. General, shouldn't we be heading on to the meeting?"

"O, there's no great rush. They can't very well begin without their chairman, can they?" Thoog-chuckles beat against the press. "Well, I suppose it is time to get the ball rolling. We mustn't keep the royal Flibitto waiting, must we? My, that Equivair gets so damn het up about every diddly

TWENTY-SEVEN. **Behind the Hanging.**

*W*hen the silence had lasted as long as he could stand, Edgar kicked open the press door. The fire still smoldered in the brazier, but a draught swept the room. The outer door stood ajar, while the inner one was a thornbrake of metal and jagged wood. The lingering stink yielded to dank cellar air. Edgar wondered where to go next. Of the two ways that offered, that leading to the Feast Hall they could not now take. With Alice nauseous and frightened, any attempt to dog Skaling's heels had to wait. "I wouldn't have dared do it anyway," Edgar confessed to himself as soon as the decision was made. They would take the other way from that by which they had come. Ganno would know if it led to an eavesdropping spot. Edgar turned to find the Slizz on his hind legs, groping the back wall of the press. He rapped lightly at the wood till it echoed. When a panel slid, Edgar almost jumped. O, two doors could never be enough for a room in this place!

"Is this a way to the Feast Hall, Ganno?"

"Yes!"

Edgar felt Alice wince. He drew her to her feet. Her fur was dusty and damp.

"Will you be all right?" he urgently whispered. "We've got to follow Ganno again." Alice looked where he pointed, and burst into tears. "Come on," he said, "we can't wait here. We've got to go through with it now." She sniffed and turned without a word. The Slizz was already in the hole; he caught Alice's wrists, while Edgar set his shoulder to her rump. A heave, and she was in. Then Edgar clambered up.

This tunnel was very like the sally port, except that it climbed. As the guardroom receded, he found himself bracing both legs against masonry to keep from slipping back down the steep grade. Rubble dislodged by Alice hit his face till his mouth tasted grit; but he bore these discomforts stalwartly. He did not feel afraid. He had been in the dark for so long, he had travelled by such secret ways, that now he felt able to go where he liked; he had Ganno.

Soon a faint light ahead outlined Alice's bulges. She was turning herself around to back out; they had pierced another wall. Edgar tried, as he approached, to smile into her unhappy face, but she gave no sign before dropping out of sight. He poked his nose out the opening, half hoping to see the Feast Hall itself. Instead, there hung, a mere arm's-length away, a wall of hairy knots and groping yarns. It curtained off every prospect but the thin strip of floor a short drop below him. Though he squinted, Edgar could see no border on either side or overhead. And as the weaving's great weight had caused it to sag, the nether selvage bunched in folds on the floor. So thick with dust was the air, it seemed a second arras, gelling behind the first. He looked for Alice. She was sidling away to the left, her back against the stone, her face turned from him. Edgar twisted around and lowered himself to the floor. Then, stifling sneezes, he followed his sister. The coarse knotting rasped his fur. Was this to be their spyingpost? He prayed not.

Then Alice halted, leaned back, her eyes closed. Beyond her, Ganno was gently palpating the folds of the hanging.

Edgar wondered why they had stopped now. The tapestry swept on as far as he could see. Laid flat, it would carpet acres! But Ganno's hands, bolder now, began to open a rent in the fabric. Beyond it swelled a wooden convexity: a huge egg the color of dried blood, whose surface, however, was corrugated like oak-bark; or else like fur. Very likely it was that, the stylized fur of a statue; or of an old piece of furniture; that was probably it. It would just suit Felipo's taste to outfit his banquet-hall with chairs imitating the forms of subject kinds. Edgar easily imagined them drawn up in rows, backed against the walls, waiting. But he still could not square the red egg with any familiar furniture. It did not seem to rest upon the floor; at the height of Edgar's shoulder, it curved sharply inward and vanished. Thus a chair-back might join its seat, but there were no legs. At this moment Ganno let go of the fabric. The rent remained open. Then the Slizz slipped through it. Edgar couldn't see what he did next, but a curving slab of wood soon detached, just at the heel of the bulge. It swung down and hung. Another trap-door! And by far the smallest yet.

"I can't get through that," Edgar silently declared. He glanced at Alice, who still leaned against the wall, eyes closed, panting. When Ganno touched her on the shoulder, she blinked and straightened. Without hesitating she stooped, thrust her arms and head past the wooden slab, then worked her shoulders in. Edgar thought she would stick but by stages her back and legs disappeared. The hole was empty, Ganno was looking at him.

It was not quite dark inside. Pale light dropping from above let him view an oddly rounded interior. It certainly was no chair; more like another cupboard. His sister had found a spot on one side of the trap-door; she was already curled up in a ball. There was room for Edgar to lie down opposite, but he wanted to *see*. He looked up toward the light. It descended a tubular shaft and glimmered on metal brackets set ladder-wise. He wriggled all the way inside, and the trap-door snicked shut. Edgar listened for any noise that would tell him what the Slizz was doing, but all he could hear was his sister's slow breathing. He turned again toward the light. There was just room enough to stand. He set a foot on the lowest of the brackets and reached for the next, hauled himself up and up, till his head passed the lip of the shaft. He emerged into yet another rounded cavity.

Unsteady daylight filtered through a serrated slot that wrapped around his field of vision. The serration's irregular cones looked so much like teeth, that Edgar almost fancied he was gazing through the rictus of a smile. This conceit led him to conclude that he was perched inside some statue's head, an element in the Feast Hall's barbaric decor. But he did not frame this idea, nor even register what he'd seen, till much later. For as his eyes adjusted to the light, he found himself staring across a wide space into the toothy snarl of a seated Crimson Bear.